SPOOKED

Elise Noble

Published by Undercover Publishing Limited

Copyright © 2018 Elise Noble

v10

ISBN: 978-1-910954-92-8

Edited by Nikki Mentges at NAM Editorial

Cover art by Abigail Sins

www.undercover-publishing.com

www.elise-noble.com

It's a miracle that curiosity survives formal education.
- *Albert Einstein*

CHAPTER 1 - KIMBERLY

MY DATE WAS going well until the dead girl in the back seat started talking to me.

At least, I thought it was going well. And I thought it was a date. The guy sitting beside me at the wheel had taken on an ethereal quality, hazy, floating in and out of my field of vision like smoke on the breeze.

How much time had passed since dinner? We *had* eaten dinner, hadn't we? I recalled a bowl of pretzels, wine, candles... But I'd gone beyond feeling full and straight to sick. Do not pass go, do not collect two hundred dollars, do not puke in the nice man's car.

He smiled at me, white teeth shining eerily in the darkness, and I tried to smile back but my face had stopped working. None of my limbs felt as if they were attached to my body either. What was wrong with me?

"Are you okay, Kimberly?"

His voice echoed around the car, words coming at me in stereo. How did he know my name? Had I told him my name? What was *his* name? Was he a cab driver?

"Who are you?"

"We're friends, remember?"

No, I didn't remember, not really.

"Where..." The words stuck in my throat. "Where are we going?"

"Home, Kimberly. I'm taking you home."

Ah, home. Home would be good. I could put on my new pyjamas, the ones with the cats on them that Annie gave me for my birthday. My birthday... Candles, lots of candles... Cake... How old was I?

"You need to get out."

Boy, the man's voice had gotten really high pitched. Feminine.

"You need to get out *now*."

Wait a second. Or a minute. Who knew how time worked anymore? The voice was coming from behind, not beside me, and I tried to twist around. A glimpse of pale white skin, a flash of shiny brown hair, that weird, translucent shimmer people got after they died.

Shoot. There was a ghost in the back seat. A ghost! The bane of my freaking existence.

"Just get out of the damn car!"

Was she crazy as well as dead?

"The car's moving," I mumbled.

The man rested a hand on my thigh. "Of course it's moving. I'm taking you home, remember?"

Don't talk to ghosts in front of people, Kimmy. My mom's words echoed in my head, and I cursed myself silently. *Don't swear out loud*—that had been another of her rules.

"Hey, hey!" the girl shouted. "Don't fall asleep on me. My name's Georgette, and I died in this car—don't let it happen to you too."

Georgette. My mom used to have a friend called Georgette, but that was before Mom got taken away. Locked up for being crazy, although nobody ever said those exact words. *Don't let it happen to you too.*

Was I crazy? I sure felt as if I'd lost my mind.

Fuzziness clouded my thoughts, and darkness nibbled at the edges.

"He killed me," Georgette said. "The man you're with killed me. He drugged me just like he's drugged you."

Drugs? I didn't take drugs. Except for that funny cigarette I smoked in high school with... What was her name? Blonde... Always carried a Twinkie in her purse... No, it was gone. But hold on, Georgette said the man drugged me. Could he have done that?

"What...should...I...do?" I slurred, every word an effort.

His hand squeezed my leg. "Just sit back and relax. I'll put you to bed."

"Did he even ask your address?" Georgette asked. "Did he?"

Did he, did he, did he? Everything before the car was a blur. What was my address? I had a nice house, ranch-style, painted cream on a good-sized lot. No pets unless you counted the orioles that hung out at my bird feeder in spring.

"My name is Georgette Riley, and I was twenty-four years old when I died. Remember that, because you need to solve my murder."

No. No way. I didn't do crime solving. I organised weddings and the occasional party. Never for teenagers because those always ended in disaster, but anniversaries, corporate functions, even the occasional bach...bachelette...bachor... Strippers. Those.

"No no no."

"Honestly," the man said. "Taking you home is no trouble."

"Look, Kimberly—that's your name, isn't it? You

need to kill this asshole to set me free, and right now, the only thing you're capable of killing is your own liver. So I'm gonna help you escape, and then you're gonna hunt him down."

That sounded good. The escape part, not the hunting. And I hated liver.

"Nod once if you can hear me."

My head didn't want to cooperate, but I managed to move it a little.

Georgette sounded shrill, her voice a mixture of desperation and excitement, and I knew why. Meeting me was a one in two billion chance, quite literally. Almost eight billion people in the world, but only four Electi, if you could even count me among them seeing as I didn't carry out any of my duties. My appearance had given her hope.

"Okay, he's locked the doors, but the button to unlock them is on the centre console. Move your left hand. More. More. Got it."

My eyes began closing all of their own accord, but I felt the smooth plastic of the button under my fingertips. A lifeline.

"Now, slide your other hand over and get ready to unbuckle the seat belt."

This plan made no sense. Georgette expected me to jump from a moving vehicle? I'd die anyway. Then the man rubbed my leg with his thumb, and a shiver ran through me. It felt...wrong. So wrong.

"Not long now, darling," he said.

Darling? Darling? Daddy always called Mom darling, and then he sent her away. For a rest, he said, but she'd never left the Spring Grove Treatment Center in the whole time before she died. And I didn't want to live in *that* place. It smelled funky, and the nurses always spoke in this weird whisper that sounded like the wind in the trees.

No, I couldn't stay with this man.

"There's a traffic light coming up, and it's just turned red," Georgette told me. "You'll have about five seconds to get out. Ready?"

I was anything but ready, but she didn't seem to care.

"Go!"

Some primal instinct must have taken over, because suddenly I was on the grass verge, looking through the open car door at the man's angry face. For a second, I thought he might come after me, but then the car behind honked its horn and he reached over, slammed the door shut, and roared off, quickly followed by Mr. Impatient.

Alone at the side of the road, I gave in to temptation and closed my eyes as a light drizzle dampened my face. The ground felt soft. Squishy. Kind of cold, but that was okay.

Finally, I could take a nap.

CHAPTER 2 - KIMBERLY

"MA'AM, ARE YOU awake?"

Define awake.

I could hear a man talking, but I wasn't entirely sure he was real. Nor did I know where I was, how I'd gotten there, or what the incessant beeping in the background was.

A car. I'd been in a car. With a murdered girl and possibly her killer, and now my head felt as if it'd been run over by a truck and squashed like a cantaloupe. Was I dead?

"Ma'am?"

I made an effort to pry open one gummy eyelid, light hit me, and I leaned to the side and threw up.

"Dagnabbit!"

The grey-haired man standing beside my bed staggered back three feet, and I groaned as I took in my surroundings. White blankets on a metal-framed bed, monitors next to me, and a green curtain all around. This was no hotel room.

"Sorry," I croaked.

"How are you feeling?"

"Who are you?"

"Officer Leopold with the Montgomery County Police Department."

"How did I get here? This is a hospital, right?"

My voice came out croaky, and I spotted a jug of water on the nightstand next to me. Thirsty. So thirsty. I reached across, but the stupid wires tugged at the back of my hand and stopped me. Leopold stepped around the pool of vomit and helped me out.

"Here you go." He passed me a glass. "A motorist found you passed out drunk at the side of the road."

"How long ago?"

"Wait a moment—I need to find a cleaner for..." He waved at the mess on the floor. "For that."

When he pulled the green curtain back, I got a glimpse of the hallway beyond. Stark white with a gurney parked in it, the occupant waiting for a bed and a massive bill, no doubt. The curtain swung back into place, and I tried to fit the jigsaw pieces together in my head. Had I been drinking? I usually limited myself to one glass when I was out. After all, I didn't want to do anything stupid. Hold on—didn't my ghostly companion mention drugs?

Officer Leopold came back with a shorter man in tow, who set to work with a mop and bucket. Guilt washed over me because he had to clean up after my bad judgement. Why on earth had I gotten into a stranger's car?

"Last night," Leopold said.

"Huh?"

"You got picked up last night."

"What time is it?"

Leopold glanced at his watch. "Almost noon."

Oh, shiznits. I'd already missed my first appointment today. And the second. And Sara Hawkins was getting married in a week and needed daily pep talks so she didn't back out. She loved her husband-to-be, but the idea of being stared at by three hundred guests, including her future mother-in-law, made her break out in hives. Literally. Last Tuesday, I'd driven her to the doctor for treatment.

And then there was...Georgina? Georgia? Georgette, that was it. More memories filtered back, of her telling me to escape, to jump from the car. Usually I ignored the dead, but last night she'd saved my life. It could have been my body in the back seat, my father getting informed of his daughter's sad demise. And then there was the bigger question—what would have happened if I'd died without passing on my strange ability? Would the buck stop with me? I had to hope so. Ghosts had been part of my life for years, you see, ever since my mom passed the gift on to me. Or rather, the burden. The first time I'd seen one, I'd been spooked so badly I hid in my room for three days, but now I'd gotten used to their presence.

Why? Because lucky old me was one of only a handful of people on earth who could communicate with the dead, and not just any old dead, but those who'd had their lives cut short by another. Murder victims, accidental deaths, casualties of war. I saw them all, going back centuries. And the worst part? They knew I could see them.

That meant everywhere I went, men, women, and children begged me for help, and I never got a moment's peace. I was the supernatural equivalent of a rock star without having sung a single track.

Usually, I blocked them out. Ignored them. I'd become quite proficient at it over the years, but now I had a problem.

I owed Georgette.

Part of me wanted to apologise to the medical staff and Officer Leopold for my mistake and walk right out of the hospital, because who would believe me if I tried to explain I'd been drugged by a murderer? He hadn't laid a finger on me. All I had was Georgette's story, and my memory was shaky on that at best.

But what if he tried to abduct another woman and she wasn't so lucky? If three months down the line, I caught sight of a newspaper and realised a girl just like me had disappeared on an evening out, only for her body to be found dumped in a forest or by a lake or beside a quiet road? Or worse, never found at all.

Could I live with myself if that happened?

The answer was no. This was the first time a murder had gotten personal for me, and even now, as I lay safe in the hospital with a policeman at my side, a shiver ran up my spine.

I had to do something, but what?

Officer Leopold smiled down kindly. "Now you're awake, the doctor needs to check you over, and we've arranged for a representative from Alcoholics Anonymous to stop by with a few pamphlets."

"I'm not an alcoholic!"

He shifted from foot to foot, uncomfortable. "Ma'am, you were unconscious when they brought you in, and when you woke up, you spent half the night vomiting. Then you locked yourself in the bathroom, and it took the nurses twenty minutes to convince you to come out. They almost broke the door down."

Really? I didn't remember any of that.

"That was..."

Dammit, how was I supposed to explain my escape? I could hardly admit to my deep and meaningful conversation with a dead girl, could I?

"That was what?"

"That wasn't like me at all. I...I think I was with a man. In his car."

"The person who called 911 was a woman, and she didn't see anybody else around."

"I think he drugged me. Honestly, I don't normally drink that much, and I've never, ever passed out."

Okay, so I threw up after prom, but I'd been eighteen. It was practically a rite of passage.

"That's a serious allegation, ma'am."

Leopold didn't groan out loud, but his reluctant expression said it all. How far off retirement was he? A year? Two years? The last thing he wanted was a tricky case to interrupt his coffee-drinking time.

"I know it is, but what if there's a man out there hunting innocent women? Do you have a daughter? A granddaughter?"

Reluctance turned back to sympathy. "Two granddaughters."

"I'm in a hospital. Can't you run a test to see if he gave me anything?"

"I think they run a drug screen as a matter of course. I'll ask a doctor."

"Thank you."

Even though I'd been unconscious for hours, a wave of tiredness washed over me, and I yawned. Leopold patted me awkwardly on the shoulder.

"I'll leave you to get some rest. Is there someone I can call? You'll need clothes to wear home, I guess. And shoes."

Shoes? I'd lost my favourite LK Bennett kitten heels? The news brought tears to my eyes, which was stupid considering everything else that had happened. I'd loved those damn shoes with their little white bows.

"C-c-can you call my friend Annie?"

"Do you have her number?"

"It's in my phone."

"You didn't have a phone with you when you arrived."

"No purse?"

"Sorry."

More to do—cancel my credit cards, get a new phone, replace all my make-up. Just what I didn't need at such a busy time of year. Then it hit me.

"I left my purse in his car! It had my phone, and my wallet, and my driver's licence. He's got my address."

"You're sure you had the purse with you?"

"Well, no, but I'd never have left it behind in a bar." Would I? I didn't recall leaving the bar or the restaurant or wherever I'd been. "At least, I don't think so. I suppose it's possible."

"I'll look into it, ma'am. Perhaps somebody handed it in. Now, about this Annie. How can I contact her?"

"We work together at Just Imagine Events. She'll be in the office by now."

Placating our clients, no doubt, and cursing my name in her sweet southern accent as she paced the meeting area with its white-and-silver furniture and artfully arranged flowers. Always fresh, never artificial.

The curtain moved back again, and I pretended not to care as Officer Leopold and the doctor held a whispered conference, probably about me peeing in a cup. After this, I was never drinking again. Not even a glass of champagne at the many, many weddings I had to attend. New, teetotal Kim had been born, and maybe

I should start going to the gym too.

Tomorrow. I'd go to the gym tomorrow when my limbs stopped feeling like overcooked soba noodles. The doctor nodded a few times then fussed around, checking out the beeping machines and making notes on my chart.

"How are you doing, Miss...? Well, we've got you down as Jane Doe at the moment."

"Miss Jennings. Kimberly Jennings. I just want to go home."

"We need to run some more tests first, but as long as you're feeling okay, you should be able to leave this afternoon."

This afternoon? Annie was going to kill me. But I smiled and did my swan impression—you know, all serene above the water but frantically paddling underneath.

"Thank you. That sounds perfect."

The doctor disappeared, and Officer Leopold stepped closer once more.

"They've taken a urine sample, but nothing showed up apart from alcohol."

Was he kidding? "I've never passed out from a glass of wine, or even two. What drugs did they test for?"

"They did a standard screening. Amphetamines, benzodiazepines, marijuana, cocaine, that sort of thing."

"What about roofies? Did they test for roofies?"

"I believe those fall under benzodiazepines."

"Well, he must have given me something else. I've read tales of those fancy club drugs on the internet. Please, you have to look for this man. If he incapacitated me, he could just as easily do it to another woman tomorrow."

"Any idea where you might have met him?"

"I was exhibiting at the Big Day Bridal Show, so I guess in the hotel where it was being held. The Park Plaza. I certainly didn't plan on going anywhere else afterwards."

"I'll ask one of my colleagues to take a look, see if they can find any witnesses."

"They have security cameras. There's a little sign in the lobby saying 'Smile, you're a movie star.'"

Leopold smiled too. I amused him.

"I'll make sure I relay that information, ma'am."

"I know how this looks. That I'm just a stupid girl who made a bad error in judgement. But I assure you that's not who I am, and it makes me sick to think there's a man out there preying on women."

His smile faded. "And I assure you we'll investigate. Honestly? I wish we had the manpower to chase down every lead, but the department budget's been pared to the bone over the last few years, and the new mayor's on our backs at the moment because burglary rates are so high. Half of the officers are investigating crimes against property. Not saying I disagree with that, but..."

"Have you ever heard the name Georgette Riley?"

Riley was her surname, wasn't it? My mind was still hazy.

Leopold looked at me sharply. "What's she got to do with this case?"

So he *had* heard of her.

"Nothing. Nothing at all. I just heard a friend mention her name as an unsolved murder the other day, and while you're here, I thought I'd ask."

"Georgette Riley disappeared from Arlington,

Virginia...two, maybe three years ago. My cousin's a cop there. But there's no evidence she was murdered. Between you and me, most of the investigating officers thought she ran away." Leopold's voice dropped to a conspiratorial whisper. "Boyfriend trouble."

"It's still an open case?"

"Can't see it ever being closed unless she reappears. Or a body turns up, I guess." He checked his watch. "I need to go, ma'am. Shift change."

Who was I to keep him from his coffee and donuts?

"Will you call Annie?"

"Right away. And you'd better write your contact details down too."

With the formalities taken care of, I flopped back against the pillow as Leopold's rubber-soled shoes squeaked their way along the hallway. I knew what the police didn't—that Georgette had died. The question was, how did I convince them of that fact without either implicating myself or coming across as a crazy woman, and more importantly, how could I prevent her murderer from killing again?

CHAPTER 3 - KIMBERLY

"WHAT THE HECK happened?"

Annie pulled back the curtain, looking perfect from her artfully twisted chignon to the manicured nails in her peep-toe pumps. As always. How she didn't freeze to death in her pastel-pink suit was beyond me. We'd met seven years ago, just after I got married and started my company. Annie had been a year older than me at twenty-two, but she'd already spent four years living with an abusive asshole before she escaped on a Greyhound bus in the middle of the night.

I'd helped her through that trauma, and since then, she'd repaid me tenfold—firstly, by being the best assistant a girl could ever hope for, then by helping to pick up the pieces when my own relationship failed, and now, once again, she was here to fix my mess. Annie wasn't just an employee, she was my best friend. Being honest, I didn't have many friends at all. I found it difficult to get close to people, and although I had hundreds of acquaintances, I never spent time with them outside work and organised social events.

But Annie? Annie was different. Once or twice, I'd even considered telling her about my strange gift, but I was too afraid of her reaction to risk it. Why upset the status quo?

"I had a small problem last night."

"Really? You think? I almost died of shock when a cop called me. When you didn't come to work, I thought something terrible had happened."

"Something terrible *did* happen."

"I meant that you'd been kidnapped, or gotten hit by a car, or drunk too much and accidentally slept with someone's fiancé at the wedding show."

"Why would you think that? You know I rarely drink."

"Well, you did go to the bar with Maria Fitzgerald."

"I did?"

Maria was one of our best customers, seeing as she was about to embark on her third marriage and to a movie mogul this time. She'd once confessed that each wedding felt more like a business transaction, although that didn't stop her from ordering expensive dresses and six-tier artisanal cakes and thousands of pure-white roses. Soon, she'd be Maria Rosenberg, and Annie and I had a secret bet Maria would be shopping for a new husband within two years. Don Rosenberg had an eye for the ladies, and Maria's prenup gave her a great settlement if he got caught cheating.

But why had I gone to the bar with her?

"She wanted to buy both of us a drink to celebrate finding the perfect table centrepieces, but I stayed behind to finish packing up the booth. Remember how last time the movers broke a vase and scratched one of the leather stools?"

I did. I also remembered that Annie didn't like Maria much. Said she was mercenary. But Annie still believed in the concept of true love, while I believed in putting food on my table, so I didn't have so much of a problem with Maria's approach to marriage. But now it seemed that Maria's approach to drinking may have put my life in danger. She always had liked cocktails.

"I don't even remember seeing her after the show. And I'd never sleep with somebody's fiancé."

"Not knowingly, but I always said that too and look what happened after Better Brides last year. If that swine's engagement ring hadn't fallen out of his wallet when he paid for our drinks, I'd have gone on another date with him."

Instead, she'd caught a cab over to my place and spent the rest of the night downing margaritas and cursing men while Margaret, the spirit of a sixty-year-old former housewife who resided in one corner of my living room, shook her head and tutted and muttered that ladies in her day would never have acted that way.

But even when she got drunk, Annie's hair had stayed perfect, and although she might have wobbled a bit on her way up the stairs, she didn't have the slightest hangover the next morning. While I, on the other hand, felt as though I'd been hit by a semi.

How many bosses got jealous of their assistants? Was it just me?

"But you did the smart thing and walked away, while I...I... Honestly? I have no idea what happened, just that I ended up in this guy's car, and he scared me, so I jumped out."

Annie's mouth formed a perfect O. "Did you hurt yourself?"

"No, but I'm almost certain he drugged me, and I feel really, really sick."

"You do look kind of green, and your hair... Never mind." She plastered on a perky smile. "I can fix it up for you before we leave. You don't have to stay here, right? I brought you yoga pants and a comfy sweater, and Kayla's going to meet with Marnie Blake and her husband-to-be so I can take you home."

Kayla was the third member of our small team, twenty years old and a little too enthusiastic at times.

"Kayla knows we can't do the live swans, right? I checked, and it's just not possible to train them to carry baskets in their beaks."

"Absolutely, it's a no on the swans. Kayla promised to look into alternatives. Maybe dogs."

Marnie Blake had originally planned on having flower girls, but a falling out with her future sister-in-law meant Daisy and Petunia's services had been withdrawn. Marnie desperately wanted to give the woman the finger as she walked down the aisle, hence her outlandish ideas for the girls' replacements. We'd already vetoed monkeys and micro pigs, and I dreaded to think what she'd come up with next.

"Dogs? I guess, but what if—"

Annie held up a hand. "Stop! You shouldn't even be thinking about work today. Everything's under control. You seriously think a guy drugged you? Did you speak to the cops?"

"As soon as I woke up."

"Maybe they'll catch him." She gave her head a little shake because she didn't really believe that. Not after her experiences with her ex. "In the meantime, forget all about what happened, and let's get you home. Dwelling on the bad things never helps. How does sushi and a movie sound?"

Awful. I wasn't hungry, and I'd never be able to concentrate on a movie.

"Perfect."

"Then I'll drop you at home so you can take a shower while I pick up dinner from Sushito. Maki rolls, kaiso nigiri, and mango ice cream mochi?"

"Don't forget the edamame beans."

Annie gave a mock salute, and the peridot ring I gifted her for her birthday flashed under the strip lights. Her birthstone. Born on August thirteenth, and when that date fell on a Friday, she took the day off and stayed in bed.

"I never do, boss."

***

"Maria? It's Kimberly."

With Annie on her way to pick up our food, I had fifteen minutes to speak to Maria and find out what the hell happened last night before my assistant came back and chastised me for living in the past. Her attitude was my own fault. I'd said exactly the same thing to her so many times after she escaped from her ex, and now she'd adopted it as her own personal mantra.

"Kimmy!" Maria sounded larger than life, as usual. In reality, she was five feet one and a size two. At six inches taller, I felt like a giant beside her, although I was slumped into an armchair in my living room right now. "How did it go last night? With that guy?"

"You saw me with a guy?"

Maria roared with laughter, and my head throbbed harder. Painkillers hadn't made much of a dent in the ache.

"You ask that after you ditched me for him? Can't say I blamed you though, hun. A hot invalid? I'd have wanted to take care of him too."

"An invalid?"

"The bandage on his arm? Hell, Kimmy, how much did you have to drink after I left?"

"I don't know. Uh, this is a bit embarrassing..."

"We've all been there. Remember right before my last wedding when I drank too many cosmos and fell off Marco's yacht?"

"I think he drugged me."

"What, the British guy? Like, you took coke?"

"Not coke. Something that sent me to sleep."

"A roofie?"

"Apparently not one of those. Wait! He was British?"

"He said he was on vacation." She put on a Bridget Jones-ish accent. "Or 'holiday.' Why do Brits use the wrong words for everything?"

"Technically, it was their language first."

"Forget language. He *drugged* you? OMG. He didn't..."

"No, thank goodness. I felt ill in his car and jumped out at a traffic light. Then he drove off with my purse and left me there."

"Do you need cash? A ride? New make-up?"

"I'm home now. Annie picked me up. But when I spoke to the police, I couldn't remember anything that happened, and I'm hoping you might be able to fill in some of the blanks."

"They're gonna catch the guy, right? No woman is safe while freaks like that are walking the streets. Or wine bars. You know what I mean."

"What did he look like?"

"As I said, he was wearing a bandage. Said he sprained his wrist snowboarding in Switzerland three weeks ago, and he couldn't drive his Porsche because it was a stick."

"Hair colour? Eye colour?"

"Brown hair, definitely. Quite dark. No idea about the eyes."

"Any distinguishing features?"

"Uh... He wore a Hermès belt."

"What shape was his face? Big nose? Small nose? Bushy eyebrows?"

"Sorry, I'm useless with faces. I remember thinking he was hot. Oh, and he drank sparkling water, which was kind of weird when he'd just bought us a bottle of champagne."

Bad with faces? No wonder Maria always married ugly rich guys. Perhaps she'd trained herself not to look at them over the years.

"Probably he needed to keep a clear head for assaulting me later."

"Oh, hun, I'm so sorry! What can I do to cheer you up? A spa day? Shopping?"

"It's sweet of you to offer, but I just want to piece together what happened."

"I wish I could help more, but when he came over and seemed interested in you, I didn't want to get in the way."

"Will you talk to the police if they call?"

"Sure I will. Maybe they can speak to the bartender too? Although the guy paid cash, I recall that much. He had a big roll of hundred-dollar bills."

"A *roll* of—"

"Oh, wait! I remember his name."

"You do? What was it?"

"Tim."

"Tim?"

That sounded so normal. Mind you, a potential rapist was hardly going to walk around calling himself Satan, was he?

"Yep, like Tim Burton."

"Did he mention his surname?"

"I'm not sure. Sorry. And probably Tim wasn't his real name either. In the movies, the bad guys always make something up."

Right. Except this wasn't the movies, this was my life. Ever since I was born, I'd been following somebody else's script, and just when I thought I might be able to write my own ending, a new scene reminded me I was nothing but a puppet here on Earth.

"I'll call you later in the week, okay? We need to go over the options for your wedding favours."

"Any time. Apart from Wednesday morning when I have yoga. Or Thursday lunchtime because I've got lunch with Don and some of his investors at the country club. Or my regular manicure slot between two and three on Friday. Any time apart from that."

"Friday at eleven a.m.?"

"Perfect."

CHAPTER 4 - KIMBERLY

GEORGETTE RILEY.

I searched for her on the internet while the locksmith ran up a massive bill. Front door, back door, garage—all of those keys had been in my purse. I'd spent last night on edge with my new phone in my hand, listening for anybody creeping around outside. The only good thing about an otherwise horrible day was the realisation that I'd left my car key in the office when I hitched a ride to the Park Plaza with Annie.

Georgette Riley had been a twenty-four-year-old retail assistant working at the make-up counter at JCPenney in Arlington before her disappearance two years ago. The last time anyone saw her alive, she'd been heading for the dance floor in Club Riviera, tipsy but not drunk according to the friends she'd been with. One girl thought she'd glimpsed Georgette later, dancing with a dark-haired man, but she couldn't be sure and he'd never come forward. The only certainty was that when the club closed at three o'clock in the morning, Georgette hadn't been in the building.

Her boyfriend at the time swore she hadn't come home, but several neighbours in their apartment building said they'd heard yelling earlier in the evening, and he admitted they'd had a fight before she went out. That the only reason she'd gone clubbing in the first place was a stupid argument over pizza toppings. Volatile, he'd called her. Flighty.

As Officer Leopold had said, the boyfriend had been the main suspect, although ultimately, the case fizzled out like a damp squib because with no body, foul play couldn't be proven. A small follow-up article a year later noted that Georgette had never contacted anyone, not even her parents or brother, and her bank account remained untouched.

Missing presumed dead.

Except for me, there was no "presumed" about it. I knew Georgette was dead, her life snuffed out in the back of a luxury car driven by a lethal Casanova.

I leaned back in my leather desk chair, hidden safely away from prying eyes in my home office. When Annie had offered to take my meetings this morning, I'd gratefully accepted, partly so I could catch up on sleep—which hadn't happened—but mostly so I could research Georgette in peace. That poor girl. How had she crossed paths with Tim or whatever his real name was?

Had he bought her a drink the way he did with me? Or offered her a lift home? Or had she genuinely liked the man, only for him to turn on her in the worst possible way? I'd never find out unless I could talk to her again, and I didn't have the first clue how to track down a dead woman. I was a wedding planner, not a detective. All I could do was hope the cops came up with a suspect.

Kayla gave me a sympathetic look when I shuffled into the office at lunchtime—a small, hesitant smile and apologetic gaze even though she had nothing to be sorry for. No, last night's events had been totally my fault. Annie had obviously filled her in on what happened, including how utterly stupid I'd been.

"Can I get you a coffee? Hot chocolate? Green tea? Fruit juice? Or a muffin? Some lunch?"

"I ate before I left home. Sorry, I should have stopped at Starbucks on the way."

"It's fine, honestly. I already had two lattes today." She paused, eyes searching my face. "How are you? Annie told me about... You know."

"You know me—I always bounce back."

At least on the surface. Inside, I'd been bottling up all my anger and fear and frustration for years. Anger that my parents had let me down. Fear that I'd be alone for the rest of my days with my strange gift. Frustration that I couldn't lead a normal life.

"Do you want a distraction? I need to find a pair of pure-white Falabella horses."

"Fala-what?"

"Like pygmy ponies."

Uh-oh. I had a bad feeling about this. "Marnie Blake?"

Kayla nodded and grimaced at the same time.

"I thought we were going with dogs?"

"Turns out that Marnie's fiancé got bitten by a shih-tzu when he was six, and he's been terrified of dogs ever since. Apparently he's got a scar and everything."

"So she wants ponies? Can they carry flowers? What happens if one of them poops in the aisle?"

"I guess we also need to order a shovel."

See? My life was a freaking disaster.

***

And the disaster only got more disastrous after lunch on Wednesday. One day since I'd woken up in the hospital, and I was trying to stay positive. At least I'd gotten plenty of exercise with the four trips I'd already made to Starbucks, even if the caffeine hadn't made a dent in my tiredness. Turned out getting drugged and nearly murdered plays havoc with a girl's sleep patterns.

"Kim, you've got a visitor." Kayla poked her head around my office door. She sat out front at the reception desk while I shared a room with Annie. We also had the meeting area for clients, a tiny kitchenette with a bathroom to the side, and a storage closet stuffed with everything from emergency shoes to superglue. "He's a cop."

Officer Leopold? I put down the dragon I was busy building out of paper clips and hurried out to meet him, only to stop short because this definitely wasn't the same policeman who'd visited me in the hospital. No, this guy was thirty-ish with dark-blond hair, a strong jaw, and eyes the colour of my ex-husband's expensive cognac.

He held out a hand and flashed a smile. "Sergeant Wyatt Banks."

I longed to wipe my sweaty palm on my skirt, but that would have been worse than just shaking his hand.

"Kimberly Jennings."

"Have you got a moment? It's to do with the incident the other night."

Well, what else would it be about? I always stuck to the speed limits, I never got parking tickets, and I'd only ever killed one person but that was years ago and a total accident.

Joey Dean.

I didn't even feel guilty about his death. Well, not after I got over my initial shock and thought rationally. Joey Dean had been a murderer. He'd pushed his girlfriend down the stairs in my freaking house, then claimed it was an accident and gotten away with it. How did I know that? Because Tiffany had whined about it every damn morning when I came down for breakfast.

Yes, yes, I know I shouldn't have bought a house with ghosts in it, but it only had two, and it was a foreclosure so I got a really good deal. And do you have any idea how difficult it is to find a place without spirits? The murdered hung around for years. Centuries even. At least Tiffany's and Margaret's deaths were relatively recent, so they understood modern life and we could have a relatively pleasant conversation. I'd toured one property with three native Americans standing semi-naked in the kitchen, and they just yelled non-stop in a language I couldn't understand. I got the gist of it from their waved gestures—*do your duty, slacker*—but in their case, it was impossible, even if I'd been willing.

As a member of the Electi, I'd been put on earth to get justice for those killed by another. Their souls got trapped, tethered to the spot where they died or sometimes an item like a car or bus or airplane if it was big enough, as if their cosmic energy or whatever made up their essence somehow became intertwined with that of the object they'd died closest to. Those who died of natural causes or self-inflicted accidents passed straight over to the other side for recycling.

Why were some souls stuck? Well, because they

were supposed to assist me and my fellow Electi. Our job was to track down the murderers and dispatch their black souls into oblivion, thereby freeing the tethered. If we didn't, the criminals got reincarnated while their poor victims hung around in limbo forever.

The trouble was, whoever created us hadn't banked on pesky things like laws and prisons, so I couldn't just go around killing people even if I'd wanted to. Which I didn't. Not only did I hate the sight of blood, I just wasn't cut out to be a deadly avenger. I liked Netflix and chill, not high kicks and kill.

Apart from Joey Dean, obviously.

But Sergeant Wyatt Banks didn't know that, so I pasted on a smile and invited him through to my office.

"Kayla, would you mind picking up a couple of Americanos—"

Banks cut in. "I won't be staying long."

"Don't worry, they're both for me." I turned back to Kayla. "Plus anything Sergeant Banks would like."

She grinned at him. "An espresso, perhaps? Since you're in a hurry."

"Okay, you've persuaded me."

In my office, I waved Banks into one of the visitors' chairs opposite my desk, where he looked a little uncomfortable amongst all the flowers and silver accents. I worked long hours and I wanted to feel at home, so I surrounded myself with lace and candles and delicate floral scents in an attempt to distract myself from the darker side of my life. Plus the brides-to-be loved it.

"Do you have any news?" I asked. He wouldn't have come otherwise, would he?

"Yes, but I'm afraid it's not what you want to hear."

"What do you mean?"

I grabbed a handful of paper clips out of habit and began twisting one. I'd started doing it as a child, a nervous reaction whenever my parents started arguing. As an adult, I'd tried progressing to copper wire and pliers in order to make jewellery, but in times of stress, paper clips were always my go-to.

"I double-checked your toxicology results, but the tests definitely didn't find anything apart from alcohol."

"What? How can that be? I've never felt all woozy like that before. Never!"

"I believe you. But these substances don't always show up. We can usually detect Rohypnol for twenty-four hours, depending on the dosage, but other drugs leave the body soon after you regain consciousness. GHB's another common one, but it occurs naturally in the central nervous system, and detecting an elevated level is something the hospital lab just can't handle."

"Then find someone who *can* handle it!"

"It's just not that straightforward, I'm afraid. A sophisticated forensic analysis in a case like this isn't in the department's budget."

"Money? You refuse to follow up because of money?"

"Not only money. I visited the hotel where you claim you met the man, and I couldn't find anybody who saw you with him."

"But the security cameras... What about the security cameras?"

"There weren't any."

"No way. The sign behind the desk specifically said there were."

"Yeah, I saw that too." Banks shrugged, apologetic it seemed. "I spoke to the manager, and the whole system malfunctioned last year. Something about a bug in the software update. It was out of warranty, so rather than fix it, they just put a big sign up telling people they were being recorded, and it's actually been more effective than having cameras in the first place."

"So there's nothing?"

"No video, no forensic evidence, no witnesses." Another shrug. "I talked with the assistant state's attorney, and he said there's no way they'd get a conviction, even if we did manage to track the guy down."

"Then that's it? You just give up? What happens if he does this again? Or worse? What happens if he murders someone?"

Like poor Georgette.

"Sorry. Believe me, I want to get men like that off the streets as much as you, but there's nothing more I can do at the moment."

"What if I paid for the extra tests?"

Might as well use Daddy's money for something useful. After all, I had plenty of it since he dished it out in lieu of love, time, or you know, actually being a father.

"You could do that, but even if one of them came back positive, we'd still have to find the perpetrator and prove he gave you the drug. Difficult with no witnesses. If we caught him with GHB, that would just be simple possession."

"What's the penalty for that?"

"Up to a year in prison or a thousand-dollar fine."

"A fine? He tried to kidnap me, and he'd get a fine?"

Banks held up both hands. "Hey, I'm on your side. I don't make the laws. Do you want me to ask the lab to keep ahold of the sample?"

He glanced at his watch. No, he may not make the laws, but he certainly had a hand in not enforcing them properly. Even if I somehow proved I'd been drugged, it was clear the case wouldn't be a priority.

"I guess. Can I think about the extra tests?"

"Sure. Here's my card. If you have any questions or remember something new, give me a call."

"I don't suppose anyone found my purse?"

"Nobody handed it in at the hotel."

Perhaps my usual approach of sticking my head in the sand was the right one. Over the years, I'd become deaf to the cries of the dead, aided in no small part by the expensive noise-cancelling headphones I wore whenever I went out for a walk alone. Georgette's was just one more voice among thousands.

But right now, it was louder than all the others put together.

Banks inched towards the door. "Unless there's anything else..."

"No, no. You go. I've got your card."

And his espresso too, seeing as Kayla returned half a minute after he left. I sipped it while pondering my latest dilemma. What, if anything, should I do next?

CHAPTER 5 - KIMBERLY

"DO YOU WANT to go out for dinner tonight?" Annie asked on Friday.

"Not really."

"Too soon?"

"Too soon."

I didn't want to cook either. Or go home. Even with new locks and an alarm system, I still felt nervous in my own house. Last night, I'd lain awake until five a.m. watching infomercials for make-up and exercise programs and blenders. I may have bought a waffle maker I'd probably never use. At the end of it all, I'd managed two hours of sleep, and I was strongly considering taking my laptop and working at Starbucks.

But first, I had my meeting with Maria to get through.

She arrived at ten past eleven, late as usual, but she'd brought a bag from the Red Door Deli down the street, so I'd have forgiven her for anything.

"Is that a strawberry cheesecake muffin?"

She held up the loot. "*Two* strawberry cheesecake muffins."

"I know I said I'd never fall in love again, but..."

Maria laughed as we walked through to the meeting area. Our offices had once been part of a hotel, and although we were only on the first floor, we had a good view over a nearby park. I'd lived on the outskirts of Bethesda my whole life, and until now, I'd never considered leaving. Tim had really messed with my head, more than I wanted to admit, and coming from a woman who had a hotline to the dead, that meant a lot.

"So, wedding favours..." I started as I settled into one of the leather armchairs. "You still want the little statues to match the cake topper?"

The little gold statues of the happy couple, Oscar-style. At least the cake was tasteful—plain white with a swath of red up one side in homage to Don's Hollywood roots. He'd lived out there for a few years, but apparently the climate and an abundance of soy lattes and traffic jams disagreed with him.

"Yes, the statues, plus a lifetime subscription to the movie-streaming service Donnie's invested in, make-up from Sephora for the ladies, and cashmere socks for the men. Do you like cashmere socks? Donnie's brother owns the company that makes them. I'll get you some."

"Uh, thanks."

"And the flowers. Do you have the options for those?"

"Absolutely. If you want to stick with the red-and-gold theme, we can build the arrangements around roses—the florist says he can dip white roses in gold glitter to add a touch of sparkle." I clicked my mouse, and the first picture popped up onto the screen opposite us. "Now, roses are the obvious choice for red, but tulips or gerbera are other options. Or you could stick with white—phalaenopsis orchids, perhaps—and add colour with ribbons. Then there's this example, using a jewelled metal cage..."

We settled on white roses in a gold cage with red ribbons, then moved on to the food. Meat, fish, vegetarian, vegan, fruitarian, gluten-free—Maria wanted it all.

"And don't forget Meredith Thompson's coming again, and she hates anything green." How could I forget? She'd freaked out over parsley at wedding number two. "And Stephanie Monroe won't eat slimy food."

"Slimy?"

"No sauce, jus, foams, emulsions, gravy, coulis, or ice cream in case it melts."

Perhaps we could send out for a burger. "Got it. I'll relay that to the catering company. Shall I arrange a tasting for next week?"

"Please."

"And we're fitting around yoga and your manicure again?"

"Plus we're in New York on Tuesday because Donnie has a meeting. Do you want anything from Madison Avenue?"

I still hadn't used the Prada purse she brought me back last time. Maria had a heart of gold, and she liked to share the spoils from her divorces, even if she could be a little abrasive at times.

"I appreciate you offering, but I have plenty of accessories now." A yawn escaped. "Sorry."

"Tired?"

"I didn't sleep well last night."

"Oh! I should have asked. How are you after the thing on Sunday night? Did the police find that guy?" She rummaged through her purse and dropped a bottle into my lap. "Here, try these."

"Ambien? Aren't they prescription only?"

"Yeah, but don't worry—I've got loads on account of Don snores. The guy? Did the police get him?"

"No, and they've given up." I gave her a quick recap of my conversation with Sergeant Banks the day before yesterday. "I'm tempted to take out an ad in the *Bethesda Gazette* just to warn people."

"Hell, you should try the *Washington Post*. Don't they realise there's a maniac out there? It's about time somebody took women's safety seriously. Tim was smooth—I bet he's drugged women before. And who knows what he'll do in the future."

"That's my fear too. Well, that and the fact he knows where I live."

"Holy shit. How?"

"I think he has my purse. It disappeared."

"What if he comes to your house? The cops should sit outside or something. Where do all our tax dollars go?"

"I don't know."

"Checking for parking violations, that's where. I got two fines last week. First, we pay the police to write the tickets, then we pay them again or they impound our cars."

"Have you considered parking in a legal space?"

Maria trilled with laughter. "Not when I'm wearing five-inch pumps, hun. Okay, okay, I've got a solution. We'll hire you a bodyguard."

"I've had the locks changed. I don't need Kevin Costner sitting outside."

Hmm, on second thought... I screwed up my face a bit, regretting my words since having a young Kevin Costner outside wasn't actually a bad idea.

"You're more of a Gerard Butler girl? We could hold auditions."

"No. No bodyguard." A shame, but what would my neighbours say? I already got enough strange looks because I lived alone in a big house, without having the Terminator's baby brother watching over me.

"Hun, if anything happens to you, my wedding's gonna be screwed, so we have to fix this. How about a private detective? Like Sherlock Holmes. Are you a fan of Benedict Cumberbatch?"

A PI? It wasn't Maria's worst idea ever. No, that was reserved for wedding number one when a fear of VPL had led her to go without panties. Except after a few glasses of champagne at the reception, she forgot and hooked her leg over her beloved's arm at the end of the first dance and gave half the room an eyeful, including the groom's mother. The whole incident was immortalised on film, and I'd had to supervise while the cameraman deleted every single frame. The only saving grace was that Maria had been too drunk to get embarrassed.

"I can hire one for you." She pulled her phone out before I had a chance to answer. "Let's find a guy right now."

"You don't need to do that."

"Like I said... Hey, there's hundreds. What we need is pictures."

"No, we need recommendations. And I can pay for myself. You don't have to keep buying me stuff."

"It's Donnie's money. He's got so much of it, he doesn't even notice."

"If we do this, I'm paying."

"Suit yourself. How about... Ugh, no. He's wearing a

toupee."

"What about his credentials?"

"I'll try the next one."

"This isn't a fashion show. I don't care what he looks like. Or she. Do any of them have testimonials?"

"They write those things themselves. Do you know anyone who's used a private detective?"

No, but I did know an actual detective. Banks. Could I call him? He'd seemed so dismissive before, and I worried he'd think I was stupid for trying to dig into this myself. But what about Officer Leopold? He'd seemed genuinely sympathetic, and I didn't worry so much about him judging me.

"Hold on. I'll make a call."

Without Leopold's direct number, I phoned the precinct and asked to speak to him. Luckily, he was at his desk, in the midst of eating by the sounds of it. If he helped, I'd have to send him a box of donuts as a thank-you gift.

"Miss Jennings? I heard about the toxicology test. I'm sorry we couldn't do more."

He sounded worried, as if I were going to ask him to take on the case by himself. At least I could allay his fears.

"I appreciate everything you've done, but I'm hoping to engage a private detective. One who can look further into my case. I was hoping you might know of somebody."

Somebody who wouldn't rip me off.

"An investigator?"

"Yes."

"That won't be cheap."

His unspoken words? *And it's a hopeless cause.*

Well, he didn't know about Georgette, did he?

"I understand that, but I still want to try. I'm just worried about hiring someone who isn't up to the job. Can you help with a recommendation? Or do you know of anyone else who might be able to?"

A long silence followed. Then I heard rustling and footsteps, as if Leopold had moved out into the hallway.

"There is one person I can think of," he said.

"Who?"

"An ex-cop. He was good. The best investigator we had. But there were some problems a while back, and he quit."

"Quit? Or got fired?"

"Quit. His sister was dating Sergeant Banks. I believe you two met?"

"He came to my office."

"Anyhow, Banks had an...indiscretion. It left Cullen in a difficult position in the department. When Banks got promoted, Cullen handed in his resignation."

"Because he couldn't play nicely with others?" I wasn't sure I wanted to deal with a man like that.

Leopold's voice dropped to a whisper. "None of this came from me, okay?"

"I promise I won't say a word."

"Banks refused to admit he'd done anything wrong. I don't know all the details, but whatever happened, it was bad enough that Cullen's sister fled the state. She contacted him every so often, and each time she did, he'd take off to try and find her. Banks gave him a disciplinary for unauthorised absence."

"That seems a little harsh."

"Like I said, you didn't hear it from me. Anyhow, Reed Cullen's good as long as you can put up with him running off to Virginia or Pennsylvania or Delaware whenever he gets a message from Emma."

"Why? Isn't she a grown-up?"

"Yes, but she's also his little sister, and he's felt responsible for her ever since their mom left."

"What about their father?"

"No longer around, as far as I know." Just like mine. "But I really shouldn't discuss his personal matters. Do you want Cullen's number or not?"

"Uh..." I glanced over at the big screen where Maria was busy scrolling through a website on which every candidate looked like a bad cliché, from the sunglasses to the hands-on-hips postures to the all-black attire. "Yes, please. I'd like the number."

CHAPTER 6 - REED

"HELLO?"

ONE WORD from the woman's mouth and I swallowed back a groan. Words that sprang to mind from her tone? Entitled. Confident. Bitch.

"Yes?"

"Reed Cullen?"

"That's me."

Three guesses: cheating spouse, one of the household staff was stealing shit, or she'd lost a pet. Probably a cat. Women like that always had cats.

"Good. A mutual acquaintance suggested you might be able to help with a problem."

"Which mutual acquaintance?"

"Officer Leopold with the Montgomery County PD."

Jerry Leopold? I hadn't seen him for over a year now, but I liked the old guy. He'd been as disillusioned with the department as me, although he'd decided to stick it out until retirement.

"Go on."

"My friend needs to find a man."

"This friend have a name?"

"Kimberly Jennings."

Nope, never heard of her. "And who are you?"

"Maria Fitzgerald."

"Conrad Fitzgerald's wife?"

"Ex-wife." An uncustomary pause. "You know who I am?"

"Lady, the whole of Bethesda knows who you are. You make the gossip pages every week."

Not to mention the fact that Congressman Fitzgerald had engaged me in an attempt to prove his wife was doing the dirty after getting caught with his own pants down. I was ninety percent sure she'd been faithful, although I'd long suspected the devious ex-Mrs. Fitzgerald had hired the call girl her husband was found with.

Tread carefully, Cullen.

On the plus side, the bitch—I'd been right in my initial assessment—had money, and I sure needed some of that.

Maria laughed, loud enough that I held the phone away from my ear. "I suppose I do get photographed a lot."

"Who's this man your friend needs to find?"

An ex? An AWOL employee? Or just a date for the evening? I choked back my own laugh at the thought of the last prospect since I hadn't had a shower in three days or a haircut in six months. Life was all about priorities, and living in my car, I didn't have a roommate around to complain about the smell.

"Someone drugged her in a bar on Sunday evening, and the police haven't made the progress we hoped for."

"Let me guess—cutbacks?"

"Can you help?"

"Did he assault her?"

"No, she thinks he tried to kidnap her. She remembers being in a car, but she jumped out. And because the toxicology report didn't show anything and the camera system in the bar was broken, the police have given up."

"If the tox screen was clear, how does she know she was drugged? What if she only drank too much?"

"She just knows, okay? Besides, she's practically teetotal. She was the only person at my last wedding who didn't get drunk."

I heard a quiet but indignant voice in the background. "Because I was your *wedding planner*, Maria."

Maria was with a wedding planner? "Are you getting hitched again?"

"In two and a half months. Do you want the job or not?"

"What's your goal with this? If I find the guy, what then?"

"What do you mean?"

"Do you want to build a case and pass the evidence to the police? Go to the man's employer? Have a quiet word?"

"We were thinking of a full-page ad in the *Washington Post*. Unless you can arrange for him to have an accident. Do you do that sort of thing?"

"I run a legitimate business here, lady."

At least, I did when there was a possibility of entrapment.

"Fine, so we'll stick with the naming and shaming. When can you start?"

"I haven't said I'll take the job yet." But I knew I would. I didn't have any choice. Since a recent client bad-mouthed me all over the internet in a hysterical reaction to finding out that her husband's mistress was in fact her sister, the phone had been worryingly quiet. And my wallet was almost empty. If I didn't work, I didn't eat—simple as that. "How about I drive over and meet with you tomorrow? We can discuss things further."

Such as my fees. A case like that—finding a stranger from a bar—could be a straightforward, half-day job or a never-ending, money-sucking nightmare. And the pauper inside me secretly wished for the latter.

"I'm not available tomorrow." Frantic whispers sounded through the phone. "But Kim is. You can come to her office. I'll text you the details."

"Ten o'clock?"

More whispers. "Don't be late."

**

At seven a.m., I rolled up my sleeping bag and stuffed it into the rear footwell. Ice had formed on the inside of the windows overnight—I'd had to keep breathing, unfortunately—which meant I had to waste precious gas heating the interior of the car. Another six dollars went on the entrance fee for the gym, not because I wanted to work out—I barely had the energy for that this week—but because I needed a shower. I could hardly walk into the office of Maria Fitzgerald's fucking wedding planner stinking of yesterday's fast food, could I?

I know the question you're asking. Believe me, I'd asked it myself many times by that point. How the hell did a guy who spent five years in the US Army and another five in the police force, both good careers, end up with nothing?

The answer was simple.

Emma.

Emma Cullen, my little sister. The rose in my heart and the thorn in my side since I was five years old. Now, at thirty, I loved and hated her in equal measure, but above all, I wanted to find her. Over two years had passed since we last spoke. A thirty-second phone call made from a truck stop near Baltimore where she'd tearily explained that she couldn't stand living in Bethesda anymore and begged me to leave her alone to make a fresh start.

At first, I thought she'd left because of the argument with Wyatt. My ex-best friend, the guy I'd known since we were in elementary school, and the one man I thought I could trust to look after the only family I had left. And the guy she claimed had cheated on her.

Then I found out about the debts.

And the drugs.

My sweet sister, the girl I'd walked to ballet lessons every Tuesday when I was a teenager, had been addicted to coke. And Wyatt knew. He fucking knew, and he didn't tell me.

Emma had skipped town owing thousands to some of the most dangerous players around, and I'd used all of my savings to pay them off. Because if I hadn't and she ever came back, she'd be a dead woman the second she passed the city limits, and the assholes would have made my life pretty damn difficult too. In their eyes, one Cullen was as good as another when it came to getting their cash.

Now? Now, I was free, or as free as a man could be with fifty bucks in his pocket and a credit card abused to its limit.

Showered, shaved, and wearing my last pair of clean jeans, I found a parking space a block from Kimberly Jennings's office and set off in the bitter wind. Living in my car wouldn't have been so bad in the summer—hell, I'd slept under the stars often enough during my time in the army—but in the winter? Even after a hot shower, I hadn't fully regained the feeling in my fingers and toes, and I'd forgotten what it was like to be warm.

The reception area of Just Imagine Events lay deserted when I peered through the glass panel in the door, but when I knocked, a slim blonde hurried through from the back. Dainty-looking. Nervous. She bit her lip as she pulled the door open.

"Reed Cullen?"

"That's right."

She let out the breath she'd been holding. "Thank goodness. I was worried you might have changed your mind."

I checked my watch. Five to ten. "I'm not late."

"I know that, but... Thank you. Thank you for coming."

After the call yesterday, I'd been expecting another woman of Maria's ilk, but Kimberly seemed a complete contrast on first impressions. Timid instead of brash, soft instead of hard, sweet instead of...slightly scary, if I was honest. I pitied Maria's new husband.

Kimberly motioned me forward into a room straight out of Barbie's dreams and my nightmares. White leather chairs with chrome legs, fluffy sheepskin rugs, candles, mirrors, and flowers, flowers, everywhere. My dick shrivelled in protest.

"Please, take a seat. Would you like coffee? Usually,

I go to Starbucks, but there's nobody else here, and... We have a Keurig in the kitchenette. Or fruit tea? Or water? Or—"

"Coffee's good. Thanks."

"How do you take it? I've got cream, skimmed milk, hazelnut syrup... The caramel ran out yesterday."

"Just black. No sugar."

She hurried off, her movements jerky. Was she always this twitchy? Or had the "problem," as Maria had so eloquently put it, left Kimberly running scared?

While she was gone, I took a better look at the room. Shit, I needed a haircut. Seeing myself reflected from five different angles made me realise just how untidy I was. Any longer and I'd be one of those guys with the ponytail. But back to the room... Real flowers. Real silver dish filled with fancy mints. Real nice view over the park on the corner. How much did an office like this cost? More than any place I'd ever lived in, that was for sure. The furniture was high end—nothing cheap here—and I checked behind me in case I'd tracked dirt over the cream carpet. My boots weren't designed for this level of sterility.

"Here you go."

Kimberly bustled back in and set a tray on the coffee table. Asymmetrical cups with handles stuck on at odd angles. Figured. Still, it was hot, as was the room. She'd heated the whole suite to tropical temperatures, probably to stop herself from freezing in that linen dress. It didn't even have sleeves. How long could I make this meeting last? If I played my cards right, my feet might finally thaw out.

"Thanks." I blew away the steam and warmed my hands on the cup. "So, do you want to start from the beginning? Maria didn't give many details on the phone."

"Okay, but there's not much to tell. Not that I can remember, I mean."

She was right. There really wasn't much. Just the vague description from her friend and a bandage on his wrist. The lack of working security cameras at the hotel would be a problem because even if I managed to track the guy, proving what he did would be difficult. Everyone was fucking cost-cutting nowadays.

"Where did the cops pick you up?"

"I have no idea. Nobody said exactly. Just that it was by the side of a road somewhere."

"We need to find out."

"Why does it matter?"

Prim. That was the word to describe her. Prim and a little frosty. Matched the decor.

"Because right now, we only know of two places for certain that this asshole, sorry, this guy—Tim?"

"Yes, Tim."

"The invisible man."

"Huh?"

"T.I.M. The invisible man. Wonder if he picked that name for a reason? Did you ever read the novel by H.G. Wells?"

"What? No."

I liked to read, the classics mainly. Better than watching TV. The whole planet was falling apart with wars and famines and politicians pitting one side of the country against the other. Ever read Orwell's *1984*? Because that's what the world felt like these days.

"Never mind. As I was saying, we only know of two places where this guy's been. The hotel, where nobody except your friend has admitted to seeing him, and the place you got out of his car."

"Somebody must know where that was."

"Who's dealing with the case? Did Leopold pass it on to someone in the Investigative Services Bureau?"

"Wyatt Banks. Sergeant Wyatt Banks."

Shit. The one person in the department I didn't want to speak to, and even if I did ask him for help, he wouldn't go out of his way to provide it. I'd have to channel my request through Leopold and hope he could get me some information.

"Okay."

"Officer Leopold mentioned you had personal problems with Banks?"

Officer Leopold had a big fucking mouth.

"It's in the past."

"Will it cause a problem?"

Yes. "No, no problems."

"Then you'll take the job?"

"Forty-five bucks an hour plus expenses." That was on the low side, but I couldn't afford for her to go elsewhere. If she balked, I'd go down to forty. "And I'd need an up-front retainer."

"How much?"

"A thousand bucks."

"Will you take a cheque?"

She wasn't going to negotiate?

"A cheque works for me. You realise this could get expensive if you want to see it through to the end? Finding a person who doesn't want to be found takes time."

A truth I knew all too well from my experiences with Emma. If she'd just phone me and have a proper conversation, I could convince her to come back, but she'd more or less cut me off. Was she embarrassed? Guilty? I'd tried to tell her that I'd paid her debts off and Bethesda was safe for her again, but she refused to talk about the difficult stuff. Other than that single call right after she left, I hadn't heard her voice at all. She'd texted, telling me she'd got a job and not to worry, but after what happened with Wyatt, I worried about her every damn day. Often, the only way I knew she was alive was because she still spent money from her bank account. Not much, just some groceries every few months, and occasionally she'd visit a mall to buy clothes. Emma always had preferred cash. Didn't trust banks or the internet after she watched some program on identity theft when she was a teenager, but I still deposited money for her whenever I had any to spare. I'd even left messages for her in the reference field. *Call me. We need to talk.* But she never did.

Still, Kimberly Jennings didn't seem to care about the difficulties in tracking a person down.

"Yes, I understand it might be difficult. Could you just keep me updated on the billing?"

"Always do. Where should I send the contract?"

"Here." Kimberly passed over a white business card embossed with gold text. Expensive-looking. The gold matched the necklace she wore—a flat, odd-shaped piece covered in strange symbols. Swirls and swooshes and pictures that reminded me of hieroglyphics.

I pointed at it. "Egyptian?"

"What?" She followed my gaze, blushing until she realised I wasn't staring at her cleavage, not that I could see much because she'd covered it up. "The necklace? I don't know. It was a gift from my mother."

"She's got good taste."

"Thank you." Kimberly stood, dismissing me. "I'll email the contract right back. I appreciate your coming, Mr. Cullen."

Well, that was easier than I'd thought. Frosty or not, if she wanted to put in the money, I'd put in the hours. Time to go hunt an invisible man.

CHAPTER 7 - REED

ACCORDING TO JERRY Leopold, Kimberly Jennings had been found lying on a grass verge beside Juniper Avenue, half-hidden by a bush, wearing one high-heeled pump and a pale-pink dress totally inappropriate for the weather. No surprise there. Leopold had been first on the scene—again, no surprise because Dunkin' Donuts was only a half mile farther along the road.

Kimberly's other shoe lay near a set of traffic lights at a lonely intersection, a T-junction bordered by a derelict warehouse on one side and an undeveloped lot on the other. The area had been earmarked for regeneration years ago, but a lack of funds meant the Bethesda Urban Partnership's vision remained a pipe dream. If I recalled correctly, the lights had only been installed after a trio of fatalities caused by drivers pulling out into the path of speeding vehicles.

The shoe's location suggested Kimberly had staggered about twenty yards before collapsing, and the medics estimated she hadn't been there longer than half an hour or hypothermia would have set in. Factoring in the distance to the Park Plaza Hotel—a fifteen-minute drive—she'd been abducted between half-past nine and ten o'clock.

Guess Tim had planned on getting an early night,

the sick fucker.

On Sunday morning, I checked my armpits passed the sniff test then drove to a cheque-cashing place, not only because I needed food and gas, but because bribes were a necessary evil in my world. People answered questions far more readily when a crisp twenty was involved.

My hope lay farther back along Juniper in the motley collection of stores clustered around what had once been a popular bar until the owner got arrested for drowning his wife in the bath and the place closed down. I'd pulled that case, one of my last, and it might have been ruled an accident if not for the fractured hyoid bone in her neck. The guy died in prison.

Now the Moon Dog Tavern lay crumbling, its lopsided sign squeaking in the breeze. The subject of an inheritance dispute, or so I'd heard. Next door, Ed's Food & Liquor wasn't due to open for another fifteen minutes, but the neon sign from Dunkin' Donuts glowed beyond. With cash in my wallet, I figured a bear claw was an excellent way to start the morning, and I could check for any watchful eyes while I was at it.

But I was unlucky. The camera outside angled down into the parking lot and only caught the edge of the road. The blonde behind the counter called her friend who'd worked the late shift the previous week, but she'd been so engrossed in schoolwork between customers, she hadn't even noticed the ambulance drive past with its red lights flashing.

"Try Ed next door," the blonde suggested, topping up my coffee. "He's always sticking his nose in where it doesn't belong."

"Care to give me an example?"

"My boyfriend was here late the other night, just sitting at the counter waiting for me to clear up because some punk spilled soda everywhere, and Ed called my manager to complain that Mason was in here after hours. Kept going on and on about debauchery and the lack of morals in today's youth."

Ed was gonna love me, then. Maybe I should have put on a button-down shirt and gotten a haircut in preparation.

He glowered when I walked in, eyes tracking me around the store as I added food to my basket. Crackers, cheese, pre-grilled chicken, apples, bottled water. Nothing that required cooking. I tried to stay healthy, donuts aside, but it wasn't easy with no fridge and no kitchen.

"That's it?" he asked when I stacked my purchases on the counter.

"Yessir."

"Twenty-three dollars and eighteen cents."

"There is one other thing."

Ed huffed and rolled his eyes. Service with a smile.

"I'm a private investigator working on a case in the area, and I was wondering if you saw anything unusual last Sunday?"

"At night, you mean? Are you talking about that drunk girl who fell out of the car?"

"Not drunk. She'd been drugged."

"Drugs, you say? That's even worse. Back in my day, we never took none of those illegal substances. Work of the devil, they are."

"No, she hadn't been taking drugs. Somebody put them in her drink then tried to kidnap her."

"Drinking's the reason why our country's in such

bad shape. All those kids, off their heads on alcohol. And just look at the place next door! A goldarn eyesore, it is."

"She was drinking juice." Sometimes, little white lies were the way to go. "Somebody spiked it."

"A man?"

I sighed because I knew where this was going. Mind you, even if I'd said it was a woman, fifty bucks said I'd have gotten a lecture on the evils of homosexuality.

"Yes, a man."

"Young women shouldn't put themselves about like that." See? "They only bring trouble on themselves."

"I understand that, sir, but at the moment, I'm more interested in catching the person who tried to abduct her. Did you happen to see anything?"

"Naw, I didn't see nothing. My wife told me what happened the next day. Her friend's husband's sister works at the police station, and she said the girl couldn't even stand up."

"Do you have any security cameras here?"

Old Ed reached under the counter and came back with a shotgun, which he waved in my general direction. I wasn't sure whether to duck or run.

"Who needs all that modern technology when a good ol' Remington does the same job? Ain't nobody gonna steal from my store."

I backed slowly towards the door, clutching my grocery sack, because the guy was obviously fucking crazy. "Thanks for your time."

"Try Luigi at the Italian restaurant. He's got one of those fancy security systems. Japanese. That's what's wrong with America nowadays. Foreigners come over here, taking our jobs, and..."

I left Ed and his gun to their conversation and headed back to my car to drop off the food. The only two places left were the Styles & Smiles hair salon and the restaurant Ed had mentioned, both on the other side of the Moon Dog Tavern.

When I checked the opening times in the window, the salon was closed all day on Sunday, so I figured I could rule it out as a source of potential witnesses. Nor were there any cameras in sight there. Luigi's was in darkness too, although a small sign said the place opened for lunch and dinner. Still only half-past eleven. I'd have to sit it out in my car.

The waiting was the worst part of this job. As a cop, I'd always had something to do, even if it was only paperwork. But working alone, often on one case at a time, I got bored. I missed the variety. I missed the camaraderie of Investigative Services. Sometimes, I even missed Wyatt.

Hell, now I sounded like a girl.

I turned on the radio to drown out past regrets and munched on an apple until Luigi's opened. I'd never eaten there before, probably because it was the kind of place you took a date and I didn't have a girlfriend. My last serious relationship fizzled out while I was in the army. After my first deployment, she complained I'd changed, after the second, we barely spoke, and when I came home after the third, I found she'd moved out. Gone back home to live with her parents, or so the note said. I'd tried dating while I was a cop, but the job always seemed more important. And now? Fucking in the back seat was for teenagers, not a thirty-year-old man, and I barely had the money to buy my own dinner let alone a woman's too.

A light in the restaurant turned on, and it was time to get to work. A tall, dark-haired guy waved from behind the bar when I walked inside. Luigi? No, Mario. I saw that from his name tag when I got closer.

"Table for..." He leaned to the side to check behind me. "One?"

"Is the owner around?"

"Is there a problem?"

"Not here. I'm a private investigator, and last Sunday—"

"That girl? The one they found by the lights? People said she was drunk, but I said at the time I didn't believe it. I mean, what kind of girl walks all the way into the middle of nowhere after a drink or two? She'd go the other way, no? Back towards town?"

"Yes, it's about the girl, and no, she wasn't drunk. It was an attempted abduction."

"Luigi. Luigi! Come here." An unintelligible stream of Italian followed in both directions. "He's coming. You want a drink? On the house? We have good coffee, better than the donut place along the street." He wrinkled his nose. "Espresso?"

Who needed sleep, anyway?

"Espresso would be good."

Luigi appeared, as plump as Mario was thin, and held out a floury hand for me to shake. "Luigi."

"Good to meet you."

"Mario said you are an investigator?"

"That's right."

"We didn't see anything. If we had, we would've told the police."

"I'm more interested in your cameras." I pointed at one on a pole in the parking lot, facing towards the street. "Especially that one."

"We already watched them. She didn't walk past. She must have come from the other direction."

"No, she was in a car, and it drove past here."

The two men looked at each other.

"I didn't think of that," Mario said. "My wife's hairdresser's friend knows a cop, and he said she walked there."

"Sometimes things get misheard." Or plain made up.

"The recordings are on my computer," Luigi said. "Please, come through to the office."

"The office" turned out to be a grandiose term for a cupboard, too small to fit more than a desk and a chair, but the two men squashed in there alongside me, and Luigi shoved some papers aside to balance a tray with three tiny cups next to the keyboard. The monitor was split into quadrants, each displaying the feed from a different camera—one covering the front, one at the rear, and two wide-angles inside the restaurant itself.

"Nice system."

"We bought it after the burglary last year. Someone stole our panini grill. What kind of *stronzo* steals a panini grill?"

"The police didn't catch them?"

Luigi flung up his hands. "They did nothing. Nothing! And I guess they're not looking into this abduction either if you're here and they're not."

"They tend to go for the easy wins nowadays."

"The whole world is *andando all'inferno*."

"Going to hell," Mario translated. "The world is going to hell."

Tell me something I didn't know. "Can we start

reviewing the footage from a quarter to ten?"

"Of course."

"Will it zoom in on the road?"

"Like this?"

"Can it go any tighter?"

"*Mi spiace*, this is as close as it goes."

Luckily, the street outside was well-lit, and at that distance and angle, I was able to make out the forms of the occupants in the vehicles whizzing past. The shades of their clothes were visible, but I couldn't see the detail of their faces. Worse, I couldn't read the licence plates either. Still, I had to take whatever information I could get, and if I was able to narrow down the make and model of the car to a handful of possibles, that could only help. Kimberly had been wearing pink, and according to Maria, Tim had been wearing a suit with a light-blue shirt.

"We're looking for two occupants, a dark-haired male wearing black and light blue in the driver's seat, and a brunette female in pale pink on the passenger side."

Luigi put on a pair of glasses, and the two men leaned forward as the footage played. Cars rolled past, most slowing for the upcoming bend. A white pickup, single occupant. A sky-blue compact, woman at the wheel judging by the bouffant of platinum hair. A green SUV, two occupants, both black. After half an hour, our drinks were cold, but we had three possibles.

"Can you play those ones again? Nine fifty-one, nine fifty-seven, and ten oh-two."

Nine fifty-one drove past, a burgundy SUV. Could that be Kimberly? The hair on the woman was the right length—past her shoulders.

"I think I know who that is," Luigi said.

Good or bad news. "Who?"

"Pastor Osmond and his wife. I recognise the decals in the side window. They're for his church."

Well, at least we'd ruled one suspect out.

Nine fifty-seven was another SUV, black or maybe dark blue as it drove under the streetlights. A definite possible. Same for ten oh-two, a big black sedan. Both had the right clothes and the right skin and hair colours.

But if I were a betting man, I'd pick ten oh-two. Something about the girl's posture was off. She'd slumped to the side while nine fifty-seven was sitting straighter.

"Can you make me copies of both of those? I have a memory stick."

"No problem."

"Play them back one more time?"

I almost missed it. At nine fifty-eight, a group of people gathered around the glowing Luigi's sign on the left-hand side of the parking lot, right in the corner of the screen. At ten oh-two, they were still there, and it looked an awful lot like one of them had a camera. What were they doing? Taking pictures of themselves for Instagram?

"Do you know who that group was?"

Mario nodded enthusiastically. "*Si, si*. They were here for a birthday party. Hundreds of dollars, they spent, and we made a giant tiramisu with candles that spelled out the name Britt."

"I need to contact them. See the camera?"

He squinted at the screen. "A clue?"

"A clue."

"They booked the table in advance. I have a phone number in the booking system. Would you like a pizza?"

"A pizza?"

"For lunch. It's lunchtime now. Twelve o'clock?"

And by the sounds of the clinking cutlery and soft chatter outside, they had more staff who were already serving diners. I didn't want to offend the dude, and pizza was my favourite food, so I figured taking twenty minutes to eat wouldn't hurt.

"Not gonna say no to that."

CHAPTER 8 - REED

"BRITT" TURNED OUT to be Brittney Lightfoot, according to a reverse lookup of her phone number, a twenty-one-year-old student at DeVry University. I figured I'd try phoning her because I didn't want to freak her out by turning up on her doorstep and risk getting arrested by Wyatt. He'd probably love that.

"My name's Reed Cullen, and—"

"The pool guy?"

"I'm sorry?"

"Rachel's pool guy? Reed?"

"No, I'm not a pool guy. I'm a private investigator."

Her squeal hurt my ears. "Are you serious?"

"Yes."

"Ooh, that's so— Wait! Why are you calling me? If it's about the weed, I swear I thought it was tobacco and I didn't have a clue until I smelled the smoke, and —"

"I'm not calling about weed."

"Then what do you want?"

"I understand that last week, you went out for a birthday dinner at Luigi's? One of your friends—"

"Mandy? I told her not to take that little statue thing. You know, the Pisa tower? But she said nobody would notice, and if we're gonna get into trouble, I'll totally make her put it back."

"It's not about the statue either. You were taking photos by the sign outside, and—"

"That freaking camera! The guy said it was legit, I swear. Like, he got two the same as Christmas gifts and that was the only reason he was selling one."

Women tended to overshare with me. An ex-colleague once told me it was my tone of voice. Made people want to spill all their secrets. Sometimes, that worked to my advantage. Other times? Not so much.

"Look, I don't care about weed or statues or cameras or anything else illegal or borderline illegal you may or may not have done. A girl got abducted, and we think you and your friends may have accidentally taken a photo of the kidnapper's car as it drove past."

Silence. Had I been too snappy?

Then, "Kidnapped? For real?"

"Yes, Brittney. For real."

"What car? Do you want me to look?"

"Is there any way you could just email me the pictures?"

"There's, like, a zillion of them. And my friends have more. Shall I call them up and get them to send all the pictures to me, and you can come to my place and look at them on the computer?"

The last thing I wanted to do was go to Brittney's apartment. At least on the phone, I could hang up in an emergency. But I'd almost used up my data allowance for the month, and even with the advance from Kimberly, money was tight.

"Okay, can you give me your address?" Better to ask, even though I already knew it.

"You sound young for a private investigator."

"I'm thirty years old, ma'am, but I assure you I have

enough experience to do my job."

"Do you wear a uniform?"

"Not since I was a cop."

"A cop? Wow. How about handcuffs? Do you carry handcuffs?"

"Brittney, I'll need your address if I'm going to visit."

"Oh, sure, sure." She rattled it off, and I jotted it on an empty coffee cup to be on the safe side.

"Tomorrow night?" she suggested. "Eight o'clock. I can get the photos together by then, and I have dance practice this evening."

"Perfect."

That gave me enough time to buy a gag and come up with a suitable excuse to get out of there once I'd seen all I needed to.

**

With little more I could do until the next day, I headed to the gym. I spent a lot of time there even though I couldn't afford a full membership anymore. Today, a big lunch had given me more energy, and a workout always took the edge off my stress levels.

Raise the Bar occupied one half of an old warehouse on the outskirts of town. The other half held a body shop and carwash, so you could get your car detailed while you lifted. The gym was a no-frills kind of a place. No fancy workout classes, no jacuzzi, no juice bar. Not even any carpet. Just sweat and a whole lot of iron. That suited me fine—I preferred to run outside for my cardio fix. It let me keep up with the city.

But going to the gym gave me company, and I didn't get much of that now I'd left the force. Unless they needed a favour, most of my former colleagues steered clear since I didn't carry a badge anymore, and the guys on the street who knew I'd once been a cop avoided me as well. At Raise the Bar, all I had to do to fit in was bench-press two-hundred pounds, and that was easy.

Want to hear a secret? Even tough guys get lonely sometimes.

"How you doin', Cullen?" Jerome asked when I walked out of the locker room.

We'd both joined on the same day, and Buzz, the owner, had taken us on the grand tour together. Weights, bikes, weights, more weights, water fountain. Buzz was a man of few words.

"Not bad."

"You gettin' your problems sorted out?"

Jerome knew I'd had difficulties with Emma's debts after she left, but I'd never let on how bad it had got. I may not have had money, but I still had pride.

"Things are getting better, Rome." He'd adopted the nickname years ago after someone kidded him that Rome wasn't built in a day. "Picked up a new case on Saturday."

"Not another one of those infidelity messes?"

"No, this one's different. Attempted kidnapping."

"Attempted?"

"The woman escaped. The cops have given up, but she wants him found and educated on the error of his ways."

"Need a hand with that?"

Rome cracked his knuckles, and several people

turned their heads. He had that effect. Five years ago, he'd worked as an enforcer for one of Maryland's most feared drug dealers, but when his boss got shot dead in a turf war, Rome had decided to go straight. Well, straight-ish. Six and a half feet tall, he weighed two-hundred-and-fifty pounds and people crossed the street to avoid him.

"Maybe. I need to find him first."

"I've got faith, brother."

"This one might need more than faith. Can you do me a favour tomorrow night?"

"What sort of a favour?"

"I need you to call me at nine thirty and pretend there's an emergency."

"Why?"

"Because I've got to visit a potential witness, and the thought of being alone with her leaves me cold inside."

"She's a dog?"

"More of a rabid cheerleader-slash-cop groupie."

**

I deliberately dressed down to visit Brittney—worn jeans, battered boots, and a leather jacket that had seen better days, say, last century. In hindsight, that was a mistake.

"Come in, come in!" She flung the door wide. "Wait —you're Reed, right?"

"Ma'am, you really should ask for ID before you open the door."

"Ma'am?" She giggled, and a boob almost fell out of her top. "You're so old-fashioned. Love the jacket, by the way. Hugo Boss?"

"No, I bought it off a guy at a truck stop."

"Really?" Her over-plucked brows furrowed. "I get it! You're joking." She reached up to stroke my face. "The stubble really suits you."

Mental note: shave every single fucking day.

"Did you get the photos?"

"Duh, of course. And yeah, some of them have totally got cars in them. I bought wine too. Do you want wine?"

"I'll pass."

"I'm allowed to drink it legally now, you know. That was my twenty-first birthday dinner the other night."

"I'm driving."

"You could get a cab. Or..." She looked me up and down, smiling. "Or you could just stay the night."

She didn't mess around, did she? "I'm almost a decade older than you."

"With age comes experience." Another giggle. Had she started on the wine already? "That's what they say, isn't it?"

"If we could just see the photos..."

"I'll get you a soda first. And nibbles. Do you like pretzels? I have, like, four different kinds plus two flavours of chips."

"I'd better lay off the snacks. I'm..." Fuck. "I'm meeting my boyfriend for a late dinner after I'm done here."

Brittney's eyes widened so much they were in danger of popping out. "You're gay?"

"Sorry."

"Wow. Not even a little bit straight?"

I struggled to keep from laughing.

"It doesn't work like that."

"Really? Because my friend Marcia had a three-way with these two guys and—"

Stop. Talking. I held up a hand. "Brittney, the photos? Please?"

"Oh *yeah*. The photos."

She hitched her top up and sashayed over to a cheap-looking dining table—chipboard and plastic, not wood—and took a seat in front of her laptop. Another not-quite-legal purchase?

"Here we are when we arrived. Travis drank half a bottle of Jack Daniels before he left home, and he was *so* trashed. Monica said he might get kicked out, so we squashed him into the corner out of the way. See?"

"You're a student?" I asked, even though research had already told me the answer.

"How did you guess?"

I pointed at the pile of study notes on the coffee table in front of the sofa.

"Oh, right, yeah. I'm a student."

"What are you studying?"

"Communications."

Heaven help us all.

"A worthy subject. Now, I'm only really interested in the pictures with cars in them. The ones you took down by the Luigi's sign."

"Right. You said that yesterday, didn't you?"

Have a gold star. "I did."

"Okay, so Lance took most of those. And Sierra took some selfies. And I think Jared may have taken a few shots at the end..."

Finally, we got to looking at the pictures. Most of them were useless, either blurred or too tightly focused on the group. But a handful showed vehicles, and one in particular caught my eye.

"Stop. Go back, would you?"

"Oh, I remember this one! Lance tripped over Jared's foot and almost dropped the camera."

And in the process, he'd gotten the perfect shot of a big black sedan. A Mercedes, from the badge on the back.

"Can you zoom in on the vehicle?"

"Sure."

There it was. The licence plate. Light blue with a darker concave stripe at the top. Fuzzy, but when I squinted, I could make out the number. DWZ 0196.

At that moment, I should have been elated, right? Brittney certainly thought so.

"Yee-haw! That's the car, isn't it? So we've got the guy? What next? Do you call the DMV? Hey, this is so exciting! We should open a bottle of champagne. Well, fizzy wine. What do you think?"

"I think there's still work left to do." Because I recognised that plate, or at least its type. And it wasn't good news. "Can you copy that picture onto this memory stick?"

"Sure I can. You don't have to do more work tonight, though? I could order a pizza."

I glanced at my watch. A quarter to ten. What the hell was Rome doing?

"Thanks, but I can't."

"You're still going out for dinner? But it's so late."

"I'll pick something up on the way home."

"There's a great—"

My phone rang. Rome calling. Thank goodness.

"Hey, sweetie," I said.

"Sweetie? What the fuck you on, man?"

"Just leaving. I'll be home in fifteen... Chinese? Sounds great to me."

I quickly turned the volume down as Rome guffawed. "Home? I'm in the damn bar."

"You know how much I love crispy beef."

"You've lost your damn mind, buddy. Get out of there."

I was only too happy to comply.

CHAPTER 9 - KIMBERLY

"YOU DID WHAT?" Annie asked on Tuesday morning.

"Hired a private investigator. I just thought I should mention it since he's supposed to be coming by with an update. I didn't want you to be alarmed since he doesn't look like our usual clientele."

Kayla put down her low-fat strawberry shortcake. "Then what does he look like?"

"Uh, big."

"Chandra Boyce's fiancé was big."

"No, he was wide." The silver medalist at last year's US Sumo Open, to be precise. We'd definitely had to go with made-to-measure for his tuxedo. "Reed Cullen is just big all over. Tall. Muscly."

Although he'd made the effort to wear a shirt, he'd risked bursting out of it at any moment the way the buttons had stretched so tightly across his chest.

"Handsome?"

"He desperately needs a haircut."

"Sometimes long hair can be attractive. Think Brad Pitt in *Legends of the Fall*."

"Cullen's more like an extra from *Lord of the Rings*."

"So dark hair?"

"Yes."

"And does he drive a cool car?"

"I have no idea. He's an ex-cop, and he was actually quite dull."

Not that we'd talked much, but he took his coffee black and plain voluntarily, which said everything. So had my ex-husband, but at least Alan had imported the beans from an ethical co-op in Kenya.

"Didn't he have any stories to tell?"

"I didn't ask. He agreed to take the case, and that was the only thing we spoke about."

Kayla nodded, grinning. "Okay, got it. He's a fit ex-cop who's here to save womankind. I'll share my desk with him any day."

"I thought you were going to put it all in the past?" Annie said.

"And I tried, really I did, but I barely slept last week. Every time I closed my eyes, I wondered if *he* was out there, selecting his next victim."

"But—"

"And he more than likely knows where I live. He holds all the power here. I just want to find out who he is and let him know that I know so he'll think twice about pulling the same stunt again."

"What if he doesn't appreciate you poking around? As you said, he's got your address."

"But it won't just be me. Cullen will know, and you, and Kayla, and Maria."

"Maria? I might have guessed she was involved."

"Think of it as an insurance policy. Please don't be mad at me, Annie."

She stepped forward and pulled me into a hug. "I'm not mad at you, just worried. I was terrified when that police officer called me last week."

"I'm never drinking again."

"Not without both of us with you to supervise, you're not. We'll be your wingmen."

Guardian angels, more like.

"Dinner and a movie at my place on Friday?"

"Wouldn't miss it for the world."

***

"Reed Cullen's here," Kayla announced, poking her head into my office. She waggled her eyebrows and mouthed, "And he *is* hot."

Annie had gone with a client to look at dresses, so at least we could talk in private, and I'd cleared the visitor's chair opposite my desk in preparation for his arrival.

"Would you show him through?"

Kayla backed away, and ten seconds later, Reed's oversized frame darkened my doorway.

"Please, take a seat."

"Coffee?" Kayla asked.

"I'll have a cinnamon spice latte. Mr. Cullen?"

"Reed. Just plain black, please."

See? Dull.

He settled back in the chair and crossed his ankles. Today, he'd worn a white T-shirt, so at least I didn't have to worry about his buttons.

"You said there was news?"

"Yeah, I did."

"Well? Is it good or bad?"

His face stayed impassive, and I couldn't read his eyes. They were an unusual greyish blue, which looked strange with his dark hair.

"It's not great," he admitted. "I've tracked down the

car."

"But that's good." A tiny shake of his head said otherwise. "Why isn't it good?"

He reached into his jacket pocket and pulled out a piece of paper. A photograph. No, two. He smoothed them out on the desk in front of me and pointed at the top picture.

"Here's the vehicle with you in it, a half mile before the traffic lights."

Whoa. I mean, I knew I'd been there, but seeing myself slumped in the car with a madman sent a shudder through me.

"And here it is from a different angle."

"The registration's blurry."

"I've got an electronic copy that's clearer." He flipped the paper over. "Here's the licence plate, zoomed in."

"That doesn't look like a Maryland plate."

"It isn't. It's a diplomatic plate."

"A diplomat? I was drugged and kidnapped by a freaking diplomat?"

"Sure seems that way."

"That's crazy! I mean, aren't they supposed to be responsible?"

"You'd be surprised by the shit...stuff they get up to."

"So what now? Can you find out who he is from the DMV?"

"The DMV doesn't register diplomatic vehicles. The Office of Foreign Missions and its Regional Offices does that."

"Then can't you call them instead?"

"They don't release the information. National

security and all that."

"There must be a way. Right? Don't you have sources?"

"Not many in Washington. Embassies take their security very seriously, and they don't like answering questions."

"Can't you narrow it down? How many embassies are there?"

"Narrowing it down is easy. See the letters at the beginning?"

"DWZ?"

"The D stands for diplomat. The two letters after it is the country code for the embassy."

"Then which one is it? Wait. Let me guess..." Maria had mentioned Tim's British accent. "The United Kingdom?"

"You should be a detective."

If his comment was supposed to lighten the moment, it didn't work. I still couldn't get over the fact that I'd been kidnapped by a damn diplomat.

"How do we find out who drives the car? How many diplomats are there?"

"The number at the end is one-nine-six. That means at least a hundred and ninety-six plates have been issued to the British embassy. Probably more."

"They must have a list."

"It'll be almost impossible to get hold of."

"*Almost* impossible. Not *absolutely* impossible?"

I realised what she was getting at. "Honestly? I wouldn't recommend continuing with this. I've only spent nine and a half hours so far, and expenses have been minimal, so you'll be due a refund."

"We can't give up. Not when we're so close."

"Miss Jennings, we're not close. Finding the embassy connection is only the beginning. Even if we managed to get photos of all their staff and asked your friend to pick one out of a line-up, the most he'd get is a slap on the wrist from the Brits. US law enforcement is prohibited from touching him, and we can't even prove you were drugged."

"Sergeant Banks mentioned a more accurate test. He promised to keep the sample."

"And say it showed something—how would you prove who slipped it into your drink?"

Why did Cullen have to be so negative? We'd narrowed down the suspects to people who worked in one freaking building. All we had to do was watch who went in and out, surely?

"We need to find him."

"Do you understand how diplomatic immunity works? Tim can't be arrested or charged with anything."

"So he's untouchable? What if he went around murdering people?"

The way he already had.

"If the British chose to, they could recall him. Or possibly revoke his immunity, but don't count on that. It rarely happens. And with the way our president's been sniping at the British prime minister lately, not to mention the other world leaders, nobody's gonna go out of their way to do him any favours. Our 'special relationship' isn't all that special anymore."

"Letting someone get away with murder? That would be crazy."

"You want crazy? In 1979, the Burmese ambassador to Sri Lanka allegedly had an argument with his wife and shot her dead. Then he burned her body on a damn funeral pyre in his backyard, and the cops could only watch because the property was designated as Burmese territory."

"He got away with it?"

"Worse. He remained the fu— He remained the ambassador."

"You're right. That *is* crazy."

"And that's just scratching the surface. Two years ago, a Saudi diplomat allegedly imprisoned two women in his apartment for two months and raped them daily with his buddies. Then there was the diplomat who ran over a cop in New York and got away with it. The Russian diplomat who killed a woman driving drunk in Ottawa. And you think us Americans aren't as bad? An American marine serving at the embassy in Bucharest ran a red light while under the influence and killed a Romanian musician. Did the US waive his immunity? No, it didn't."

I felt sick inside. Was diplomatic immunity just a licence to commit crimes?

"How do you know all this stuff?"

"While I was a cop, I investigated a paedophile ring, and one of the monsters we tried to arrest had a diplomatic passport. European. He was as smooth as anything, and we couldn't stop him from climbing on board a plane and flying home. After that, I read up on the history of the Vienna Convention."

"It sounds like something out of the Dark Ages."

"Believe me, I'm as pissed as you that there's an asshole out there messing with women, and I could use the work, but my conscience won't let me take your money when I know you won't get any closure in return. Shall I email you the final invoice?"

No, no, no, no, no. I couldn't quit. Georgette's picture flashed up in my head, her pretty smile and green eyes full of life. I'd made a promise to myself that I'd find her killer. Cullen mentioned immunity being revoked? Maybe with enough publicity... I could even beg my father to take time out of his busy schedule and help. He was a lobbyist, powerful in Washington, even if I did hate almost everything he stood for.

"No, I still want you to carry on."

"Miss Jennings..."

"If you won't help, I'll just have to find someone else."

"Why is this so important to you?"

Because I'd failed in every one of my duties as a member of the Electi. I was supposed to get justice for the dead, and instead, I spent my days planning parties and making animals out of paper clips. Perhaps I wasn't cut out to be a deadly avenger, but for once in my life, I could do the right thing.

After all, it was only money. My house was paid off, I had a trust fund I rarely touched, and paper clips didn't cost that much. Georgette had saved me, and I owed it to her to help.

But I could hardly explain that to Cullen, could I? I was trying to sort out the jumble of words in my head when a tear popped out. Then another, and another.

"I'm sorry, I..."

He patted his pockets, then spotted the box of tissues on my credenza and grabbed a handful.

"Here." Reed knelt beside me, but our heads were still almost level. "Miss Jennings... Kimberly... Is there something you haven't told me? *Did* he touch you in the car that night?"

It would have been so easy to lie, but I'd been doing that my whole life, or at least avoiding the truth.

"I don't know. I just don't know. P-p-please, don't quit on me. You've got so far in two days, and Officer Leopold said you were the best."

Cullen sighed, and it was clear he'd rather have been anywhere but stuck in an office with a hysterical female.

"How about I dig into things for a couple of weeks and see how far I get? Then if it still looks hopeless, we can call things off."

That was better than nothing, and it gave me extra time to convince him to see the case through to the end.

"Okay." I gave a shuddering sniff. "Thank you."

A soft gasp at the door made me look up, and I saw Kayla standing there with our drinks.

"Is everything okay?" she asked.

"Uh..."

"Getting emotional's perfectly normal in situations like this," Reed told her. "Kimberly'll be fine in a few minutes."

"I just need coffee."

Reed climbed to his feet, leaving my eyes level with his stomach. The bumps of his abs strained against his T-shirt, and I fought to keep my eyes from straying downwards. Why did he buy all of his clothing a size too small?

"I'll keep you updated with the billing," he said.

Be still my beating heart. No, seriously. The stupid thing was threatening to punch its way out of my ribcage.

I forced a smile. "I'd appreciate that."

Chapter 10 - Reed

THE BRITISH EMBASSY in Washington, DC was located on Massachusetts Avenue NW, otherwise known as Embassy Row. It was also one of the largest embassies in Washington, employing around five hundred people, over two hundred of whom were diplomats. Not only would all of those diplomats have immunity, certain members of their families enjoyed the privilege too, as well as consuls and other staff going about embassy business. Even the damn chauffeurs.

With the amount of shit going on in the world—a terrorist incident in London and a recent attack on the Italian consulate in São Paulo that had left everyone twitchy—security was at an all-time high. The three buildings that together made up the embassy—the old and new chanceries and the ambassador's residence—were located behind a high metal fence and surrounded by trees and gardens designed by the wife of a previous ambassador that may have been nice to look at but which made surveillance hell.

Information was difficult to come by. Embassies tended to be quite insular, since they were a little slice of foreign territory located overseas, and without a British passport, I couldn't easily get inside. They didn't run tours. Even the fucking White House ran tours.

For the first day, I donned an *I heart Washington* T-shirt and played tourist, taking a bus ride around the area and snapping hundreds of pictures while I was at it. Not the usual shots of Ford's Theatre and the Lincoln Memorial, but entrances, exits, positions of security staff, and structures I could use as cover for snooping. It was tricky—the embassy compound had more than one entrance and exit, and if I hung around for too long without a good purpose, I'd probably get questioned.

The nearest cafés were right at the far ends of Massachusetts Avenue, which left me with two options. Either the parking spaces open to the public opposite the embassy's main security gatehouse on Observatory Circle, or the park on the other side of Massachusetts with its jogging trails and benches over near the Khalil Gibran Memorial.

The parking spaces were ideal, but if I sat there all day in between the British Embassy, the New Zealand Embassy, and the Naval Observatory which included the vice president's official residence, I'd look sketchy as fuck. No, I'd have to leave my car there with a covert camera filming, then review the footage remotely. That would cover one exit.

I'd have to get more creative for the other.

Literally.

***

On Thursday morning, I drove to Washington before most of the world was awake because I wanted to secure a prime parking spot. My plan worked. By seven thirty, I'd got my recording equipment set up as I wanted it, and I strolled off along the street, carrying my phone, a compact camera, a pad of paper, and a tin of graphite pencils.

Back in my teens, I'd been a keen artist before life and the need to earn money took over. Nowadays, I rarely got the time to draw, and I might have looked forward to a quiet day outside, doodling trees, if it weren't so damn cold.

Think positive, Cullen. At least I'd have plenty of choice when it came to benches.

By four p.m., I had eight and a half hours of video plus seventeen sketches of trees, the memorial, and a squirrel, none particularly good since most of my focus had been directed towards the gate of the embassy. Another vehicle nosed past the barrier as I watched on my phone, which I'd propped on my leg out of sight of passers-by. A white Honda with a woman at the wheel who waved to the security guard before driving off along the road. Did I mention I also had frostbite?

Then I saw a possible target. A black sedan, a Mercedes, edging out of the gate. I quickly zoomed in. Yes! That was it. The car that drove past Luigi's, with a man at the wheel. Only this guy was black. Brittney's friend's photo may have been blurry, but the guy driving that night had definitely been light-skinned.

So who was today's mystery occupant?

The plot only thickened over the next week. Each day, I watched both entrances, and I counted four different people driving that same car. The black guy on one more occasion, plus three others, all white. I discounted the man with light-blond hair because that didn't fit with Brittney's photo either. Were any of the drivers chauffeurs? Was it some kind of pool car? Or did a particularly generous diplomat just lend the Mercedes to all of his friends?

The following Friday, it pulled out of the gates just as I arrived, and I decided to follow. One of the dark-haired men was driving, and he wove through the traffic, cutting in front of people and generally behaving like an asshole. Guess he thought *diplomagic* gave him a free pass on courtesy too. Finally, he abandoned the car outside Manny's Delicatessen, skewed across a handicapped spot.

He'd driven three miles to get breakfast?

I parked properly and followed him inside, and sure enough, he was at the counter ordering a breakfast roll with everything plus freshly squeezed orange juice.

"Don't forget to strain the pulp out this time," he told the girl behind the counter, who didn't seem all that thrilled to see him judging by her gritted teeth. Was he a regular?

"You want ketchup in the roll, sir?"

"And HP sauce. And extra napkins. Last time you didn't give me any napkins."

I grabbed a smoothie from the chiller and got into line behind him, and when he reached out to pay, I leaned to the side and got a look at his credit card. Simeon J Dobkins.

Suspect number one had a name.

He left as the girl rang up my smoothie, turning right out of the parking lot, back towards the embassy.

"Can I get a roll like the last guy had too?" I flashed her a smile. Candy, according to her name badge. "I promise I won't get upset over napkins."

"I did put the napkins in, honest, but that man always likes to complain about something."

"He comes in often?"

"A couple of times a week."

"Well, he can't be that unhappy if he keeps coming back."

"I guess, but I'd rather he just kept his six dollars and went someplace else." She sighed. "Sorry. I shouldn't say things like that. My boss gets mad if I complain about the customers."

Especially to other customers, I bet. "Don't worry; I won't say anything. I already decided he was a dick when he parked in two handicapped spots."

"One of his colleagues came in last month and reversed into another vehicle as he left, then denied the whole thing."

"What an asshole."

"They all are. Want a coffee? On the house?"

"That's real kind of you."

Back in the car, I took my time eating breakfast. After all, I didn't want to appear too eager for the next part. I had one name, and I wanted more. Once I'd finished my roll—and now I understood why Simeon-the-dick drove the whole way out here to get his fix—I looked up the general enquiries number for the British embassy.

"Hey, I stopped off to buy breakfast this morning, and a guy walked past me out of the door and dropped a glove. At least, I think it was his. I couldn't catch him before he left, but he was driving a car with British diplomatic plates. Number one-nine-six. I'm with the state department, so I know how the codes work. Normally I wouldn't bother calling, but the glove looks expensive. Leather, cashmere lined. I could mail it back if I knew who to send it to."

"Hold on, let me check. One-nine-six, you say?"

She sounded upper class, although most Brits did to me. At least she hadn't blown me off.

A minute later, she came back. "That vehicle belongs to our head of management affairs, but he's out of the country at the moment."

Head of management affairs. Thanks, sweetheart. I could work with that.

"I definitely saw someone driving it this morning. White guy, dark hair."

She gave a dainty laugh. "Robert's always been generous with the keys, and the staff in his department do tend to borrow it. Consuls mainly. Between you and me, they're not really supposed to do that."

Because consuls didn't have full diplomatic immunity. Could this be a lucky break? What if one of them was driving that night?

"Happens all the time."

"If you want to leave your number, I can send an email around about the glove."

"I'll be flying overseas myself this afternoon. Tell you what, why don't you give me your name, and I'll mail the glove to the address on your website. Hopefully you can trace its owner."

And hopefully, she'd forget about this phone call by the time the glove didn't arrive.

"That's ever so kind of you. Yes. I'm Felicity Barnwell."

"No problem. I'll send it before I leave."

"Have a lovely day."

"You too."

***

Our management officer, Robert Turner, heads up a department of twenty to oversee all diplomatic mission operations from real estate to people to budget.

The photo underneath showed a sixty-year-old man with a forty-year-old wife and two children who must have been in high school. A polished-looking girl who took after her mother, and a younger boy with braces on his teeth. *Robert Turner and family at last year's garden party.*

Robert Turner. Simeon Dobkins. Two names. Nineteen left to find, assuming Robert didn't decide to lend the car to one of his buddies in economics or political affairs. That was a possibility, of course, but I had to start somewhere. Kimberly Jennings was paying me to keep digging, and quite handsomely since I was working on the case full-time. I glanced at myself in the rear-view mirror. Perhaps I should invest in a haircut now.

After all, a haircut might help with the next part of my plan. I needed to get up close and personal with the embassy staff, and if there was one thing diplomats enjoyed more than collecting traffic citations, it was partying. Now I just had to find out where they drank.

I went to the Georgetown library to warm up and borrow their internet connection for an hour, and then I headed back to the embassy. Suspect number three tossed his hat into the ring just after lunch. Another white, dark-haired guy behind the wheel of diplomatic vehicle number one-nine-six. I'd only just left my own car, so I turned back to follow him.

This must have been the chauffeur, because five

miles outside of DC, he turned into the forecourt of a luxury car wash and handed the keys to a teenager in coveralls. From the expression on the kid's face, which matched the girl at the deli's exactly, one of the modules in the UK's diplomatic training manual covered how to be a dick. The staff who worked with Robert Turner had all passed with flying colours.

Suspect three didn't stick around, though, just sauntered off along the road, whistling, as I parked and stared after him.

"He's going to the strip club along the road," the kid supplied. "Does it every time."

"That's one way to spend the wait."

"Can't go in the evenings or his wife would get pissed."

"He's married?"

"Yup. I've heard him on the phone to her. She keeps him on a short leash."

So possibly she'd have noticed if he spent the night with Kimberly Jennings.

I stuck out a hand. "Reed. Any chance you could wash my SUV?"

The guy gave me a fist bump. "I'm Tyrone. Sure, I'll do yours first. That guy won't be back for hours, and he always complains no matter how much time I spend cleaning his damn Benz."

"Really proud of it, huh?"

"It's not even his. He's just the chauffeur. Comes in every week, regular as clockwork."

Well, that answered one question. I nodded at the diplomatic plates. "Reckon I should get me one of those cushy government jobs."

"You and me both, brother. You and me both." He

waved at my car. "Want me to do the inside too?"

"Nah, it's full of my girlfriend's shit. Just the outside."

While Tyrone got his hands dirty, I waited in the rusty cabin that served as an office, messy as hell and heated by a single-bar electric fire. Regular as clockwork, he said? I found the invoice file and flipped back a week. Last Thursday, Paul Lincoln had brought the Mercedes in for detailing, and a scrawled note at the bottom of the receipt said he'd complained the wheels weren't clean enough.

One more name to add to the collection.

After the visit to the car wash, I turned my gleaming SUV back towards the embassy at the end of the day to pick out a likely candidate for after-work drinks. A youngish guy in a BMW left at five on the dot, and I figured he may be the type to hang out in the bar, but he drove over the Fourteenth Street Bridge and headed for Virginia. Unlucky. I headed back for a second try, another guy in his twenties, but after I trailed him into a bar downtown, he kissed his girlfriend on the cheek and ordered them both glasses of wine.

Another strike. Well, I did warn Kimberly this would be a long process.

After an hour in the gym, I decided to grab a chicken burger from the Sunrise Diner. I'd been eating there since I was a kid, and Becky who owned the place knew how to cook good food without adding a vat-load of grease. Except when I drove past Just Imagine's office, the light was still on, glowing from behind the filmy drapes someone had pulled across the windows of the reception area. A shadow passed in front. Was that Kimberly? What was she doing there so late?

Before I had time to think about it, I'd pulled over and parked at the kerb. It was almost nine o'clock. She should be at home with candles and bubble bath or whatever slightly icy women with a penchant for shiny things did in the evenings.

I knocked softly on the door, only to stiffen when the sound of breaking glass echoed from inside.

"Kimberly? Are you okay?"

"Who's there?"

"Reed Cullen. Are you okay?"

The door flew open. "What are you doing here? You scared me half to death!"

I didn't have a proper answer for that. "I saw the light on."

"So? I'm working."

Coffee spread across the tiled floor behind her, edging dangerously close to the fluffy cream carpet.

"Let me clean that up."

I didn't wait for her to protest, just strode through to the kitchenette and snatched up a roll of paper towel. She started sputtering behind me.

"I can do that."

"Let me fix it. And I apologise for scaring you."

Stupid, Cullen. I should have known she'd be skittish after what happened.

"It's okay."

"I'll get you a new cup too."

"I don't care about the cup, just... It doesn't matter. Did you want something important?"

Shards of china were everywhere, and I wrapped a paper towel around my hand to sweep them into a pile. She'd got more of that caramel syrup judging by the sickly aroma. Did I want something important? Not really. I just didn't want her to be alone at that time in the evening, especially in winter.

"Thought I'd give you an update. What doesn't matter?"

"Nothing. Everything's splendid."

"Splendid? Splendid's like 'fine' but for rich people."

"You think I'm rich?"

"You own a business, your home's paid off, you come from a good family..."

Kimberly clenched those dainty fists and crouched beside me, eyes flashing.

"You researched *me*? How dare you?"

"Standard procedure. Been stiffed on the bill too many times."

"That's...that's...*invasive*."

"Invasive would be if I rummaged through your nightstand or got ahold of your medical records. All of that other information's publicly available."

She looked kinda cute when she was angry. Like a pissed-off kitten. Shit.

"Will you just finish up and leave?"

"Don't you want an update?"

"Well, yes, but I'm busy right now."

"I thought everything was splendid?"

A roll of the eyes. "*Fine*. There's a small problem."

"What kind of problem?"

"One of my clients is getting married tomorrow, and the gift bags arrived this afternoon. They're supposed to be white lace with pink ribbon ties woven through the top, but they arrived with red ribbon instead."

"And?"

Red and pink were pretty much the same, weren't they?

"The bride's ex-boyfriend was called Red, they had a bad break-up, and she insisted there be no red in the wedding whatsoever."

"I guess I see how that could cause an issue. So, what are you doing about it?"

"I have pink ribbon, and I'm redoing all the closures."

"How many bags?"

"Three hundred and twenty."

"And how many have you done?"

A long sigh. "Sixty-three."

"What about the other girls? Can't they help?"

"Annie's on a date, and Kayla's got a family dinner."

"Show me what to do, and I'll help."

"You?"

Yeah, my offer surprised me too. Weaving ribbons wasn't what I'd planned to do when I left the gym, but when the alternative was falling asleep in my car a few hours earlier, I figured I might as well lend a hand.

"I'm not a complete Neanderthal."

"You've certainly got the right hair." She clapped a hand over her mouth. "I'm sorry. That was rude."

"You're right. It needs a cut."

Now I had some cash, I'd get it done soon.

Chapter 11 - Kimberly

SALVATION CAME IN many forms, but I hadn't expected it to stomp through my door in Reed Cullen's cracked leather boots. After a day spent hunting down lemon-yellow bridles for the Falabella horses, the red ribbons had been the last straw.

My heart was still racing, and part of me wanted to chew Reed out for turning up so late at night, but I really did need the help. I'd gladly pay him forty-five bucks an hour if he knew how to tie a darn bow.

I was desperate, okay?

"I'll show you what to do."

Each bag needed the red ribbon pulled out, then pink ribbon re-threaded through the holes in the lace to make a drawstring. A fiddly job, and I worried Reed's fingers would be too big, but they seemed remarkably nimble. In fact, he was faster than me.

We'd reworked another fifty bags between us, sitting at the glass table in the meeting area, before I dared to interrupt our progress.

"Thanks for doing this."

"It's splendid."

I ignored the dig. "Did you say you had an update?"

"Yeah, I do, but don't get too excited." He told me about his week, about seeing the car and all its drivers and his trips to the deli and the car wash. "My next step is to start talking to these people, then I'll get better pictures so we can do a line-up with your friend."

But I was more interested in the Mercedes. Georgette was in the Mercedes, and the chauffeur took it to be cleaned every week. Regular as clockwork, Reed said.

"Where was this car wash?"

"Why?"

"My car's dirty, and the last place I took it to scratched one of the panels. You said Tyrone was good?"

"Good at giving out information."

"But he didn't do a bad job on your SUV? Did he polish the glass and put that black stuff on the tyres?"

"Yeah."

"So can you tell me the name of the place?"

"Auto Shine Express. But promise me you'll avoid going there until after the case."

"Mmm-hmm." I kept my fingers crossed behind my back. A little white lie never hurt anyone, did it?

He rattled off the address, and I tapped it into my phone. What did I have going on next Thursday? A dress fitting, but that was only in the morning. I quickly blocked out the afternoon. Yes, I'd go and visit Georgette. That could solve this whole mystery. If Reed had already followed the chauffeur to the car wash once and eliminated him, he wouldn't need to do so again.

"Why are you smiling?" Reed asked.

Darn it. "I just counted up in my head and we're more than halfway through. We might get to bed before midnight."

Just then my stomach grumbled. No, of course I hadn't had time for dinner.

"Have you eaten?" Reed asked.

Oh, thank goodness, a change of subject. "Not yet. Shall I order something? Pizza? Chinese? Japanese? Burgers? I think there's a new Lebanese place opened a few blocks away, but I haven't been there yet. Have *you* eaten?"

"Only a protein bar at the gym."

"I tried one of those once. It tasted like sawdust."

"Most of them taste like sawdust."

"Do you run in the gym? Cycle? Lift weights?"

"Weights."

"Doesn't that earn you proper food? Like a steak or something?"

For a second, Reed looked wistful. "Only on cheat day."

"Well, I must have walked twenty miles this morning, so I deserve dessert."

"Twenty miles? What were you doing?"

"Scouting photography locations with a client." Who ran marathons for a hobby. "She wanted somewhere rustic, but not shabby, at one with nature, but no bugs, mud, or ryegrass because apparently her fiancé's allergic to that. I twisted my ankle falling over a log."

"Did you put ice on it?"

"I didn't have any time or any ice." And the biggest injury had been to my pride.

"You should rest it."

"If I stopped to rest after every problem, I'd never get anything done. This morning's accident was just a little hiccup." That I didn't want to be reminded of. "Chinese. Shall I order Chinese?"

"I'll eat anything," Reed said.

Good to know. No! Bad Kimberly. I shouldn't be thinking about Reed that way. Before my dirty mind could come up with any new ideas, I grabbed my phone and ordered two portions of my favourites. Sweet-and-sour pork balls with chicken chow mein and spring rolls, eaten straight from the carton. Food always tasted better when there was no washing-up to do, and at least if Reed had the same menu items, he wouldn't get tempted to steal mine.

By the time the food arrived, we only had fifty bags left to finish, but I was too hungry to wait.

"Chopsticks or a fork?" I asked Reed.

"Chopsticks."

Show-off. I was a fork girl; otherwise, I ended up with more food in my lap than in my mouth. But Reed once again proved how good he was with his fingers when he managed to eat like a native.

"What's the worst thing that's ever happened in the world of wedding planning?" he asked between mouthfuls.

"Why?"

"Just curious."

Where did I start? Most issues could be salvaged without the bride ever finding out—that was my job, after all, to make everything run smoothly—but sometimes, a disaster of epic proportions arose.

"The saddest day was when the bride's father had a heart attack and died right after the vows."

She'd been inconsolable, poor girl, and even though the bride and groom insisted the rest of the guests stay and enjoy the reception while the family followed the ambulance to the hospital, the event had turned into more of a wake.

"At least the old guy died happy, right? Seeing his daughter get married."

"I guess that's one way to look at it."

"Have you ever had a couple not get married?"

"A few times. Only one where they split up at the altar."

"What happened?"

"The bride had been really worried all day. All week, in fact. But I thought it was just last-minute nerves, even after she threw up on the groom when the officiant asked if anyone knew of any reason why they shouldn't get married."

To this day, I vividly recalled rushing forward with a packet of wet wipes while the priest leapt out of the way.

"I guess puking's a good reason to call the whole thing off."

"That wasn't the problem. It turned out she had morning sickness, which she admitted in front of the whole churchful of guests."

"Let me guess; it wasn't the groom's?"

"Her fiancé was a devout Christian who'd insisted they wait until after the wedding to...you know."

"Did you find out whose it was?"

"*Everyone* did. She started looking at the best man funny, then the groom put two and two together and punched him. Once he got up, he grabbed the bride's hand and the two of them escaped in the wedding car."

Reed began laughing. "Bet that was awkward."

"The most awkward part was sending them my final bill afterwards. I almost wrote it off, but I hadn't been in business for long and that would have left me in the red."

"Did they pay it?"

"The bride's parents did. They moved in the same circles as my father, and I guess they didn't want people whispering about how they'd stiffed me."

"Wish it was that simple to get money out of my clients. Half of them don't have a reputation left to worry about."

"Have many of them screwed you?"

"Over cash? A couple this year."

No wonder he'd wanted a retainer. "I promise I'll pay. If you want more up-front...?"

He shook his head. "No, I trust you." He picked up another pork ball with his chopsticks and popped it into his mouth. "So, that's the worst thing that's ever happened?"

Oh no. There was a clear winner in that category. I shoved the remains of the food away, unsure whether to laugh or cry. Even the memories of that day filled me with horror.

"Nuh-uh. That was the shart bride."

"The what?"

"The shart bride." I screwed my eyes shut. "She'd just walked into the reception with her new husband when she got this really odd look on her face. Surprise mixed with horror. Then she dashed off to the bathroom. It turned out she'd needed to pass wind, only a little more came out than she'd intended. She'd been drinking these weird slimming shakes all week, and they'd wreaked havoc with her digestion."

"So what did you do?"

"This was a big wedding. Huge. *Hello* magazine had a photographer there. And we had a horribly tight schedule—cake-cutting, dinner, the first dance, speeches, toasts. A famous band playing in the evening. I ran after her and found her in the bathroom, crying, and the smell... Imagine swimming in a lake of raw sewage."

"I don't think I want to." Reed pushed his carton of chow mein away too.

"Oh, and it gets worse."

"How?"

"She was wearing latex shapewear, and the poop had kind of filled it, like a giant balloon. Her dress had hoops and layers of netting and organza, and we couldn't fit it into a bathroom stall, and the designer had sewn her into it so we couldn't just take it off. Kayla blocked the door while Annie ran off to find cleaning supplies, and I had to crawl under there and unsnap the panel in the crotch."

Horrible memories flooded back and when I say flooded, I mean it literally. A river of stinking goo ran out, the colour of chocolate and the consistency of vegetable oil. I pushed the takeout carton farther away and began laughing hysterically.

"Are you making this up?" Reed asked.

"If only."

"What happened? What did you do?"

"Cleaned up the mess with toilet paper and baby wipes. Some had squished up under the bodice, and there was a brown stain on the back of the dress, so Annie sponged it off as best she could and we took Kayla's chiffon scarf and tied it so the ends trailed down the bride's back. I fixed her make-up and changed into my backup outfit, then she headed out and cut the cake."

"The wedding went on?"

"The wedding always goes on, barring examples one and two. Everyone was polite enough not to mention the stench, and the magazine photos came out lovely. We had to pretend there was a plumbing problem and close down the ladies' bathroom, though."

Reed shook his head, incredulous. "I had no idea. I thought you just arranged flowers and stuff."

So many people did, and it trivialised my whole job. "Weddings are a very serious business."

"I'm beginning to understand that."

"And so often, the groom doesn't want to be actively involved. Like when I got married myself, for example. My husband-to-be was happy to write cheques, but even trying to get him to go to a suit fitting was a challenge. Still, at least his mother didn't try to take over. You have no idea how many times that happens."

"But you're not married anymore?"

Of course his research would have turned that up, but it wasn't something I liked to discuss. Who enjoyed admitting to their mistakes?

"It turned out we weren't as compatible as I thought. How about you? Do you have a girlfriend?"

Reed shook his head. "I'm not in a place where I could consider a relationship at the moment."

"Too busy?"

"Something like that."

"You're still searching for your sister?"

He looked as if he'd seen a ghost. "How do you know about my sister?"

"Officer Leopold mentioned she was missing."

Until then, Reed had always seemed larger than life, but now he shrank into the leather chair.

"I haven't heard from her in months."

"Do you want to talk about it?"

"Not really."

Our earlier laughter was nothing but a memory, and an uncomfortable silence settled between us. I snatched up a fortune cookie and shoved it towards Reed in an attempt to lighten the mood.

"Here. Open this." I tore the wrapper off my own and pulled the tiny strip of paper out. "'All things are difficult before they are easy.' What does yours say?"

"'You have rice in your teeth.'"

"Seriously?"

Reed showed me the piece of paper, and I had to thank the person at the fortune cookie factory with the warped sense of humour because at least we were able to laugh again.

Chapter 12 - Reed

"YOU'RE SURE IT'S not any of these?"

Maria shook her head, and I cursed under my breath. I'd spent the whole week tracking potential suspects and gathering names and background information, culminating in the six mugshots spread out on the table in front of us, and now it seemed I'd been wasting my time.

She pointed one French-tipped talon at picture number three, who happened to be Simeon, the asshole from the coffee place.

"This one's got similar hair, but the face is wrong. Tim had thinner lips. At least, I think so. Maybe it was just the way he smiled. Did any of them have a bandage?"

"Not that I could see, but they were all wearing sleeves."

Kimberly looked as disappointed as I felt, and she twisted the paper clip in her hand until the metal snapped with a quiet *click*.

"So we've gotten nowhere," she said.

I tried to cheer her up. "Not nowhere, exactly. We've eliminated six suspects."

"But now we need to start again with new ones. What happens if he takes another girl in the meantime?"

"Don't blame yourself, hun," Maria told her. "You're doing more than anyone else would have done. More than the police. Mr. Tough Guy here will just find us more possibles, and quickly. Right?"

She stared at me with laser eyes, and I resisted the urge to flinch.

"Right. I'll head back to DC tonight."

The management people from the embassy tended to drink in two bars plus a private members' club. The bars were easy. I'd spent the past week hanging out in one or the other, apart from Tuesday evening when I went on a date with a blonde chick from the HR department and narrowly avoided her swallowing my tonsils. She wanted to see me again, while I wanted to run a hundred miles in the opposite direction, but I couldn't turn her down outright in case I needed to use her in the future. Welcome to the awkward world of stringing a girl along by text. I might have felt guiltier if I hadn't gotten a look at her phone while she visited the bathroom and found messages from the other two guys she was involved with.

The private members' club was more of a challenge. Even if I could have convinced Kimberly to put the joining fee on expenses, the waiting list was over a year long. Getting inside would require ingenuity, and I was all out of that this week.

Tonight, I'd go back to bar number one, The Penalty Box Bar & Grill, because as well as being a font of information, the place served great nachos and I really needed a beer.

***

Thursday morning, I started off with a run. Not because I needed the exercise, but because I was so damn cold. My trip to The Penalty Box the night before hadn't yielded anything new, and after I got back to the car, temperatures had dropped below freezing and I'd woken up to a layer of ice on every window.

Once I could feel my feet again, I went to the gym and stood under a hot shower for as long as I dared—too long, and the guys began muttering about me being a girl. Last week, Jerome had bought me a bottle of bubble bath—Moroccan Rainforest, it was called. I was pretty sure Morocco didn't have any rainforests, but it smelled okay. Then it was off to visit Candy at the deli—I'd developed a liking for their breakfast rolls, and Candy always gave me extra bacon and a free coffee while she bitched about life in general and diplomats in particular.

All that meant I was late getting to the embassy, and my favourite parking spot was taken by a Toyota Prius with Alabama plates, but it didn't matter, because before I had time to decide on a different space, the black Mercedes drove out with Paul Lincoln at the wheel and a previously unknown companion in the passenger seat. White with dark hair and a scowl on his face as he stared at the phone in his hand. Who was he, and where were they going? The car wash? It was Thursday, after all. Or did they have other plans?

I trailed them through the city, and when the pair stopped outside a barbershop to get their hair cut, I almost followed them in. Despite what I'd said to Kim, I still hadn't gotten around to having a trim.

But I had to keep a low profile today. If I needed to eavesdrop later in a bar or restaurant, I didn't want them to recognise me and start asking questions. Once they'd gotten their short back and sides, Paul headed towards Auto Shine Express, and I nearly turned back because my car was clean enough and I had no desire to sit in a half-empty strip club at lunchtime. But then I happened to glance in the mirror. Two cars back, a cherry-red BMW moved into the outside lane, and I spotted a familiar face behind the wheel.

Kimberly.

Why the hell was she in Washington?

And more to the point, why was she heading towards Auto Shine Express? Yes, she'd mentioned wanting to get her car detailed, but why now? A coincidence, or...? I groaned out loud when I remembered my debrief last week—*comes in every week, regular as clockwork.*

Was she checking up on me? Or did she want to get a better look at Paul Lincoln? Why would she when we already knew he wasn't our guy? But his friend...

Shit. I couldn't let the passenger see her. If he was the culprit, that could blow the whole case.

I stabbed at the screen on my phone, and the sound of ringing filled the cabin.

"Hello?"

"What are you playing at? Have you lost your mind?"

"Excuse me?"

"You're behind me in the red BMW."

"Oh. That."

"Yes, that. Pull over."

"Why? I'm only going to get my car washed."

"You promised you wouldn't go near the place until this was over. If somebody recognises you, you could be in danger."

"But you already said the chauffeur wasn't the man who drugged me."

"No, but he's got a friend with him today, and as of this moment, I have no idea who that person is."

"Oh. Then I'll be careful."

"Just go home, Kimberly."

"I can't."

"What? Why? Why have you come at all? I'm following down every damn lead I can."

"I know, but... It doesn't matter. You wouldn't understand."

"Try me."

Kim made a little choking sound. "I wish... I wish... I just can't, okay? I'm sorry, but I have to do this."

We were getting closer and closer to the car wash. Only one more turn, and if Kim steamed in there behind the two embassy staff, there was no telling what might happen.

"Stop right now, or I quit. I already told you pursuing this case was a bad idea."

"You can't just quit. We have a contract."

"Really? Watch me."

I jerked the wheel, and my SUV skidded into a supermarket parking lot. An old lady pushing a shopping cart gave me a dirty look.

Fuck. I was breathing hard, exasperated, and I didn't even understand the conversation we'd just had. Why was Kim so determined to screw this up? I mean, the way she kept her office, her late-night obsession with getting every ribbon exactly right, I knew she had to be a control freak, but this... This was a whole other level.

A flash of red caught the edge of my vision, and I glanced across to see her BMW nosing into the space alongside. Big blue eyes stared back at me, watering slightly if I wasn't mistaken. Why was she so upset? She'd seemed fine yesterday evening.

Neither of us moved. A stand-off.

A minute passed. Two, and Kim focused on the steering wheel. I'd never met such a stubborn woman in my life, and since I'd grown up with my sister, that was a strong statement to make. Kim didn't even look at me when I slid into the passenger side of the BMW, just kept staring straight ahead.

"What was that all about?" Nothing. I reached out and turned her head towards me. "Kim? Kimberly?"

"I thought... I thought that if I could see the car, you know, in person, it might jog my memory. Help me to picture the man who drugged me. I read this article on the internet about associative memory, and... Like I said, it doesn't matter."

A tear rolled down her cheek, and when her hands stayed in her lap, I reached out and wiped it away with a thumb. Sometimes, smart clients were the most difficult to deal with. I'd read studies on associative memory too, and even made use of it in the past, like the time a rape victim recalled extra details about her attacker when she smelled his cologne. He'd gotten fifteen years as a result.

"I understand that you want to help, but we need to be sensible about this."

"I'm sorry."

"Look, I'll try to get you into the car, but we need to do this my way, okay?" Yes, it was official. One emotional woman and I lost my fucking mind. "I don't want you getting hurt."

"You'll help? Really?"

"My way."

She nodded and even managed a half-smile. "Just tell me what to do. I promise I'll follow instructions."

Giving her this would mean losing the chance to follow Lincoln's companion, but more than likely they were only heading to the strip club. I felt Kim's pain. And I also needed the money.

"Right, let's get this over with. I'll do the talking—you just follow my lead and try to look happy."

CHAPTER 13 - KIMBERLY

I WANTED TO get into the car, but at the same time, I didn't. In daylight, I could see Georgette through the window, watching me with a mixture of surprise and happiness. It was an expression I'd seen many times before, usually on a bride as she walked down the aisle and realised her husband-to-be had scrubbed up better than she thought he would.

Reed's arm tightened around my waist, getting dangerously close to my ass, but I'd promised to behave so I couldn't slap it away.

"What do you think of the Mercedes?" he asked the Latino guy he'd introduced as Tyrone, jerking his head towards the car I'd been abducted in. So far, they'd discussed the merits of steam cleaning the upholstery versus merely vacuuming, last night's ball game, and which chain restaurant sold the best fries. "We need to replace the SUV sooner rather than later, and we're thinking of going for a sedan instead. Right, honey?"

Honey? Oh, yes, that was supposed to be me. In Reed's hastily created plan, he'd admire the Mercedes with a view to buying one similar, and I'd balk at the idea. If Tyrone was the helpful guy Reed thought he was, he'd let us take a closer look at the car to settle the argument.

"I'm not sure. Now I've seen it up close, I think it's

too big."

"It's no bigger than the Jeep."

"No, it's longer."

Tyrone shook his head. "It only looks longer because it's not so high, ma'am."

"Really?"

Reed gave me another squeeze, and I began to sweat a little. Purely because of the situation, nothing whatsoever to do with the fact that I was plastered against a muscular private investigator who admittedly wasn't butt ugly. I'd perhaps been a little disingenuous when I compared him to an orc.

"I bet it comes with parking sensors," Reed said to Tyrone. "Am I right?"

"And a backup camera."

Thank goodness—Tyrone was acting the way we'd hoped. I took a step closer and stooped to peer inside the car.

"You came back?" Georgette asked. "You came to find me?"

I ignored her for now. "I'm not sure about the headrests. Remember how the ones on the BMW used to push me forward and give me a neck ache? These look the same."

"They're adjustable," Tyrone said. "So are the seats. They've even got those lumbar rests you can inflate. Why don't you try sitting inside?"

"Your clients won't mind?" Reed asked.

"They won't even know. When the two of them go to the club together, I'm lucky if they come back before closing. Last month, I had to hang around for an extra hour and my girlfriend got so pissed." He glanced sideways at me. "Upset. She got upset."

"Can't you just close up anyway?" Reed asked.

"Tried that. They complained to the boss."

"Sound like a pair of dicks. Okay, honey, you sit in the car, but don't touch anything. Here, I'll hold your purse." He turned back to Tyrone. "Reckon I *will* try that steam clean, buddy. Twenty bucks extra, you said?"

Reed led Tyrone away, leaving me to investigate the peculiar phenomenon of associative memory. Or so I claimed. At that moment, I wished I'd studied ventriloquism instead of flower arranging.

I slid into the driver's side, feeling sick as I realised that Tim had sat right here the night he tried to kidnap me. What thoughts went through his mind? Any guilt? Or just sick vignettes of what he planned to do to me?

Stop it, Kimberly. Concentrate on the job.

"Georgette?"

She nodded. At least this time, I could twist around to look at her on the pretence of admiring the leather seats. She appeared older than in the photos I'd seen, perhaps because of the make-up she wore. Dark lipstick, eyeliner, layers of mascara, all running down her face. There were no obvious marks on her, though.

She hovered an inch above the leather in a seated position, although that was only a pretence. Ghosts couldn't really sit, you see. Or lie down, or lean on things. Their souls may have been tethered to physical objects, but they could pass right through them. I'd never quite worked out the mechanics of it, but I guess it was so spirits who died in the middle of a road, for example, didn't get splattered by a hundred cars every freaking day. If I'd had to watch that, I'd have moved to a desert island. As it was, they just floated in their assigned spots while the world went on around them, waiting for one of the Electi to turn up and do our thing. Or not, because whoever created us had seriously miscalculated. Four Electi for the whole of the earth? Even if I *had* done my job, that was a woefully inadequate number. Either the world had been a nicer place back then, or, more likely, our creator had been a pathological optimist.

Anyhow, back to Georgette's hovering. I'd noticed that some spirits liked to pretend they were still human by arranging themselves in an appropriate position, and she was obviously one of them. Better than having her head sticking out through the sunroof, though.

"How did you die?"

"What, no small talk? I haven't had a proper conversation in two years."

"There's no time for that. I risked a lot to come here today..." Reed's wrath, my sanity, my reputation. "And I need to catch the man who did this to you. To us. Please, just answer my questions. How did you die?"

"Would you believe an asthma attack? The guy...the driver... Whatever he gave me, I think I had an allergic reaction because I woke up and I couldn't breathe properly. I asked him, no, begged him to take me to the hospital, but he just put me in the back seat and held me down until I died." She turned to show me the dark bruises marring the skin under one thin strap of her sparkly dress. "See?"

Was it better or worse to have died in that way rather than facing what would have come next? I didn't want to think about it.

"The guy with me today—Reed—he's a private detective. The police aren't taking what happened to me seriously, and obviously I can't tell them about you, so I hired him to help me find the man who hurt us. But it's not easy. Do you know anything that can help? His real name? His address?"

She shook her head. "Not his name or address. I only saw him, like, three times. Once when I met him, once when he took another girl, and then with you. He doesn't speak much, just—"

"Wait. Wait! He took *another* girl?"

"Jacqueline. At least, that's what he called her. About three months before he tried to take you. Maybe four. I lose track of time."

"Jacqueline what? Do you know her surname?"

"Sorry. She was totally unconscious by the time they pulled out of the parking lot."

"What parking lot?"

"Uh, a club. Studio Nine. Do you know it?"

I only went to clubs for bachelorette parties, and that was solely to ensure the bride didn't get arrested. Even then, I usually sent Kayla.

"No, I've never heard of it. Is it in Arlington? That's where you're from, isn't it?"

"You looked me up?" Her voice cracked. "When you left, I thought you'd gone for good. I can't believe you came back."

"That man shouldn't get away with what he did."

"Are you gonna...you know? The whole Electi thing? Some spirit guide told me about it when I died, and honestly, I know I could get reincarnated in, like, Alaska or something, but I really don't want to be stuck in this car for all eternity. Some guy picked up a hooker and had sex right next to me a few months back. Totally weird."

"You mean am I going to kill the man? Sorry, but I don't do that. This is the twenty-first century, and we've moved on. It's jail or nothing."

"Normal jail? Or is there a special supernatural jail for their nasty souls?"

"Just normal jail, I'm afraid. And to do that, I still need to find the guy. Where did he take Jacqueline?"

"I'm not exactly sure. Somewhere in the countryside, but it was dark, and these windows are tinted so I didn't get a real good look. Studio Nine's in Falls Church, and we drove for maybe half an hour after that."

"Okay, the countryside. To a forest?"

"No, a house. A big house. I saw the outline, and one of the windows had a light on."

Outside, Reed was watching me as Tyrone turned the hose on our SUV. *His* SUV. I leaned forward and opened the glove compartment in the Mercedes. Empty except for the owner's manual, a single condom, and an empty Reese's Pieces packet.

"Did you see a name? A number? What was it near?"

"I don't know! I wasn't thinking straight, okay? Jacqueline kept groaning in the front seat, and I shouted at her just in case she could hear somehow, but there wasn't a damn thing I could do. Have you ever felt utterly helpless like that?"

More times than I cared to count.

"I understand how difficult it was. But you've got to give me something. Anything. At the moment, all we know is that the man has dark-brown hair, a British accent, and he's around thirty."

"I'm not certain about the hair. When he picked up

Jacqueline, he was blond. Oh, and he wore a cast on his arm, but I think that was fake because he only slid it on in the parking lot before he went into the club."

"He had a bandage on his wrist when I met him."

"Yeah, he took that off after you jumped out. Guess he was looking for sympathy or something."

"Seriously? So now we're actually farther back than when we started."

"The car's from the British embassy. Sometimes other people take it home, but mostly it stays in the parking lot there. The owner's an old guy—Robert something—but he doesn't use it much. Mostly because he drinks. One of the times he did try driving, he ran a red light then got stopped by the cops, and even though he was so drunk he couldn't walk straight, he claimed diplomatic immunity, and they had to let him go. I watched the whole thing. Oh! The person he called to pick him up that night was the guy! The guy who kidnapped us. Does that help?"

"I don't know. Did they say anything to each other?"

"Barely a word. The younger guy seemed furious."

"Can you remember where he picked Robert up?"

"I'm, like, really bad with directions. Even with satnav, I always used to get lost. One time, it told me to turn left, so I did, only I was towing my horse trailer and we went down this narrow lane and got stuck. Did you know I had a horse?" She gave a quiet sniffle. "I miss him."

No, I didn't know, and I didn't want to know either, because that would make Georgette all the more human, and I found this hard enough already without emotions getting involved.

"Which state? Do you recall that much? DC? Maryland? Virginia?"

Georgette fell silent for a minute, thinking. "Virginia, I'm almost sure. Near the Potomac. We drove over a bridge not long before."

"Do you remember anything else from the night I was in the car?" I needed something to give to Reed. A little snippet of information. Anything. "He called himself Tim. Have you heard that name before? Maybe from the other people who drive the car?"

A few seconds passed as Georgette thought. "No, I don't remember ever hearing it."

"Did he go anywhere else that day? Or straight to the hotel where he met me?"

"He stopped at an apartment complex first. The parking garage was underground, but he pulled into a spot near the back."

"Do you remember where the building was? The name?"

"Sorry. But I saw a girl walking her dog outside, and it reminded me of my Rosie. Did you know I used to have a dog? A Maltese, and she—"

"Can we stay on topic? Please? Was there anything else distinctive about his appearance that night? I told Reed I wanted to sit in the car to jog my memory."

"Wait—he doesn't know you can see me? You haven't told him about your...you know...abilities?"

A hysterical giggle bubbled out of my throat. "Of course not. He'd think I was crazy."

"Maybe not. You should confide in somebody," Georgette said. "A problem shared is a problem halved. My mom always used to tell me that."

"Well, my mom confided in my dad. He had her

committed, and she spent the rest of her life spaced out on all the drugs they gave her at the so-called treatment centre, barely able to think or speak or move. That's where sharing gets people like me."

Although she still kept enough faculties to save up her pills and overdose. I wasn't supposed to know that, but I'd found the report in my father's study, hidden away in a drawer. That I might have picked open with a bobby pin.

And I'd never forgive him for what he did to her.

"Perhaps she just shared with the wrong person. This guy's a detective, right? Just tell him you're psychic. Sometimes they work with psychics. They made a whole TV program on it."

"What TV program?"

"*Medium.*"

I rolled my eyes. "That was fiction."

"But based on a real person."

"Who loads of people think is a fraud."

"You should open your mind."

"I'm sitting here talking to a freaking dead person, and you tell me to open my mind? What happened to staying on topic? Clues. We need more clues."

"No offence, but you don't seem very good at this."

"You think? I'm only doing it to help you out. It's not as if I've had any practice."

"What do you do for a living?"

"I'm a wedding planner."

"Figures."

"Figures? What's that supposed to mean?"

"Nothing. But you definitely need help here. That detective looks kind of nice too. I like his eyes."

"How can you see—"

Tapping on the window made me jump, and I hit my knee on the steering wheel.

Shoot. Reed was looking down at me, one eyebrow raised. "Who are you talking to?"

"Uh, nobody. Just myself. It's a nervous habit."

"Just tell him," Georgette said.

"Shut up," I muttered under my breath, then plastered on a smile for Reed. "I'm done here." A few fumbles, and I found the handle to open the door. "The seat isn't very comfortable. How about we test-drive a Lexus? Kayla has a Lexus, and I like the seats in that."

"Sure, a Lexus. Are you okay? You look as if you've seen a ghost."

I jolted upright. Oh, if only he knew. "I'm fine."

"You're shaking."

I lifted a hand and stared at it. So I was.

"Come here." Reed stooped and half lifted me out of the car, holding me steady with one arm around my waist once I had my feet back on the ground. I curled my fingers around the edge of his leather jacket to stop myself from trembling.

"Will you come back?" Georgette asked. "Please? I've got nobody else to talk with."

I couldn't speak, and even if I'd been able to, she wouldn't have wanted to hear my answer. Instead, I leaned on Reed as he led me towards a rickety little shed filled with a desk and papers and a chunky laptop that had to be ten years old.

Once again, Reed had been right. This was a bad idea. A terrible idea. All my life, I'd avoided talking to spirits wherever possible and with good reason. It hurt. Hearing their stories and thinking of the people they'd once been—it hurt. Georgette was right too. I was awful at my job, and I'd never solve this mystery on my own.

I shouldn't even have tried.

But I *had* tried, and now I needed to see it through to the bitter end or *my* soul would never rest either.

Chapter 14 - Reed

TALKING TO HERSELF? That wasn't just a few words. That was a whole damn conversation. I'd been watching Kim for the last five minutes, and her mouth hadn't stopped moving. Nor was it a habit, because I'd never seen her do it before. Whenever she got nervous, she picked up a pile of paper clips and began twisting.

At first, I'd thought she was on the phone, but when her mobile chirped in the purse in my hand, I realised she couldn't be. So what the hell had she been doing in the car?

Should I press her? A gentleman would have backed off and let her calm down, the way she was shaking, but I had a feeling if I did that, she'd never tell me the truth. And no mistake—she was lying to me about something. I'd seen all the signs before. Cagey. Hesitant. Unable to make eye contact.

There was only one seat in the office, and tempting though it was to sit her on my lap, I lowered her onto the cracked plastic and knelt in front of her.

"Kim? Did you remember something in the car?"

Now she looked at me, but her expression was kind of...glazed.

"Not really." A pause, another lie. "Just how terrified I was that night."

Tim *had* put his damn hands on her, hadn't he?

Why else would she be so upset? Although that didn't explain the talking, unless she'd just relived the whole experience in the car. I didn't know how to comfort her. She looked as though she needed a hug, but what if another man touching her freaked her out?

"Shall I take you back to work? Maybe one of the girls...?"

She shook her head, almost violently. "How long ago did you leave the police force?"

What did that have to do with anything? "A year and a half ago. Why?"

"It doesn't matter."

"It clearly does, or you wouldn't have asked."

"A girl called Jacqueline went missing from a nightclub called Studio Nine. I just thought that if you left recently, you might have heard of the case."

Well, that came out of left field. "I saw it on the news. Does that count?"

"I guess. I never watch the news—it's too depressing. Did they ever find her?"

"Not that I know of, but I don't understand why you're asking?"

Nothing.

"Kim, why do I get the impression there's a lot about this case you're not telling me? How is Jacqueline involved? *Is* she involved? I can't do my job if you keep me in the dark about everything."

Her only answer was a tear that rolled slowly down her cheek. Shit. This woman was seriously fucked in the head, and I didn't know whether to stick around and dig deeper or run as fast as possible in the other direction. If I hadn't been so strapped for cash...

"Let's get you home."

"There's no need..."

"Yeah, there is." I lifted Kim to her feet and held her up. "Hey, Tyrone? My girl's just remembered she has a salon appointment. Can you do the steam clean next week instead?"

"Sure, bro."

Kim didn't speak on the way home, not a word until we turned onto her street.

"My car... It's still outside that supermarket."

"I'll pick it up later."

Honestly? She was scaring me a bit. Something had obviously clicked in her head, and it wasn't good. Maybe she needed a therapist? Once I'd got her inside, I could phone Kelly, one of the police psychiatrists. Things had been awkward between us since she drunkenly groped me at the last departmental Christmas party I attended, but Kim was more important than my failed love life right now. If Kelly recommended a therapist Kim could talk to, I'd set up an appointment and drive her there myself.

"Do you want me to call someone?" I asked as I took her key and shoved open her front door. "A friend? A relative?" The alarm beeped away at me. "What's the code?"

"Zero-three-zero-four. And I don't have anyone. Not really."

"Isn't your dad still alive?"

Now I got hysterical laughter. "Believe me, my father isn't a person I'd ever talk to about my problems."

"Then talk to me. I promise I won't judge."

What was I even saying?

"You will. Everybody judges."

"Everybody? How many people have you told about this particular issue?"

Silence.

"You haven't told anybody, have you? I'm sure it's not as bad as you think. Now, do you want a drink? Coffee? Tea?"

"My mom had the same problem, and my father sent her to a psychiatric hospital and she died there," Kim blurted.

Cancel the coffee. We both needed something stronger. Shit. I knew her mother was dead—it came up in my research—but I hadn't seen any mention of a psychiatric hospital.

"I'm sorry about your mom. Uh, where's your wine?"

Kim burst into tears.

"Forget it, okay?" she sobbed. "Forget I said anything. And forget the whole case. I just want to go back to planning weddings and pretend none of this ever happened."

"Hey, hey, don't get upset. Let's go and sit down." I tried to steer her into the living room, but she grabbed the doorjamb and hung on.

"Not in there. I don't want to go in there."

"The kitchen?"

She stumbled along beside me, leaving her pumps behind in the hallway, and I sat her on a stool at the breakfast bar. When I first joined the police force, they sent the new recruits on a psych 101 training course, but that was six years ago and I'd forgotten almost all of it. I opened a few cupboards, but the strongest thing I found was a bottle of Mountain Dew.

"Kim, what can I do to help?"

"Nothing."

"Look, I'll keep investigating, but you have to understand it's difficult when I've got one hand tied behind my back."

For two whole minutes, I thought she wasn't going to speak, but then she whispered so quietly I barely heard her.

"Do you believe in ghosts?"

Huh? Every time I tried to guess what was going on in Kim's head, I got it totally wrong.

"Ghosts? I don't follow."

"Ghosts. Spirits. Tethered souls. Do you believe in them?"

There were two answers I could give. The truth—that I thought the supernatural was a TV program and rumours of the afterlife were bullshit—or a lie, which was what she seemed to be angling for.

Or I could play it sort of safe.

"I'm open-minded. I've never seen any evidence for or against their existence."

"What if I told you there's one in my living room?"

Whoa.

"I would be...surprised?"

Her head dropped forward, and those slender fingers began twisting together in the absence of paper clips.

"You don't believe in them."

"Kim, it's not a question I've ever been asked before. But you clearly *do* believe in them." I lifted her chin so she had to look at me. "Don't you?"

"Yes." Another soft whisper.

"Okay, so now we've established that we have different views on the paranormal, can we get back to the case? I'm at a loss here, sweetheart."

"There's a ghost in Tim's Mercedes."

Oh boy. Tell me I hadn't deleted Kelly's number by accident. Could psychiatric problems be genetic? I was fairly sure I'd seen a program on the Discovery Channel that concluded exactly that.

"Are you on any medications? Do you have a doctor I can call?"

"Just leave. And do me a favour, would you? Write everything I said off as the ramblings of a madwoman." She slid off the stool, rummaged through the nearest cupboard, and pulled a roll of hundred-dollar bills out of a sugar canister. "Here. This should cover what you've done so far." More rummaging, and she came back with a bottle of cranberry vodka. "I need a drink."

"Kimberly, I'm not leaving you alone in the middle of..." Was she having a psychotic episode? "Whatever this is. You really shouldn't keep that amount of cash in your kitchen."

And who the hell drank cranberry vodka?

Kim, it seemed. She unscrewed the cap and poured the contents of the bottle down her throat until I made a grab for it. For the first time, I wondered if Tim mightn't have had the right idea by drugging her.

"Put that down."

"No!"

She tried to hold the bottle out of my reach, but it slipped between her fingers and smashed on the tiles. Fuck. Now I had a hysterical, barefoot woman plus a pile of broken glass to deal with. Right, Kim first. I picked her up and carried her into the living room whether she wanted to go in there or not.

What the fuck happened today? She'd seemed so

put-together when I first met her, and now this.

"If I go and clear up the mess, are you going to stay here?"

Her response? She curled into the foetal position and refused to look at me. I decided to take that as a yes.

A dustpan and brush, a thick layer of newspaper, a garbage bag... I soon had the glass swept away and took a moment to reflect. Kim obviously had problems, but she'd managed to function in society and run a successful business for years. Was this just a temporary blip? I didn't want to ruin her reputation by calling in professionals if I could help it. After all, she hadn't been an awful client to work for, and she'd paid in full. More than full. I thumbed through the roll of notes she'd shoved at me. Ten thousand dollars, and she kept it lying around? Definitely unhinged in more ways than one.

Back in the living room, she was sobbing quietly to herself. Perhaps if I could get her upstairs and then call Annie or Kayla...

"Can you stand?"

She looked up at me with unfocused eyes. "I'm sorry, I'm sorry, I'm sorry..."

"Forget that. Let's just get you to bed, okay?"

"My bed?"

Well, it was hardly going to be mine, was it?

"Yes, your bed."

Another stumble, so I picked her up again. She didn't weigh much at all. Her shoes were already gone, so once I found her bedroom—the pink one with piles of fancy shit on the dressing table, I assumed—I peeled her out of her jacket and tucked her under the covers in her dress. It didn't look too comfortable, but no way was I about to try removing it.

"He's gonna... He's gonna take another girl, you know," she mumbled. "Three so far, at least. Maybe more."

"Who's gonna take another girl? Tim?"

"Who else? Me, Georgette, Jacqueline... He won't stop. Why would he stop? Nobody can catch him."

I knew I was going to regret asking this, but... "Who's Georgette?"

"Georgette Riley. The dead girl in the car. In the back seat. He killed her. Well, she had an asthma attack, but he made it happen. And now she's stuck there forever and Jacqueline's gone and I'm the only person who knows and nobody will believe me."

"Georgette was who you were talking to earlier?"

"Hahahahahahahaha! Yes! She likes to talk to me because nobody else can see her. You can't see her, right?"

"And Jacqueline? Is she in the car too?"

"Nope. Nobody knows where Jacqueline is. Not even Georgette, because she's reeeeeeally bad with directions." She looked at me again, and those eyes tugged at my damn heart. "Do you believe me now?"

"I believe that you believe that."

"So you don't believe me?"

"You have to admit, it does sound slightly...absurd."

"Yes, but that doesn't mean it's not true." Her eyes began to close. "I'm not...I'm not a liar."

"Sleep, sweetheart. Get some rest."

Amazingly, her eyes closed, and within a few minutes, her breathing deepened and became more rhythmical. Perhaps her downing half a litre of vodka in one go wasn't such a bad thing, after all, although I didn't want to leave her alone in case she woke up and started puking. I'd done that once or twice myself in the dim and distant past—the joys of a misspent youth followed by a stint in the military.

I headed downstairs and checked the doors and windows were secure, then fetched my laptop from the car. If nothing else, I could finalise my bill in the warmth while Kim slept.

The total came to a little over six thousand dollars, which seemed too much considering the outcome. But I couldn't afford to undercharge. By the time I deducted expenses and paid off the last of my credit card debt, I'd have fifteen hundred dollars and a clean slate to go on with. I ran a hand through my hair. No, I still hadn't gotten around to visiting the barber.

While I had my laptop open, I dug a bit deeper into Kimberly's parents. I couldn't get at her mother's medical records, but her obituary showed she'd died after a battle with cancer. No mention of any psychiatric problems but there wouldn't be, would there? Not when Kimberly's father was an influential lobbyist used to twisting the truth in Washington. Kim said they weren't close, and after reading some of the stories about Mr. Jennings, I wasn't surprised. He was the thunder to her fairy dust.

Before I could stop myself, I'd typed another name into the search engine: Georgette Riley. Not many hits, but a girl by that name had disappeared from Arlington the year before last. After a brief investigation, the police came to the conclusion that she'd most likely run away. Trouble at home, relationship problems, blah, blah, blah. But she'd never shown up. I found her

Facebook page and scrolled through it. Georgette had lived her life through social media until one day her postings suddenly stopped. Apart from a few dozen messages from friends asking where she was, the account was dead, just like Kim claimed Georgette was.

A pretty girl, a brunette, she didn't look much like Kim although they both had heart-stopping smiles. She'd owned a horse by the looks of things, and half of her photos featured the palomino's antics. Then one snap made me pause. A candid shot, Georgette and a group of friends at a barbecue with flames coming out of the grill. But that wasn't what caught my eye. I squinted, then enlarged the picture. Yes, Georgette had an asthma inhaler in her hand.

Georgette Riley and the mysterious Jacqueline. Two girls only connected in Kimberly's head. What if...? Hold on. *I* hadn't been drinking. How could I even contemplate that she was telling the truth? Ghosts? That was crazy talk.

Psychics and mediums and clairvoyants—they all belonged in the asylum Kim claimed her mom had been locked up in. Several years ago, the Montgomery County PD had a captain who was a little odder than most, and when a medium called to offer her services on a murder case—for a fee, of course—he'd actually taken her up on it. She'd led half a dozen officers on a wild goose chase through a forest only for an escaped dog to unearth the kid's body in a neighbour's backyard. Like I said, crazy.

Except Kim hadn't asked for money. In fact, she hadn't even wanted to discuss Georgette and Jacqueline—I'd had to pry the information out of her with the assistance of alcohol. What did she gain by telling me? Nothing, only my utter disbelief.

What time was it? Only seven o'clock. I picked up the phone and dialled an old friend in the Arlington County PD, not really sure what—

"Brett? It's Reed Cullen."

"Long time no see. You hear anything from your sister, buddy?"

"Not for months, but that's not why I'm calling."

"Oh?"

"I have a question about one of your cases. Do you have a minute?"

"Shoot."

"Georgette Riley. She disappeared almost two years ago now."

"Have you picked that one up?"

"Her name was mentioned in connection with another investigation. Did you ever find out what happened?"

"It's still open, technically."

"What do you mean, technically?"

"I mean, she never turned up, but ten months ago, she started using her debit card every so often. Never buys much. Last time, it was a donut."

"Any witnesses?"

"The first couple of times, we sent the locals to check, but they never found her."

A chill ran through me because I was all too familiar with that scenario. Except with Emma, it was different. She'd called me after she left. Only once, but I'd sure as hell recognised her voice when she sobbed out her story about Wyatt Banks and another girl. A little of the tension seeped away.

"So you're not actively investigating?"

"I shouldn't say this, but no. Before she disappeared, she told a friend she'd had enough of living with her boyfriend, and she hated the idea of moving home since her father always seemed more interested in the animals than her."

"Animals?"

"Horses, cattle, chickens. The family's got a ranch. Why all these questions, Cullen? Have you found something?"

"I'm not sure. One more question, though—did anyone spot a black Mercedes near the scene of Georgette's disappearance?"

"How did you know that? We never released that detail to the public."

"I can't say right now, but if it comes to anything, you'll be the first to hear."

Well, shit. I hung up and stared at the phone. How had Kimberly known about the Mercedes? The options were limited.

Either she'd been there, or someone had given her the information. A cop? Tim himself? Or...she was being truthful and Georgette had communicated from the afterlife.

For Pete's sake, Cullen. Have you been smoking something?

Next, I typed "Jacqueline" into the search engine, together with the name of the nightclub she'd disappeared from. Studio Nine, if I recalled correctly. Sure enough, there she was. Jacqueline Springer, a pretty redhead whose hobbies included ballet dancing and playing the flute, according to the tearful statement her parents had given. Her father was a pastor in Falls Church, and the evening she'd disappeared, she was paying her first ever visit to a nightclub for a college friend's bachelorette party. Sometime after midnight, she'd gone outside to get some air, and apart from a doorman who thought he glimpsed her talking to a blond guy on the other side of the parking lot, nobody ever saw her again.

The only person I knew in Falls Church was Wyatt Banks's cousin, and I didn't relish the thought of calling him. But since I wanted to solve this mystery before Kim woke up, I didn't have much choice. Trent had been a reasonable guy on the dozen or so occasions we'd met; I just had to hope he hadn't turned into a dick like my former best friend.

"Reed Cullen?" he asked when I introduced myself. "Reed Cullen who used to be friends with Wyatt?"

"That's me."

"Gotta say, I'm surprised to get a call from you."

"That makes two of us, but I have a question on one of your local cases."

"Ask away. Always felt bad about what happened between you and my cousin. He can be pig-headed when he wants to be. Say, did your sister ever come back?"

"No, she never did." And talking about her hurt. "Anyhow, I'm calling regarding the disappearance of Jacqueline Springer."

"The pastor's daughter?"

"That's her. Rumour says there haven't been any further developments?"

"Not a thing, but that case always did bug the hell out of me. Nobody heard her scream, and nobody saw her struggle. What made a conservative twenty-three-year-old get into a car with a man rather than going back to her friends? Because that's the only thing that could have happened. She didn't walk anywhere from the club—her girlfriends said her shoes were pinching and she'd already sat out most of the dancing."

"Did you trace all the cars parked nearby?"

"Not all of them. A half dozen are still on the query list from what I know."

"Any of them a black Mercedes?"

"Not sure. Why? You got a lead?"

"Right now? I've got a whole lot of pieces I can't fit together. But if you could check on the car, I'd appreciate it."

"Give me half an hour."

I may have accused Kimberly of being absurd, but at that moment, I felt like the lunatic. Asking questions of law enforcement officers based on a ghost story? Had I lost my damn mind?

Maybe so, but Kim had seemed so matter-of-fact in what she was saying, even while drunk. And what reason did she have to lie?

Back when I was a kid, I used to love *The X-Files*. Aliens, ghosts, conspiracy theories... I even had a poster of a spaceship above my bed. Only as I got older did I stop believing in the supernatural as grown-ups and the mainstream media taught me their view of our planet. There was no evidence for the spirit world, so how could it exist? But there'd been no proof of radiation either until William Herschel's experiments in the early nineteenth century. I'd claimed earlier to be open-minded, but in truth, I'd become closed off to anything I couldn't see, hear, taste, touch, or smell since my teens.

But what if ten-year-old me had been right? That

there was a whole other universe out there that we didn't know about? My mind teemed with questions as I lay back on Kim's sofa. Were ghosts real or all in her head? Had science been missing a trick for years? And worst of all, was there a serial killer out there, lurking behind a devilish smile and diplomatic immunity?

Chapter 15 - Kimberly

"HEY."

THE FIRST thing I heard when I rejoined the land of the living was Reed's voice.

"You're awake?" he asked.

Yes, but I didn't want to be. Little snippets of my antics last night flittered back to me—my stupid confession about Georgette, the vodka, Reed carrying me upstairs to bed. What was he still doing here? Tell me he didn't plan on having me committed.

"I have a headache."

A glass of water and two pills appeared beside me, as if by magic.

"Try these."

"Thanks, but the issue is more fundamental."

A ghost-induced headache. Or perhaps a tumour. What if I pretended to have a tumour? That could explain my outburst yesterday in a much more believable way.

Or perhaps I could just jump off a bridge?

"Why are you still here?" I asked Reed.

"We need to talk."

"That's not necessary. I've had a think about things, and you were absolutely right before. I should forget the case and carry on with my life."

"I've been thinking too, and you shouldn't forget

the case."

"Is it the money? I gave you cash last night, right? Do I owe you more? I can wire you any amount that's outstanding."

"It's not the money. About what you said. The ghosts..."

I forced a laugh. "Oh, just ignore me. I talk complete garbage when I've been drinking."

"You hadn't actually drunk anything at that point."

"I hadn't? I guess I was just tired. Maybe I saw a movie on TV, and—"

"Kimberly, stop talking. I think... I mean, it all sounds insane, but I think I believe you. Either that or you're in cahoots with Tim and I'm the biggest idiot that ever lived."

"And sometimes movies can seem really real, and— What?"

"Yesterday evening, after you passed out, I did some research on Georgette Riley and Jacqueline Springer. A black Mercedes was seen nearby at the time of both their disappearances, and the driver's never been identified."

"Even Jacqueline's? I was hoping it wasn't true, but..."

"I put a call in to an acquaintance in Falls Church, and he got back to me late last night. A witness claimed she saw a black Mercedes drive out of the parking lot after Jacqueline went missing, but the witness had been drinking and was considered unreliable." Reed sat on the edge of my bed, and the mattress dipped towards him. "I don't know how or why you can see ghosts, but I do believe there's something going on with you that doesn't have a rational explanation." He tucked a stray lock of hair behind my ear. "Okay? Please don't hit the vodka again."

All my life, I'd wished for one person, just one person other than my mom to believe in my weird abilities, but now I'd heard those very words come out of Reed's mouth, I was the one left struggling to believe.

"Are you winding me up? Pretending? Because if you are, it's not funny."

My father had played along with my mom at first, encouraging her to tell stories of what she saw and heard before he called the men in white coats. The only thing worse than people's disbelief was a betrayal of trust.

"I swear I'm being straight with you. Kim, will you tell me more? More about what you saw in the car yesterday?"

I tried to speak, but no words would come out, only tears. When Momma was in the treatment centre, she'd told me I'd find somebody to talk to about the gift— even after all the misery it caused her, she still called it our gift—but until now, I'd always doubted her. Could Reed really be that person? I'd spent so long holding the world at arm's length that I didn't know if I had it in me to let him get close.

What if this was a game to him? I'd get hurt.

But what if it wasn't?

I'd lose the one chance I had to ease the horrible burden I'd carried for years.

"Kimberly, what's wrong? What did I say? I thought you wanted to get to the bottom of this?"

"I did, I mean, I do, but... I'm just so confused. The only person I could ever speak to was my mom, and now she's gone, and... Why can't I stop crying?"

"How about I go downstairs and make us both breakfast while you take a shower? You didn't eat dinner last night, and trying to deal with this on an empty stomach can't be good."

"Breakfast?"

"Toast, cereal, coffee. Whatever you want." He put a hand over his mouth as he yawned. "Sorry. I was up for half the night looking into this."

"Okay." This was weird. "I'm not fussy. Anything you want to make is fine."

"Then I'll meet you downstairs."

Reed's footsteps padded away along the landing, and I had a minor freak-out when I realised it was eight thirty on a Friday and I was still at home. Then I remembered I'd cleared today in case I needed time to process Georgette's revelations, and we didn't have a wedding on this weekend. Phew.

Another panic came in the bathroom when I caught sight of my face, which mirrored Georgette's with make-up smudged everywhere, and once again, I wondered why Reed hadn't run for the hills. If all my talk of ghosts hadn't scared him off, surely my tear-streaked mascara should have?

As I got dressed, I couldn't help pausing every so often to listen. Was he really making breakfast? Or had he snuck out to get a straitjacket? After all, that was what my father did to Mom. She came back from her yoga class, took a shower, then walked downstairs into the arms of the waiting doctors. Father had hustled ten-year-old me back to my room so I never even got a chance to say goodbye, and three months passed before I was allowed to speak to her again.

But today, when I plucked up the courage to tiptoe into the kitchen, I found Reed cooking scrambled eggs.

"Hey."

He saw me in the doorway and smiled. "I feel as though I should have made some cheesy crack about how you like your eggs in the morning."

"I appreciate that you didn't."

"Scrambled okay?"

"Scrambled's fine."

"You like bagels? I found a package in the fridge."

"I was the one who bought them."

"Yeah. Of course."

I took a seat at the breakfast bar, feeling decidedly uncomfortable in my own home. Reed had already set out cutlery and two glasses of orange juice, and I took a sip from the closest.

"So..." I said.

"So."

"I'm not sure where to start."

"How about at the beginning, with the truth this time? I need to know what we're dealing with. There's a whole different level of danger involved if we're hunting a murderer instead of just an asshole who likes to spike girls' drinks."

"I'm sorry. So, so sorry. I should have told you, but I just... I didn't know how."

"Don't dwell on it. If we're going to work together on this, we both have to move on."

"I don't understand why you're still helping."

"Honestly? Two reasons. Firstly, I need the money, and secondly, I don't want a killer roaming the streets any more than you do. You would have been his third victim, and so far, he's been clever enough that nobody else suspects a thing."

Two bagels popped out of the toaster, and Reed put them on plates then divided the eggs in half and spooned them over the top. Today was the first time anyone had cooked for me in this kitchen, and if I hadn't been so antsy inside, I might even have enjoyed it.

"Have you always been able to see ghosts?" Reed asked.

"Can I take a mouthful first?"

"Sorry."

Wow, these eggs were good. I never managed to get them fluffy like that.

"Uh, not always. Only since I was seven. But I knew it was coming."

"How?"

"My mom told me. It's something that gets passed down to your firstborn child, and there was a crossover point, a few years when we could both see the spirits, then her gift began to fade as mine got stronger."

"So now you're stuck with it until you have a kid?"

"Nuh-uh. I'm never having kids. Not biological ones, anyway. You really think I want to burden someone with this?"

My only hope was that this horrible ability would die when I did.

"I suppose when you put it that way..."

"Do you know, you're the first person I've ever told that. With my ex-husband, I kept my mouth shut until we got divorced."

Oh, the arguments it had caused... Before the wedding, Alan swore he didn't want children, and since he was twenty years older than me and therefore should have had plenty of time to consider these things, I'd accepted the ring when he proposed. Yes, I was a trophy wife, okay? But I thought he was the safe option, and I didn't want to be alone for the rest of my life. Except six months after we tied the knot, he changed his mind. His sister had a baby, you see, and he kept going on and on about wanting an heir to leave his fortune to.

"You split up over kids?"

"The lack of them? Yes."

That and the fact he'd taken matters into his own hands and gotten his secretary pregnant when I refused to acquiesce to his demands. Was I bitter? Not really. I'd never loved him enough to hate him, and he offered a generous settlement if I agreed to end things quickly and waived my right to alimony. A clean break had suited me just fine, and after I bought my house, I'd tucked the remainder of the cash away in equities and bonds and funds, the income from which would provide me with a perfectly comfortable lifestyle even if I chose not to work. And Alan? The last I heard, the secretary had given birth to her second set of twins and he'd taken up fly fishing just to get out of the house.

"I'm sorry," Reed said.

"Don't be. If nothing else, it confirmed what I already knew deep down—that serious relationships aren't something I can entertain."

"And Tim?"

"Apparently, he was good looking. Don't judge me. Thousands of men do exactly the same thing."

Reed chuckled. "I'm not judging. It's just that I can't picture a girl like you having a one-night stand."

"What do you mean, a girl like me? What's wrong

with me?"

"Nothing. Nothing at all. It's just that you've got this prim thing going on with the frilly skirts and the bows and the little heels."

I felt the neck of my blouse. What was wrong with a pussy bow?

"Just because I don't like letting my cleavage hang out..."

He held both hands up. "Hey, I like it, okay? But no one's gonna mistake you for a hooker."

"Oh. That's good, I think. But I'll have you know I still enjoy a good party."

"Champagne and canapés?"

"Shut up."

"I'm sorry." He was still laughing, the pig. "Georgette. Let's go back to Georgette. Start at the beginning."

"Well, I met her after Tim drugged me. I didn't even notice her before I got into the car, what with the windows being tinted, but then she started speaking. And she told me..."

Reed's phone buzzed, and he pulled it out of his pocket.

"She told me her name, and that she'd died in the car after... What is it?"

He was staring at the screen with a mixture of apprehension and excitement if his expression was anything to go by. Was it a lead in the case?

"It's a message from my sister. Wishing me a happy birthday." Now he shook his head in disbelief. "Nothing for months, and now this?"

"When's your birthday?"

"Three weeks ago."

"Oh. I guess it's sweet that she remembered, even if it's a bit late."

"She's ignored every message I've sent asking if she's okay, whether she needs anything, how she's coping... Our great aunt died, and she didn't even send a damn card. And now this?"

"You sound angry."

"I guess I am. She's my sister and I'll always love her, but sometimes she can be so damn selfish."

"When she left, was it on bad terms?"

"It was...difficult. But I've never blamed her for anything she did. I've told her that a thousand times. Voicemails, emails, text messages. And this is all I get back. *Happy Birthday, Reed. Enjoy being thirty! Love, Emma.*"

Put that way, Emma's actions did seem a little thoughtless. "What are you going to do?"

Reed sighed, pain leaching out on his breath. "What I always do; go and look for her. I'm sorry, but I need to take a few days."

"It's okay. There were three months between Jacqueline and me, so Tim will probably stay quiet for a while. Don't you think?"

"I hope so. He didn't get the ending he wanted with you, though. Remember?"

An icy chill washed through me. "You don't mean...?"

But Reed had already turned away with the phone pressed to his ear.

"It's Cullen. I need another location trace." He read out a number. "Same price as last time? ... Yeah, I'll wire the money ... Thanks."

"You're bribing somebody for information?" I asked

once he'd hung up. "At the phone company?"

"A necessary evil now I don't carry a badge anymore. Why? Does that bother you?"

"Not really. How long does it take?"

"Usually a half hour, give or take."

"Is it expensive?"

"Two hundred bucks. I used to have a cheaper guy, but he went to work at HBO. Kim, can you do one thing for me?"

"Is it legal?"

"Sweetheart, I'd never ask you to do anything illegal. You gave me a bundle of cash last night, but could you transfer the money electronically instead? I don't have time to go to the bank right now."

"Of course. How much do you need? All of it?"

"You only owed me six thousand, and you gave me ten."

"Consider the rest an advance. Give me two minutes, and I'll transfer it from my phone."

"I meant what I said last night—you shouldn't be keeping that much cash in your kitchen. Statistically, that's the first place a burglar will look."

"I've got an alarm, and my next-door neighbour's an insomniac so he's always looking out the windows at odd times of night."

"A surprising number of break-ins happen during the day when everyone's at work. Bet you've got a lot of commuters in a neighbourhood like this, and you never know who's around when you're not in."

"Yes, I do. Margaret tells me."

"Who's Margaret?"

"The ghost in the living room. She stands near the window."

The look on Reed's face said he wished he hadn't asked. "What does she do? Scare them away?"

"No, she memorises the registration numbers and descriptions of all the people who visit. It's like a game for her."

"Do me a favour. Next time you meet a potential kidnapper in a hotel wine bar, take Margaret with you instead of Maria."

"That's not possible. Ghosts can't move."

"What do you mean?"

"They're stuck to the spot where they died. Or in Georgette's case, a car."

"Stuck forever?"

"More or less."

"What about really old ghosts? Like civil war soldiers?"

"Yes, they're still around. Some places are horribly crowded. When I was looking to buy a house, one property I viewed had half a dozen charred teenagers lounging in the front room, and they all started yelling at me when I arrived. Apparently, there was a fire there in the fifties."

"Is that the worst thing that's happened?"

"No, that was the time my ex-husband surprised me with a minibreak to New York and insisted we visit the 9/11 memorial. I was sick for three days straight after that."

I could still see it now. Thousands of broken bodies, twisted at unnatural angles from where they'd hit the ground. Some floated in mid-air, staring down at me from twenty floors above. I'd closed my eyes, but I could still hear them, moaning and wailing and crying and begging and cajoling and shouting and...

"Kim, it's okay. I'm here. Shall I get more tissues?"

I swallowed down the lump in my throat. "I won't cry; I promise."

Reed's phone rang, and I thought it would be the person from the phone company, but then he started talking about transactions.

"Her debit card? Where did she use it?" He looked around wildly and mimed writing, so I passed him a pen from the drawer under the microwave. "Forty dollars? Okay, thanks... Sure, the same amount as last time? I'll transfer it today."

Another clue?

Reed closed his eyes for a second after he hung up. "Emma's been busy today. She just spent forty bucks at a grocery store in Cincinnati."

"And another bribe?"

"It's how the world works, Kim, from the government to the guy on the street."

Oh, I got that. I may even have been guilty of slipping a dress designer a Louis Vuitton purse to bump my client to the front of the line for a custom fitting.

"How can I help? Want me to book you a plane ticket while you go pack a bag?"

"Thanks, but I'll drive. By the time I go to the airport and check in, then rent a car at the other end, I won't save much time anyway. I've got everything I need in my car, and that way I'll have wheels when I get there."

"But Cincinnati's eight or nine hours away. You'll be exhausted."

"I'll be fine. Not my first rodeo, sweetheart."

"Yes, I'm aware of that, but you're already tired.

Why don't you sleep for an hour or two first?"

"Because every delay gives Emma more time to disappear again. I'll try not to be long. Just a couple of days, and I can do some more research into your case remotely." He yawned again. "But maybe I'll just grab a coffee before I go."

I smiled sweetly because an idea was forming in my mind. Reed planned to drive eight hours when he was already worn out? Visions of crumpled metal flashed through my mind, and I wouldn't even be able to tell his unfortunate soul what an idiot he was because if he killed himself through his own stupidity, he'd skip straight to the line for reincarnation.

That would happen over my dead body.

CHAPTER 16 - REED

"WHAT'S THE BAG for?" I asked Kim when I tripped over a small duffel in the hallway.

After downing two mugs of strong instant coffee, I was waiting for the caffeine rush to hit, and boy did I need it. Why did everything have to happen at once?

"It's my overnight bag. I'm coming with you."

Was she serious? "No, you're not."

"Why? Think about it—we can share the driving and take it in turns to sleep. I don't have a wedding this weekend, just a meeting to discuss floral arrangements, and I already spoke to Annie and she said she'd take that and also pick my car up."

Kim had really thought this through, hadn't she? A strange warmth spread out in my chest because nobody had ever done that for me before—dropped everything to help—but I still couldn't let her come along. Not when I planned to sleep in the back seat and skulk around the bad parts of Cincinnati where I feared Emma had ended up. My sister's best traits were also her weaknesses—her sweetness and kind heart meant she was easily led, and more than once, that had landed her in trouble. Landed the whole family in trouble. Mom blamed Emma for the break-up of her previous marriage, and our current stepfather refused to have anything to do with my sister.

"I appreciate the offer, sweetheart. More than you'd think. But I can do this on my own."

"I'm sure you can, but why should you have to? Besides, I hardly ever leave the state, so it'll be fun. I hate heights, you see, so I never fly unless I absolutely have to, or stay in high-rise hotels, and even tall staircases make me feel a bit sick. Sorry, I'm rambling now."

"Kim, this isn't a vacation. It's work."

"I can stay in the hotel while you do your thing. I promise I won't get in the way."

"I'm not staying in a hotel. I'll sleep in my car."

Her lips formed into a perfectly plump circle. "But it's freezing outside."

"I'm used to it."

"Used to sleeping in your car? What, like on stakeouts?"

Oh, fuck it. If we carried on with the invisible man case, she'd find out about my living situation sooner or later.

"I'm between homes at the moment."

"You're what?" Determination morphed into pity, exactly what I didn't want. "You're homeless?"

"It's temporary. Just some cash flow problems."

"But...but..."

I backed towards the front door. "See you in a few days, okay?"

Outside, I heard the door slam and too late, I realised Kimberly was on the wrong side of it. She ran past me, clutching her flowery pink bag, and leapt into my passenger seat. Shit.

"Kim, didn't you hear a word I said?"

"Yes. I just chose to ignore it."

"What's it gonna take to get you out of my vehicle?"

"A dozen firemen, an Ines di Santo bridal gown at ninety percent discount, or an act of God."

For a moment, I actually considered the firemen. I knew a couple at the gym, and... *Forget it.* That would take time I didn't have.

"You're crazy."

"We've just established I can talk to dead people, and now you tell me I'm crazy because I want to go to Ohio?"

Think positive, Cullen. If I did find Emma, maybe she wouldn't create such a scene if I had a stranger with me.

"Fine. Come if you must, but if I do anything remotely dangerous, you're staying in the car."

"Okay, I'll agree to that."

Kim clipped her seat belt on, and I wanted to kiss that smug little smile right off her face. *What? Where did that come from?* Too long without a woman and I'd turned into the crazy one.

"And stop looking so damn pleased. I'm only taking you under duress."

Although as we drove across the edge of Pennsylvania, I began to change my mind. I'd grabbed a couple of hours' sleep while she drove and begun to feel more human again.

"Want me to take another turn yet?" I asked.

"Swap after we get gas? We need to stop soon."

I took the opportunity to watch her out of the corner of my eye as she concentrated on the road. Kimberly Noelle Jennings was a whole bundle of contradictions: brave yet nervous, smart yet naïve, organised yet impulsive. How much of her personality stemmed from the secret she'd been holding inside for so long?

"Where do we need to go when we get to Cincinnati?" she asked, interrupting my thoughts.

"The mall where Emma bought groceries, and the area she sent the text message from." My contact at the phone company had emailed me the details while we were en route, and the locations weren't far apart. "Then we ask around to see if anyone knows her."

"How many times have you done this?"

"What, dropped everything and gone running across the country after my sister?"

"Yes."

"Maybe a dozen."

"Always Ohio?"

"A few times. Also Pennsylvania and West Virginia."

"Don't you think it's odd that she moves around so much? Why doesn't she settle down?"

"For anyone else, it would be odd, but Emma's always had her problems. I'm afraid that unless I catch up to her, she'll always be running."

"Running from what?"

"Long term? Her past. Short term? A bunch of drug dealers she owed money to."

Kim's gasp reminded me once more that she didn't belong to that world. "Drug dealers?"

"Don't worry; I've paid them off. Why do you think I'm living in my car?"

"My goodness. I had no idea..."

"How would you when I didn't tell you?"

"What about her past? What happened to her?"

Kim had trusted me with her secrets; now I had to

trust her with mine. Partly, at least. "Our father abused her when we were kids."

"Holy crap. What happened? I mean, is he in jail?"

"He left town."

Feet fucking first. Emma had been eleven years old when I walked in on them in her bedroom, and I'll never forget the expressions on their faces. Emma's a mixture of pain and fear. My father's a combination of pleasure and shock. Even at seventeen, I'd been strong, and it only took three punches to make sure he didn't get up again. That night, Emma had refused to leave my side, clinging to me in tears while we rode to Seneca Creek State Park in my old truck to bury him.

Did I feel guilty for killing my own father? Not after Emma told me how long the sick fucker had been creeping into her room at night. Six years. Six damn years, and I hadn't had a clue. I liked to think our mother didn't know either, but I'd never be sure about that. She'd definitely turned a blind eye to the asshole's infidelities and his drinking.

Of course, questions were asked. The cops sniffed around after Mom reported him missing, but back then, I'd still been on good terms with Wyatt, and he gave me an alibi. Helped with the aftermath of Emma too, help that was desperately needed because when Emma confessed our father's sins to Mom, rather than give my sister the support she needed, the weak-willed bitch had made excuses for the piece of scum she'd married and suggested we'd misinterpreted his motives, seemingly more worried about the loss of grocery money than Emma's mental state.

I'd already committed to the military by then, and I ended up sending half of my wages home to support the two of them, not that Mom ever offered any thanks. She seemed to view the income as a right since we'd "driven away" the asshole she married. Do you understand why I never spoke to her now? As soon as I got out of the army, Emma had moved to live with me, and nothing had given me greater pleasure than cancelling the standing order to my so-called mother.

"That's terrible," Kim said. "Not that your father left town, but that he never had to answer for his actions."

"Do you believe in karma?"

"Honestly? I don't know, but I hope it exists. Do you?"

"Yeah, I do. I like to think he realised the error of his ways." Then I had another thought that left me cold. If Kim was right, my father's ghost was stuck in Emma's old bedroom, and the chances were, another little girl was sleeping in there at night. "Back to ghosts for a second. You said people's spirits stay where they died. Is there any way to get rid of them?"

"Well, it's not all people, just those who died at the hands of another. Can you imagine how crowded it would be if every single soul stayed on earth? And as far as I know, souls get recycled, so there'd be a shortage. Although the world's population's going up, so I guess new ones must get created somehow. I only got snippets of information from my mom, so I have no idea."

Died at the hands of another? Well, shit. Daddy dearest was definitely still around, then.

"But they're here forever? The ghosts?"

Kim sighed. "Not exactly. That's where I'm supposed to come in."

"You're gonna have to elaborate."

"Okay, so if you think the ghost thing was insane..."

She hesitated and glanced across at me as if she wasn't sure whether she should tell me the next part.

"Go on."

"Promise you won't call the men in white coats."

"I promise."

"We're supposed to work with the ghosts to solve their murders, and when we banish the black souls by killing the killers ourselves, it frees the tethered spirits to continue to the afterlife." She snuck another glance. "Now do you think I'm looney tunes?"

Truthfully? I was still absorbing that latest revelation. She was supposed to kill me to free my father? What was she gonna do? Beat me over the head with a bouquet?

"You said 'we.' Who else does this?"

"I have no idea. Mom said there are four of us, but I've never met the others, and she didn't either. The Electi. That's what we're called. In Latin, it means 'the chosen,' plural, but I think some Roman made that up because we've been around for longer than that. Apparently." She fingered the gold necklace she wore. "This is part of the puzzle. The others each have a piece, and they fit together."

Looney tunes didn't even begin to cover this. The ghost thing I could kind of accept, but the idea that Kim was some sort of avenging angel?

"How did your mom know this?"

"Grandma told her."

"And your grandma also..."

"Yes."

"Did your mom ever, you know, test the theory out?"

"No! She couldn't even squash a bug. She used to catch them in an upside-down drinking glass and put them outside."

"So it could all be made up?"

"It's...not."

She whispered the last word, and I began to get a bad, bad feeling.

"Kim... Did *you* test it out?"

"It was an accident, I swear." Her knuckles turned white on the steering wheel. "I swear."

"What happened?"

"You're a cop. What if I incriminate myself?"

Oh, dammit, another tear leaked out of her eye. "Sweetheart, I'm hardly gonna tell anyone about this conversation. Who would believe it?"

Plus I'd be a complete fucking hypocrite if I berated her for killing an asshole then covering up their death.

"*You* believed me. Or at least, you said you did."

"Stop twisting things. What happened?"

She took a deep breath. "When I moved into my house, there were two ghosts. Margaret and Tiffany. Tiffany died when her boyfriend threw her down the stairs, only he said she tripped, and it got ruled an accident."

"And you believed she was telling the truth?"

"Yes, because she wouldn't have been there otherwise. Accidental deaths get a free pass if they're self-inflicted. Anyhow, I got a flat tyre one day, and I really needed my car because I had a cake tasting to attend, so I went to the nearest auto repair shop instead of my regular one. And this...this pig... He was so darn rude. First, he wouldn't even look at me, just kept working under a car on one of those little wheeled plank things. Then he finally rolled out and told me they were closed, even though the sign said open, and I'm sure he looked up my skirt as well."

"Let me guess. This was Tiffany's boyfriend?"

"Joey. Yes. He was so rude that I got a tiny bit angry on my way out and kicked the bumper of the car he was under. I'll admit there was a bit of a crash as I walked away, but I honestly didn't realise I'd done any damage until I arrived home and found Tiffany gone. And then I heard that a local mechanic got crushed when the car he was working on fell off its jacks. Apparently, he died instantly."

"Karma at work."

"I guess. The car was rusty, and I scuffed the toe out of a pair of Jimmy Choo pumps." She chewed the corner of her lip for a second. "So you see, I know the Electi thing works. But I only ever tested the process that one time. Do you believe me?"

"Yes, Kim. I believe you."

CHAPTER 17 - KIMBERLY

WHAT DO YOU know? Georgette was right. Confiding in someone did make me feel better, even if I wasn't a hundred percent convinced that Reed wouldn't drop me off at the nearest police precinct or "treatment centre" the next time I fell asleep.

It was his turn behind the wheel, and taking off for an impromptu weekend away felt oddly liberating, even if the circumstances were somewhat unusual. Normally, I only travelled for work, and my last vacation had been a two-week break in Aruba with Alan. I'd spent the previous month dreading it, the flight drunk, the day after we arrived hung-over, and the rest of the trip freaking out about the return journey. This was much better. Reed had even bought me a package of Reese's Peanut Butter Cups when we stopped for gas.

While he concentrated on driving, I consulted Trip Advisor. Where was the best place to stay? No way would I be sleeping in the car, and neither would Reed. I glanced into the back seat. How was it even logistically possible? He was over six feet tall, and the car really wasn't that big. And where was all of his stuff? How did he stay clean? He didn't smell like a homeless person. I took a surreptitious sniff. More a mix of cedar wood and man with a hint of something floral. A rainforest?

"Where do you shower?" I blurted. "Sorry. I need to remember to think before I speak."

"Hey, you told me your secrets, I should tell you mine, right?" He was smiling. Phew. "I go to the gym most mornings." Which also explained the muscles. "Since we're asking questions, what made you become a wedding planner? It seems like an odd choice for you."

"Why?"

"Because you've sworn off relationships, yet you spend all day helping couples to commit to each other."

"I guess when you look at it that way, it must seem strange... But I like organising things."

And I was good at it, even if I said so myself.

"How did you get into it?"

"When I got married, I organised my own wedding because I wanted everything to be perfect. And it was. It really was. We said our vows outside, the sun shone, all the children behaved, the food was served to perfection. A friend who came as a guest asked me to help plan her ceremony since I wasn't working at that time, and because I was bored at home, I agreed. Then her cousin wanted to book me, and so did another acquaintance of theirs, and it just snowballed. Eventually, there was too much for me to do on my own, so I hired Annie and Kayla."

"You've built up a good business."

"Honestly? I earn more from my investments, but I like to keep busy. And I do love weddings, even if I'll never get married again myself."

Speaking of busy, I still needed to find somewhere for us to stay tonight. Hotels, motels, self-catering apartments... Nope, I didn't need a swimming pool because I hadn't packed a bathing suit. And I'd never use a gym, although perhaps Reed would like one. No way, that one had too many floors... I picked out a couple of possibles and fired off emails. What did they have available? Nobody put their best rates on those booking websites—I knew that from organising wedding accommodation.

"How long until we get there?" I asked Reed.

"Another hour. You okay?"

Yes. Strangely, I was.

CHAPTER 18 - REED

EMMA HAD BOUGHT her groceries from a dusty dump called Joe's Spend 'n' Save. A fucking oxymoron if I ever heard one. Located at one end of a crumbling strip mall, it was only one step away from demolition, and I spotted mouse shit in the chiller aisle.

"Now what?" Kim asked, sticking close by my side as she skirted a puddle of something sticky on the grimy floor.

I nodded towards the checkout clerk, a blonde with nails so long it was a miracle she managed to work the register.

"Once she's finished serving that customer, I'll have a chat with her."

Gaudy banners still advertised last summer's barbecue specials, and unsurprisingly, the hot dogs were out of date. How did places like this survive? The cynic in me said it was a front for money laundering, but in reality, the proprietor probably just preyed on desperate people like my sister.

The grubby teenager pocketed his package of candy and disappeared out the front door, leaving back-alley Barbie to stare at Kim and me with a mix of incredulity and curiosity. Yeah, we must have looked like a strange pair, me in my jeans and a beat-up leather jacket and Kim in a pale-pink shift dress and another pair of those prissy little heels. Today's had fancy rosettes made from ribbon on them.

"Hey, my name's Reed, and this is Kim. I'm a private investigator from Pennsylvania, and we're searching for her sister. We've got reason to believe she was shopping in here this morning. Were you working then?"

The blonde nodded and carried on chewing her gum, eyes vacant.

"She's a little shorter than Kim here, and she's got red hair. Green eyes, a stud in her nose, pierced ears. Do you remember her?"

Blondie shook her head. "Ain't seen nobody like that."

"Early, about eight o'clock."

"Bin here since seven. Ain't seen no redheads."

"Sometimes she dyes it. Brown, usually. She spent just over forty dollars on a debit card in the name of Emma Cullen."

The girl shrugged infuriatingly. "Like I said, I don't remember."

"Do you have cameras?"

"Mister, does this look like the type of place to have a security system? Kids steal stuff all the time. The boss don't care, and as long as I get paid, I don't care neither."

"Is there anyone else working here that I can talk to?"

"Billy called in sick. Left me with everything to do, the asshole. He's not sick, he's hung-over."

Like the place was so damn busy. Another thread of hope fluttered away, going the same way as all the others. Whether deliberately or by coincidence, Emma always popped up in places with no cameras and nobody who remembered her. Sometimes, as in this case, the witnesses didn't seem all that switched on, and other times, there were too many people around for one small redhead to make an impression. Especially if she'd gone brunette or worn a hat.

She'd always hated her hair colour, and if I cared to admit it, which I didn't, I'd had doubts about her parentage more than once. Our mother gave birth to her, that was for sure, but I'd long suspected she didn't always keep her legs together where her marriage was concerned. Did I ever want to find out for sure? No. In all the ways that mattered, Emma was my sister, full stop, and genetics aside, that didn't make what our father did to her acceptable in any way.

"Just leave it," Kim said, giving me a gentle tug towards the back of the store. Tell me she didn't have a sudden urge to catch E. coli?

"What is it?"

"Can you distract the clerk for a few minutes? Get her away from the register?"

"Why?"

"Because then I can talk to the other clerk."

"What other clerk?"

"The one bleeding from the bullet wound in his chest."

Oh, fuck. Another ghost? "He's dead?"

"For some years, judging by his attire. She keeps walking through him. It's most disconcerting, although I suppose he's used to it."

Even though we'd already had the ghost discussion, every time Kim said something like that, it made me question all over again whether I'd stumbled into a parallel universe.

"Uh, okay. Do you think he can help?"

"Who knows? I'm new to this detective thing, remember? But there's only one way to find out."

She was right, and if I wanted to find Emma, I had to grab every chance, no matter how slim.

I sidled up to Blondie again. "There's an empty spot for pancake mix. Do you have any more out the back?"

"How should I know?"

Because it's your job. "Would you mind looking?" I forced a smile. "I'd be grateful."

She shuffled off, and I followed her to keep watch while Kim did her thing. This reminded me of the time I had to testify in a murder case, and the poor dumb schmuck of a public defender asked the witness whether he'd become acquainted with the victim before or after he died. At the time, we'd all laughed. I wasn't laughing now.

Kim picked up a box of candy and pretended to read the back, but I could see her lips moving. How often had she done this? Pretended to concentrate on banalities while she talked to a dead person?

Her head tilted to one side and she looked up, ingredients and calorie content forgotten. What had the former clerk said? Was it important? Kim seemed to hate her gift, as she called it, but at times like this, I envied her. Detectives dreamed about this shit. How much easier would it be to solve a murder when you could ask the victim anything you wanted?

Kim was still engrossed in conversation when I heard Blondie's footsteps returning. *Think quickly, Cullen.* I shoved a jar of spaghetti sauce off the shelf and leapt back when it splattered everywhere.

"Shit! Sorry. Here, let me help you clean that up. I'll pay for the damage."

Blondie shot me a filthy glare and retreated into the storeroom. Clattering suggested she was hunting for cleaning materials, and I raised an eyebrow at Kim.

"Two minutes," she mouthed. Then, "Emma had a boyfriend, didn't she?"

"Wyatt Banks. I believe you met him."

Had the spirit, as Kim called him, seen something? Was Emma with a man?

Blondie came back with a filthy mop and bucket and began spreading tomato sauce all over the floor while I stooped to pick up the shattered glass. A few moments later, Kim came over too.

"Let me help with that."

"You'll get your shoes dirty."

She glanced down at her feet, undecided.

"We've got this. Why don't you wait in the car? I'll be out in a minute."

"Okay."

Was it my imagination, or did she look paler than usual? I watched her ass—no, her back—when she walked away, pausing as she went to turn to the empty air by the register and mouth, "Goodbye."

My heart began to race as I grabbed the mop and washed the floor properly. Were we any further forward than when we arrived?

***

"And?"

I slid back into the driver's side, clutching a packet of pancake mix and the six-pack of beer I'd bought out of guilt.

"I've booked us a hotel suite," Kim said. "It's three miles away."

"I meant, what happened with the dead dude?"

"Clyde. He lost his life in a robbery in nineteen seventy-two. Two men walked in with guns, and he couldn't get the money out fast enough so one of them shot him. He thinks they were on drugs."

"And Emma? Did he see her?"

"Can we talk about this in the hotel? Please? I'm not sure what to make of everything, and I don't want to have this conversation in a parking lot."

That didn't sound like the news I'd been hoping for. "Can you at least tell me if he remembered seeing Emma?"

"No, he didn't see Emma."

Shit. Kim had already programmed the satnav, and it didn't take long to arrive at the Wentworth Inn. I could see right away why Kim chose it—from the outside, it looked like an English manor house, and even in winter, there were flowers everywhere. When we got closer, I realised they were made of plastic.

"Isn't it pretty?" she exclaimed. "And the best part is that it's only got two floors."

"Why does that matter?"

"My vertigo. Anything higher makes my head spin."

My head was already spinning and my feet were still on the ground. What had Kim found out? I grabbed both of our bags from the trunk and followed her into the hotel, where yet more flowers were accompanied by elevator music and a dozen uniformed staff.

Kim hurried up to the desk, heels clicking on the polished wood floor.

"I made a reservation in the name of Jennings. A suite."

The receptionist adjusted her glasses and peered at the screen. "Ah, yes, Mrs. Jennings. Congratulations."

Congratulations on what? Making a hotel booking? Kim looked as confused as I felt.

"I'm sorry?" she said.

"Congratulations on your marriage."

"Marriage? I'm not married."

The receptionist peered past her to me, brow furrowed. "But you reserved the honeymoon suite."

"No, I didn't. Just a standard suite with two bedrooms on the first floor."

The woman turned a shade paler. "Excuse me a moment. I need to check into this. Won't be a minute."

She fled through a door marked *private*, and Kim turned to me.

"I don't believe this."

"The honeymoon suite?" She looked so horrified I had to laugh. "Does that make me Mr. Jennings?"

"Well, I'm certainly not Mrs. Cullen."

"I don't know... Kimberly Cullen has a nice ring to it." I waggled my eyebrows. "How do you feel about a one-night stand?"

I was kidding, but the way she bit her lip right then made my cock twitch, and if she'd said yes, I might actually have considered it.

"Don't be such a pig."

The receptionist reappeared, this time with a manager in tow.

"I'm terribly sorry," he said. "There seems to have been a mistake. Your email signature said you were a wedding planner, and our intern got her wires crossed."

"Can't you just put us in a different suite?"

"We're fully booked. The honeymoon suite was the last room available."

"Then we'll have to find somewhere else."

Which would take more time, and I wanted to find out what happened in that damn store.

"Kim, you take the suite. I'll sleep where I planned to stay all along."

Her mouth set in a thin little line. "No, you will not."

"If it helps, we could put a cot in the room," the manager offered. "And discount the price by fifty percent."

"Perfect." She gave a tight yet triumphant smile. "We'll go straight up."

A cot was better than the car, and half price made an obscenely expensive room marginally more affordable. I'd have preferred to save the money towards a rental deposit, but I also wanted to avoid having an argument with Kim in the hotel reception. I went to pick up the bags, but a porter got there before me, tutting.

"I'll take these right to your room, sir."

Kim walked after him, leaving me to bring up the rear.

"Pleased with yourself, Mrs. Cullen?" I asked.

"Stop calling me that. You're not my type, anyway."

That stung more than I thought it would. "What *is* your type?"

"Do you ask all your clients that?"

"Just the pretty ones."

"Ugh."

CHAPTER 19 - KIMBERLY

"DO YOU ASK all your clients that?"

Deflect, deflect, deflect. One of the few useful things I'd learned from my father. Once, I'd have described my type as older, refined, with a good sense of humour and enough money to keep us both comfortably. After Alan, I'd changed my views somewhat as I embarked on my new life as a single girl who didn't want to be tied down. Looks became more important because like all girls, I appreciated shiny things, and he had to have an excellent working knowledge of his equipment and preferably mine too.

Reed Cullen was certainly easy on the eye if not a little brutish, but the question was, had he studied the operating manual?

Kim, don't even think about that.

"Just the pretty ones," he said.

"Ugh."

Hold on—he thought I was pretty?

The porter held the door open, and I handed him a tip as I walked through. The living area was beautifully decorated with flocked cream wallpaper, a pair of dusky-pink sofas, and a vase of fresh roses. Reed could sleep in here, and at half price, we'd gotten a bargain.

At least, I thought so until I carried my bag into the other room and saw the dead girl lying on the bed.

"What the actual heck?"

Her eyes widened. "OMG! You're one of those Electi people! I've heard all about you! Listen, you have to help me. My name's Erin Roxbury, and my husband poisoned me on our wedding night. Our freaking wedding night! I was literally sitting right here when he told the doctor I'd clutched at my chest and then keeled over from a heart attack, the lying bastard. He pretended to do CPR and everything. It was money, that's what it was. My trust fund and the house my parents gave us as a wedding gift. He couldn't even wait until after the honeymoon, the needle-dicked asshole."

No, no, no. I couldn't even... Slowly, I backed out of the room, dragging my case behind me.

"New plan. You get the bedroom."

"What? Why?" He must have noticed my resigned expression. "Tell me there isn't a ghost in there."

"Her name's Erin, and you may want to avoid letting it all hang out because I have a feeling she'll describe everything to me in excruciating detail."

"Where is she?"

"On the bed. Wedding night blues. I hope they didn't splash out too much on the ceremony."

"Noted. I'll keep my boxers on. Now can we talk about what happened in the grocery store?"

"I suppose."

Reed took a seat on the sofa, and I perched on the edge of the cushions. Would it be rude if I took my shoes off? These ones were new, and the toes were a little narrow, and— *Kimberly, just get on with it.*

"Clyde's been standing in the same spot for more than four decades, and he gets real bored. So he makes up stories to amuse himself, mostly about people who come into the store. And this morning, he saw E Cullen."

"Emma?"

"No, this was a man. But Clyde was certain of the name because Ashleigh mentioned it, even if she'd totally forgotten by the time we arrived."

"Ashleigh?"

"The blonde girl working the register. Apparently, she's a fan of the Twilight books. Clyde reads them over her shoulder sometimes, but he's not so keen on them. Anyhow, when E Cullen came in this morning, she made a joke about him being a vampire, like Edward Cullen."

Blank look.

"You know, Edward Cullen? He's a vampire in Twilight?"

Nope, nothing. Guess Reed wasn't a fan either.

"And what did the guy say?" Reed asked.

"Looked puzzled for a few seconds, then laughed and said, 'A vampire? Not far from the truth.'"

"So are you telling me vampires really exist?"

"How should I know?"

"Well, I just thought as you've got a direct line to the underworld..."

"I see ghosts. That's it. And never once has one of them told me they got bitten to death by a pointy-toothed freak wearing a cape. Clyde's never seen one either. We discussed it, and Clyde got the impression the customer was speaking more metaphorically. Like he preys on the innocent, and he was making a sick little joke."

Reed sat stock-still for a moment, then visibly shuddered. This was why I hadn't wanted to have the conversation in a dirty parking lot. Clyde had told me there was something malevolent about the man in the store. Something dark. I had a horrible feeling Emma Cullen was in trouble, and not just in the way Reed thought.

"And he had her debit card? Then where the hell is my sister?"

"I don't know." I gripped his hand in both of mine. "I don't know, but we'll find her, okay? I'll help you to find her."

"What if this asshole corrupted her? Brainwashed her? What if he's got her locked up in a basement somewhere? Shit." Reed leapt up and began pacing. "I bet he took her phone too. What if he's been the one sending me messages all these years and not her? She could be dead. Buried in a hole while—"

"Stop it! Stop thinking the worst. The message this morning wished you a happy birthday, right?"

"Yeah."

"How many people know you had a birthday recently? Is it on Facebook?"

Reed's eyes widened. "Oh, fuck."

"What? What is it?"

"Where's my phone? I need my phone."

"In your jacket pocket? Reed, what's wrong?"

His movements were jerky as he tapped away at the screen, and his Facebook page popped up. The last post was from almost a year ago. Guess he wasn't all that social.

About... Contact and basic info... Date of birth...

Today.

It said his birthday was today.

"I forgot until you mentioned it. Emma made me

set up a Facebook account years ago, and I just put some bullshit date of birth in the box. No way would I put my real one online."

I made a mental note to change mine when he wasn't looking. "So, what? Emma got a reminder of your birthday on Facebook and sent you a message?"

"No. Whoever's got her phone did that, pretending to be her. She doesn't have her fucking phone, Kim. Someone else has had it all along."

"Wait, didn't she call you after she left?"

"Yes, but only once." He tore a hand through his hair. "Shit. I've been so blind. My own damn sister's either dead or being held by a madman, and I didn't even realise."

Or maybe he didn't want to realise. Sometimes, it was harder to see the truth when you were close to somebody. For years, I'd seen the best in my father, but only because accepting the worst would have hurt too much.

Reed continued to pace, muttering. Well, didn't this little jaunt suck balls? The grocery store from hell, a ghost in the bedroom, and a ghoul with a stolen debit card. Next time, I'd go for a lighter atmosphere and take a minibreak on Alcatraz.

Okay, Kim, you can cope with this.

"What about the message? Didn't you have somebody at the phone company tracing the origin?"

"Yeah, but it's not like on TV. Unless it's a live trace, they can't pinpoint it with any accuracy. Historical data only tells you which cell tower it got routed through, which gives a radius of a few miles. Usually, I take the tower as a centre point then visit the type of places she might hang out—clubs, bars, fast-food places—and ask around. But I've never found any sign of her, and now I know why."

"Because the ghoul had her."

"The ghoul? Fuck."

Well done, Kim. Way to set his mind at ease.

"The, uh, man. But I have a description from Clyde. Dark-blond hair, a square jaw, about six feet tall." Just like a certain cop I'd met. Officer Leopold had told me Emma Cullen and Wyatt Banks used to date, then Reed confirmed it earlier. "He spoke with a local accent, but it sounded off. Fake. And although he wore jeans and a leather jacket, they looked too expensive for the area, as if he was trying to fit in but hadn't quite pulled it off."

Reed headed for the door, but I made it across before he got it open.

"Where are you going?"

"Back to Maryland."

"Why?"

"Wyatt fucking Banks, that's why. Blond hair? A square jaw? Not from around here? He was the last person to see my sister, and I know he lied about what happened that night."

Dammit, he'd gone through the same thought process as me.

"And what do you plan to do? Beat a confession out of him?"

"If it comes to that, yes."

Oh no. No way. I liked Reed, and I didn't want to see him locked up in prison for assaulting a police officer.

"But it's late. You can't just drive eight hours back home on no sleep."

"Watch me."

Watch him crash, more like. Reed was pig-headed, that much was obvious, but Alan once told me I'd turned being stubborn into an art form. I knew all the tricks. And I also knew I'd never win this argument. No, I'd need to try a different approach.

"At least have something to eat before you go, and a cup of coffee. I can call room service. Please? You haven't eaten since this morning."

He almost said no. I could see him wavering. But even Reed Cullen realised he couldn't operate effectively on an empty stomach.

"Ask them to make it quick, yeah?"

"Absolutely."

I scooted into the bedroom to use the phone there, out of Reed's earshot, but before I did, I muttered a silent plea at the ceiling. *Please forgive me.*

"Hello, room service? Could you send up two club sandwiches and a big pot of decaffeinated coffee?"

CHAPTER 20 - REED

HOT. I WAS hot, and man did that feel good.

Yawning, I stretched my arms above my head and my feet out as far as they would go, then realised there was something wrong with this picture. Why hadn't I hit my car doors at either end?

I was in a bed. An enormous bed. What the...?

White satin sheets, chiffon drapes at the windows, a bottle of champagne sitting warm in an ice bucket... The honeymoon suite. I was in the fucking honeymoon suite, lying next to a female ghost with a penchant for gossiping, if Kim was to be believed.

Snippets of last night's conversation filtered back to me. Emma's disappearance, my fake birthday, the blond ghoul. Wyatt Banks.

I'd been about to drive back to Bethesda, so how the hell did I end up sleeping for—I glanced at my watch—for eleven hours? And why did I feel so damn groggy?

She didn't.

Tell me she didn't.

I rolled out of bed and strode through to the living room, then bent to yank Kim's quilt off with one swift tug. She rolled over in a pair of pink silk pyjamas and pushed her frilly-ass eye mask up onto her forehead.

"What the heck?"

"Isn't that my line? What did you do to me?"

"Uh, decaf?"

"Kim..." I growled.

"Okay, so I may have mixed a couple of Ambien into it. You weren't fit to drive last night, nor am I bailing you out on a murder charge."

"You... You..." Rarely was I at a loss for words, but Kim had that effect on me.

"You can thank me later. Give me fifteen minutes to get ready, then we can drive back." She checked her watch, a dainty gold thing with no numbers. "Breakfast will be here in ten. Don't eat all the croissants."

That damn woman. I couldn't decide whether to thank her for saving me from myself, strangle her, or kiss her into oblivion. Thankfully, she disappeared into the bathroom, so I didn't have to make that decision.

**

"Promise you won't do anything stupid," Kim said as we walked up the stairs to Wyatt's apartment.

"I promise."

The doorbell hadn't worked since he moved in, so I hammered on the wooden door instead. I knew he was in. His truck was parked outside, and he never walked anywhere when he wasn't on duty. Heavy footsteps clomped towards us, the door swung open, and there he stood. Wyatt Banks, up close and personal for the first time in six months, rubbing his eyes as if we'd just woken him up.

I punched him in the face, and fuck, that felt awesome.

At least, it did until Kim jumped in between us and Wyatt's return swing caught her jaw. She crumpled at my feet in slow motion, and I wasn't sure whether to finish the job on Wyatt or call an ambulance.

But then she began groaning, and I dropped to my knees.

"Kim, are you okay? Sweetheart?"

She looked up at me, eyes unfocused. "You promised not to do anything stupid, you asshole."

"I didn't."

"You hit him."

"That was the most sensible thing I've done all year."

Of course, Banks didn't see it that way. "That was assault on a police officer. I could arrest you."

"Just go and get her some ice."

"I think you've broken my nose."

"Good. I'll break your whole fucking face if you don't go and get her some ice."

Wyatt must have realised from my tone that I was serious, and he retreated inside. I heard him moving towards the kitchen as I turned my attention back to Kim.

"Where does it hurt? Do you want me to take you to the hospital?"

"No, I want you to start acting like a grown-up." She gingerly touched her fingers to her jaw. "We'll never get anywhere if Wyatt Banks is unconscious."

"He needs to understand I'm not taking his shit anymore."

"You've made your point, okay?"

I helped Kim to her feet as Banks returned, pressing an ice pack to his own face as he held out another. When he got a good look at Kim, his eyes lit up in recognition.

"Hey, I've met you before. You're that party planner."

"Wedding planner."

"What are you doing with this prick?"

"I hired him to work on the case that you seemed so unwilling to solve."

"Look, lady, there was no evidence. Do you know how many women claim to have been drugged every week?"

"Do you know how many of the men who drug them turn out to be murderers?"

Now isn't the time, Kim.

"Enough," I mouthed.

"Murderers?" Banks asked.

"Different case. Today, we're here to discuss Emma."

"What about her?" Defensive. Just like he always was when I mentioned her name. "Is she back in town?"

"You know damn well she isn't. How was Ohio?"

"Ohio? What the hell are you talking about?"

If I hadn't seen so much evidence to the contrary, I'd have said his look of confusion was genuine.

"Your little trip to Cincinnati to impersonate my sister. What did you do to her? All that bullshit over how she'd left and you couldn't tell me why. I know about the drugs, Wyatt. A hooker downtown saw you driving when Emma stopped to pick up her fix. And I know about the cheating too."

Banks winced as he shifted the ice against his face. My knuckles stung too, but it was a good pain.

"Cheating? I didn't cheat on Emma."

"Don't lie to me!" I took a step forward, but Kim

pulled me back. "She called me once after she left. Once! And she told me you'd had a fight over a girl."

Now he sagged against the wall.

"Fuck. It wasn't *a* girl, you idiot. It was just girl. Cocaine."

Finally, he admitted to something, even if it wasn't quite what I'd expected. "Why the hell didn't you tell me?"

"Because she begged me not to. Said she didn't want to cause you any more problems."

"And you listened to her? Even when she'd lost her mind, you listened to her?"

"I loved her!"

"Bullshit! What did you do to her?"

Something didn't add up here. *Nothing* added up. Wyatt's caginess after Emma left, how upset she'd been, the fact that she'd run in the first place when she knew damn well I'd always support her no matter how bad things got.

The next door along the hallway cracked open, and a grey-haired lady peered out.

"Is everything all right? Should I call the police?"

I forced my fists to uncurl as Banks tried a smile.

"Everything's fine, Susan," he said. "And I *am* the police."

"If you're sure..."

"I'm sure." Then he glared at me. "You should leave."

"I'm not leaving."

We stared at each other, toe-to-toe until Kim pushed between us.

"Can we talk like adults now? No matter what happened between you and Reed's sister, we think she's in trouble and we need to find out what happened to her. The past is the past. You two need to put your differences aside and work together because we need every scrap of information we can get."

"Emma's in trouble?"

I nodded. "I've been trying to track her via her debit card payments since she left, and yesterday, we found a witness who saw a man using her card, not her."

Yes, I neglected to mention that the witness was dead. Information on a need-to-know basis only.

Banks fell silent, considering, then stepped back and opened the door wider. "If we're gonna continue this, we should do it inside."

Over two years had passed since I set foot in Wyatt's apartment. He'd redecorated. Blacks and greys had turned to creams and browns, and he'd bought a new couch.

"Take a seat," he told Kim, and she looked to me.

I shrugged and sat down, and the way she squashed against my side suggested that, like me, she didn't remotely want to be there.

"Okay," I said. "Speak. What the hell happened that night?"

CHAPTER 21 - REED

WAS I FINALLY about to find out the truth?

"First, you need to understand that I didn't take keeping her secret lightly," Wyatt said. "But that thing with your father hit her harder than she ever admitted to you. Even ten years on, she still cried herself to sleep while she pretended everything was fine on the surface. That was why she started taking the drugs—as an escape."

"Why didn't she just talk to me?"

"Because she didn't want you to think she was weak."

"But she talked to you?"

"Yeah, she did. Whether you like it or not, Emma was my girl. In my head, she always will be."

His voice hitched, and just for a second, I remembered the old Wyatt and Emma. Happy, laughing, thick as thieves. Then I pushed that image out of my mind because he'd betrayed both of us.

"Still, you had no right to keep that from me."

"When I found out, I told her I'd only keep quiet if she quit. If she got help. And she did. Those two weeks you thought we were in Florida three years ago? She was in rehab."

Again, that didn't add up.

"She had photos of her on the beach. Of the two of

you swimming with dolphins." All over fucking Facebook.

"Photoshop. We were in Virginia. I stayed nearby while she was at the treatment centre."

Treatment centre. At those words, Kim shivered beside me, and I felt beyond guilty for dragging her into this mess. She was supposed to be my client, not my sidekick. Although she felt more like a lifeline at the moment. I squeezed her free hand, something that didn't go unnoticed by Wyatt.

"If you were so close, why did she leave?" I asked him. We needed to keep on track.

"I caught her snorting a line in the kitchen, and I'm not gonna lie—that fucking hurt. I guess I'd suspected for a while, but it was easier to keep burying my head in the sand and pretend everything was fine. Anyhow, that night I told her it was me or the drugs, and we got into an argument. Then she walked out."

"You didn't go after her?"

"She needed time to cool down. We both did. Emma was always wild—you can't deny that."

"How did she even get the coke? She had debts with every dealer in town. I've spent the past two years paying them off."

Wyatt's eyes widened. "They came after you?"

"Yeah, they did. And I paid because when she comes back, I don't want them or their associates going after her."

When she comes back... Right now, I was terrified that would never happen.

"But you were a police officer," Kim said. "Why didn't you just arrest them?"

"Not that simple, sweetheart," I told her. "The guys

at the top, the ones holding the markers, they're smart. They distance themselves from the whole operation. Legit businesses as a front, mules to carry the drugs around... We'd never have got a conviction, and not only would Emma still have owed them, they'd have been pissed at me too."

"And that's why you're sleeping—"

"Yes." Wyatt didn't know I was homeless, nor did I want him to.

"I'm so sorry. I'm so sorry this happened to you."

Kim was too damn good for this world.

"It's done now. I'm more worried about finding my sister." I turned back to Wyatt. "And you didn't answer my question. How did she get hold of the drugs? Did someone give them to her?"

Wyatt opened his mouth. Closed it again. He glanced at Kim, and I knew what was going through his mind.

"It's okay. Kimberly can keep a secret."

"Are you sure? How long have you known her?"

"Only a few weeks, but yeah, I'm sure."

Wyatt scrubbed a hand through his hair, an old nervous habit of his. "The drugs were mine."

"Yours?" This just got better and better. "You were addicted too?"

"Never even tried it. No, I had half a kilo of coke in my closet because I planned to set up Emma's main dealer. Like you said, we all knew what he did, but he never carried the drugs around himself."

"You were gonna plant that shit on him?"

"Exactly."

"Where the hell did you get half a kilo of cocaine? What's the street value on that? Forty thousand dollars?"

"Something like that." He closed his eyes briefly. "Fuck. I got it from the evidence locker. Replaced it with powdered lactose. And when we had the fight, Emma worked that out and threatened to tell the captain."

"She wouldn't have told him."

"You didn't see her that night. She was off her head, ranting like a crazy woman before she stormed out, and when she didn't come back, you know what? I was glad at first. But I swear I didn't realise anything had happened to her."

"What about a week later, huh? When she was who the fuck knows where with no money and no clothes and no food?"

"She said she needed space. Until you asked me where she was, I thought she was with you. And she had money. She took two grand out of my lockbox."

Dammit, Emma. I loved my sister, but she wasn't easy to deal with by any means.

"And after that?"

"I was scared, okay? I had a brick of coke I couldn't get back into the evidence room because the dragon lady in the admin department had tightened up procedures, and I was still worried Emma would tell someone. But I asked around. She went out clubbing the night after, and she looked fine then."

"How do you know? Who saw her?"

"I got camera footage from the manager in the club. Pretended it was for an investigation." Now Wyatt slumped forward, all his fight gone. "I never realised that was the last time I'd see her. You've got no idea how many times I've watched that tape."

"You still have it?"

"On my laptop." He took a deep breath. "I'm sorry for the way I've behaved since she vanished. I was so damn worried my whole career would get pulled out from under me, and I panicked. But it's no excuse. I shouldn't have shut you out."

I saw in his eyes how difficult that was for him to say, but it still didn't erase the last two years. And it didn't bring Emma back either.

"I didn't just lose my sister that day. I lost my best friend too."

"I know."

"And I can't forget that."

"I'm not asking you to."

"I'm not sure if I can forgive you either."

A sigh. "I get that. But can't we try to work together to find Emma? If she really is in trouble, we both need all the help we can get."

Kim squeezed my hand. "He's right, Reed. We've got so little to go on."

"You're probably wondering why I care so much, huh?" I said to her. "Emma must sound like a nightmare to you. But she wasn't always difficult. Most of the time, she was sweet and kind and smart. But sometimes, life just got the better of her."

"She had some problems growing up," Wyatt said.

"Kim knows."

"What? About the...?"

"Yeah. About that."

He raised an eyebrow, and I couldn't blame him because usually, I wasn't big on dredging up my family history. But Kim was different. That was the moment I realised she was more than just a client. She was a friend. And one day, if I ever got my life sorted out, I hoped she'd be more.

Go figure. I'd fallen in... Lust? Like? *Love*? with a woman about as far from my usual type as it was possible to get. I normally went for a girl who was easy-going, compliant, not at all clingy, and I'd ended up with an uptight, stubborn princess who'd invited herself along to fucking Ohio. Worse, she liked flowery, sparkly, fluffy shit.

But if we hadn't been in the middle of investigating my sister's disappearance, I'd have been doing everything I could to fuck that stick out of her pert little ass. Boy, that was some revelation.

And Wyatt was still staring at me.

"Can I see the tape?" I asked. "It could be a starting point."

"Yeah, but don't get your hopes up. I know the crowd of people she was hanging out with that night. They said she walked outside for a smoke in the early hours, and when she didn't reappear, they figured she met someone else and...and went back to their place."

I knew what he was thinking, but Emma never slept around. After our father ruined her, it took her years to hook up with Wyatt, and even though I wanted to kill him when I first found out he was screwing my little sister, I also knew she wouldn't find anyone better. Or at least, I'd thought so at the time.

"I doubt she'd have done that."

"Well, she walked outside, disappeared out of camera shot, and never came back."

"Can I see the video?" Kim asked, and I knew what she was thinking too. If we found out where Emma was last seen, could we find an other-worldly witness?

Much as I hated to admit it, that could be our best prospect.

"Wyatt?"

"I'll get it."

With Banks out of the room, I turned my attention to Kimberly.

"How's your face? Do you need more ice?"

"A bit sore, but I think it was the shock more than anything else. Nobody's ever hit me before. Well, apart from a drunk bride trying to do the funky chicken, but I don't think that counts."

And nobody would hurt her again if I had anything to do with it.

"Do you want a drink? Coffee? Water?"

She shook her head and put the ice pack on the side table. "I'm not thirsty. Is this good or bad? I guess it's good that you're speaking to Wyatt again, but Emma..."

"I'll try to work on your case too. We still need to find Tim, but—"

"Of course you have to look for Emma right now. She's your sister. Tim seems to take a break in between his crimes, and even though he failed with me, as you pointed out, I'd hope we've got a little leeway."

"He might have waited three months after Jacqueline, but he's escalating. Georgette disappeared years ago, and the intervals are getting smaller unless there are other victims we don't know about."

Kim's gasp said she hadn't considered that possibility. "You really think there might be? Georgette didn't mention any other girls."

"He could have used a different vehicle."

Kim went rigid beside me, and I wrapped an arm around her. It felt like the natural thing to do. As did kissing her hair.

"More girls... If that's true, he's a monster."

"The world's full of monsters, sweetheart. Some just wear human skin. But we'll find him; I promise."

Wyatt came back with his laptop, and I finally got to see my sister again. She'd never been fond of having her photo taken. Braces and pimples as a teenager meant she'd shied away from the camera, and even when she turned from an ugly duckling into a swan, she still hid her face behind her hair or a hat or other people. Most of the pictures I did have of her had Wyatt in them too, and I couldn't bring myself to look at them before today.

But now, Emma danced on a table in Illusion, a club in a sketchy part of DC, before falling off into the arms of a man I didn't recognise.

"You know that guy?" I asked Wyatt.

"Lena's older brother." Lena had been a grade ahead of us in school. "He went home with Sara Masterson that night." Another old classmate.

Emma looked happy in the video. A little too happy, if anything, which didn't bode well for her judgement. After ten minutes, she walked towards the bar, and Wyatt switched to a different camera.

"Here's where she goes outside."

She'd been wobbly by that point, fumbling in her tiny purse for a pack of cigarettes. Another habit she'd been trying to break. It seemed as though everything had fallen apart for her that night, but how badly?

It was Kimberly who spotted it first. A black Mercedes nosing through the parking lot at the top of the screen. Shiny under the lights, one occupant in the driver's seat. The resolution of the tape didn't allow us to see the registration number, but the dark, concave arc at the top told me what I needed to know. Either more diplomats than we thought liked slumming it in seedy nightclubs, or Tim had been out hunting for longer than we'd thought.

"Fuck."

Kim squeezed my hand. "Do you think it's him?"

"Who?" Wyatt asked.

Could it be true? Were the two cases connected? Georgette, Jacqueline, Kim... Emma would have come first, and there were differences. Emma had called a week later, to start with, and she'd also sent ongoing messages while the other two girls had never been heard from again. But there were also similarities. Both Emma and Georgette still used their debit cards, for example.

"I don't know. But what are the chances of it all being a coincidence? We're positive he's taken girls from clubs before."

Wyatt leaned forward, elbows on his knees. "What are you guys talking about?"

"I've been investigating Kim's case for the last couple of weeks, and we suspect it's tied to the disappearances of two other girls—Georgette Riley and Jacqueline Springer, both of whom vanished from nightclubs. And the man who tried to drug Kim drove a black Mercedes with diplomatic plates."

Now Wyatt wound the footage back and took a closer look at the parking lot.

"Shit, you're right. That's an embassy car. You really think it's the same guy?"

"I can't say for sure. But I do think it's a possibility we can't afford to ignore."

CHAPTER 22 - KIMBERLY

MY HEAD FELT as if it were about to explode as Reed drove me home. Another girl taken by Tim, and this time, it was Emma Cullen? If Georgette hadn't warned me, if I hadn't jumped out of the car, I could have been the one lying cold in the ground somewhere, and nobody would have a clue there was a predator on the loose.

"How has Tim gone undetected for so long?" I asked.

"He picked his victims carefully. Georgette and Emma both had problems at home. When they disappeared, people assumed they needed space."

Reed's knuckles turned white on the steering wheel, and I knew he blamed himself for not looking harder. Wyatt had done the same thing back in his apartment. At one point, I thought he'd punch the wall in frustration.

"What about me? I wasn't in a nightclub."

"That, I'm not sure of. I guess if I were our guy, I'd vary my methodology after three abductions to avoid a pattern emerging. Or perhaps he just saw you and acted on impulse."

"If I'd finished that drink five minutes earlier... Or if he hadn't stopped at those lights... Or if—"

"Don't. You escaped, and you're safe. I won't let

anything happen to you; I promise. I'll sleep on your driveway tonight."

"No, you won't." What would my neighbours say if I had a handsome homeless man camping outside my house? "You can use one of my spare rooms."

"Kim, you're a client. I can't impose like that."

A client. Yes, technically I was, although for the past couple of days, it hadn't felt so much like a business relationship. I could still feel the ghost of his hand on my hip from earlier. A week ago, I'd have been indignant at him for taking liberties like that, but today, I'd itched to reciprocate.

"You were the one who said working on a murder case was dangerous. I'd feel much better with you inside. The bed's already made."

When I moved in, I'd furnished all four bedrooms. One for myself and the rest for my non-existent guests, because having three totally barren rooms would have reminded me just how empty my life was. Only Annie had ever slept over. Once or twice, my father had mooted the possibility of visiting, but he'd yet to turn up.

"Are you sure?"

"Yes, I'm sure."

And now I had a new roommate. Well, not in my room, exactly, but it was a start.

***

Seven a.m. on a Sunday, and the aroma of bacon drifted up the stairs, disturbing the dream I absolutely shouldn't have been having about a certain private investigator. Would he look as good with his shirt off as

I imagined?

Stop it, Kim. He's not taking his shirt off.

But it seemed as though he was making breakfast. Again. I hurried into the bathroom and made myself presentable, thankfully minus the mascara streaks today, then pulled on some clothes. A pretty wrap dress from Diane von Furstenberg. The casual look since it was a Sunday and we were still at home.

Then I hurried downstairs and found that my dreams had come even truer than I hoped.

"I ran out of clean shirts, so I borrowed your washing machine. Hope you don't mind."

If he kept standing in my kitchen half-naked, he could borrow my washing machine every minute of every hour of every day. I made a conscious effort not to drool.

"That's fine. Did you find the laundry detergent?"

"On the shelf right above the machine."

"Yes. Of course." Great. Now I sounded like a fool. "You're cooking?"

Oh, that was so much better.

"Figured if we're going out to hunt for ghosts today, we could use a good breakfast. I found the bacon in the freezer."

Great, which meant he'd also found my secret stash of vodka. "The Stolichnaya is for medicinal purposes only."

"Hey, I'm not gonna judge. Do you want waffles or pancakes? I see you have a waffle machine, but it doesn't look as though you use it much."

"Whatever's easiest. The waffle machine was an impulse purchase, and I don't even know how to turn it on."

"Pancakes it is, then. I'll make you waffles when we've got more time. We also need to stop by the store later because your fridge is kind of empty."

"I usually pick up takeout."

"My budget doesn't run to takeout right now, but I'll make you dinner. Does that work?"

I almost asked if he'd do that shirtless too, but I managed to bite my tongue just in time. "Dinner sounds lovely."

When we'd talked last night, we'd agreed to head to Illusion this morning to look for witnesses while Wyatt went to work. While he was there, he planned to get ahold of the files for Georgette and Jacqueline as well as searching the database for any other similar crimes in Maryland and the surrounding states. I dreaded the results. More clues would certainly be helpful, but the thought of additional victims left me sick to my stomach, even when Reed slid a plate of food in front of me. Crispy bacon and pancakes drizzled with maple syrup.

"Emma's favourite," he explained. "She'd have lived on this stuff if she could."

"Did you cook for her often?"

"Every day until I joined the army. Mom wasn't so good at that sort of thing."

I tried a forkful. My mom had been more of a low-fat yogurt and muesli person. "It's delicious. I'd live on it too if I thought I'd still fit into my clothes."

Oh my. I hadn't seen that dirty grin before.

"Better get more bacon, then."

"Pig." I couldn't let that one pass, even if I secretly liked Reed being vulgar now that I knew he was kind-hearted underneath.

"Yeah, bacon comes from pigs. Somebody listened in school."

"You know what I meant."

He just laughed. "You want coffee too?"

"Yes, please."

"Extra cream?"

"Stop it."

He did stop teasing, but I wished he hadn't when he sat opposite me with his serious face on.

"Are you sure you're okay to do this? Visiting the club, I mean."

Chatting with murder victims wasn't my favourite pastime for a Sunday morning, but if it helped Emma...

"I'm sure."

"I just want you to know how much I appreciate everything you've done to help these past few days. I understand how difficult it must be."

"In a strange way, it feels good. I mean, it's not good that people have died, but I feel better for helping. For doing a small part of my duty."

"Don't take this the wrong way, but whoever handed out these powers couldn't have picked a worse person."

At last, someone understood. "I know, right? I imagine a bona fide member of the Electi would be a woman like The Bride out of *Kill Bill*."

"A sword-wielding assassin who's not afraid to kill in the pursuit of justice?"

"Exactly. But I'm better at wielding flowers. Although I did almost kill somebody with a bouquet once. Nobody realised one of the wedding guests was severely allergic to lily pollen, and the poor lady went into anaphylactic shock."

"Better stop off and pick up a bunch of flowers on the way to Illusion."

"Or one of those Japanese katanas."

"I can't picture you watching a Quentin Tarantino movie."

"It was my ex-husband's choice. I wanted to watch a romcom."

"I promise I'll take you to see a romcom when this is over."

A date? Did Reed Cullen just suggest we go on a date? Judging by the hot flash that ran through me, my libido certainly hoped so.

"Really?"

"It's the least I can do." He checked his watch. "But for now, we have a nightclub to visit."

Wyatt hadn't wanted me to go when we discussed our plans yesterday. Too dangerous for a girl like me, he said. He'd offered to go with Reed himself after his shift ended, and we could hardly explain why that wouldn't work. Luckily, when Reed promised to stay by my side and carry a gun, Wyatt had acquiesced.

"This area's gotten worse in the last two years," Reed said as we drew closer to Anacostia. Even though Annie had retrieved my car and parked it neatly in one side of my double garage, we'd taken his SUV because it blended in better. "Boundaries have shifted, and Illusion's disputed territory between three rival gangs."

Wasn't that the truth? Boarded-up buildings, a burned-out car, youths on street corners watching us through dead eyes as we drove past. Not a place I'd have wanted to venture alone.

On the sort-of-positive side, three people had been murdered outside Illusion that we knew of. Two stabbings and a shooting. Plenty of options, although I couldn't help hoping for an older spirit. They were easier to deal with and sometimes even managed to make pleasant conversation. The younger souls still thought they could convince me to set them free, so they were less willing to help without strings attached. Demanding. That was the best way to describe them.

Although if a spirit was too old, they had little understanding of how the world worked now, and that could be difficult as well. A few months ago, I'd talked briefly to a gentleman who died in the American Civil War, and he'd been convinced that airplanes were some kind of witchcraft.

"Well, we're here," Reed said, pulling into a parking space. "Place looks even worse in daylight."

Peeling black paint, a cracked sign with the N hanging off, and unless I was mistaken, a pool of vomit outside the door.

"Isn't this just charming," I muttered as Reed opened my door.

"I take you to all the best places, sweetheart."

I tugged my coat tighter around myself as we crossed the lot. At Reed's suggestion, I'd changed into jeans and fur-lined boots, and boy was I glad about that as the icy wind nipped at my face.

"Where to first?" Reed asked.

"Over there." I nodded towards the door, where I could see a young blonde woman with blood seeping from her chest. Surely she'd be sympathetic to Emma's cause? "The camera on the video was above the exit, right?"

"Ever thought of changing career? I could use an assistant."

"Isn't that my question? You're amazing at remodelling gift bags."

The blonde did a double take as we got closer. Apparently, the Electi emitted some sort of glow and the air around us crackled too. The spirit guides told them this, which was the reason I couldn't play dumb and go about my daily business in peace.

"Hi."

She looked me up and down. "Are you one of those elected things?"

"One of the Electi? Yes. And you're Shana Conway?"

"About time you showed up. You're three years late."

"I'm afraid I don't keep an appointment book."

"Maybe you should. Anyhow, the bitch that stabbed me is called Keesha West. That's Keesha with two e's. Do me a favour and make it painful, okay?"

"I'm not here to kill Keesha." From what Wyatt told us, Shana had started the fight in any case. "I'm hoping you can help with an ongoing investigation. A girl disappeared from the parking lot here just over two years ago."

"Wait. You want *me* to help *you*? No, bitch, that's not how it works. Some angel thing told me it's your job to waste murderers."

"Two thousand years ago, perhaps, but the world's moved on. We have police and jails now, and I understand Keesha's already served her sentence."

"What about my sentence? I'm fucking dead!"

"Yes, I see that, but—"

"Just get lost if you won't get off your fat ass and do what you're supposed to."

"My ass isn't fat!" Was it? I mean, I hadn't used the StairMaster since I split up with Alan, but I still fitted into a size eight. "And a girl's gone missing."

"Not my problem."

I'd never met Keesha, but if I did, I'd buy her a big box of chocolates. The good ones with caramel centres. Shana was one of the most vile spirits I'd ever had the misfortune to come across.

"You won't get anything out of her, lady," a voice said from behind a nearby dumpster. "All she does is whine."

Shana put her hands on her hips. "Shut up, Shawn."

"Bite me."

Reed followed as I ventured around the dumpster, which smelled like something had died inside. Another ghost who liked to do the pretend-sitting thing was lounging on a rickety chair, looking more relaxed than most spirits I saw. His clothes were modern, and Shana had called him Shawn, so this was most likely Lil Shawn Merit, the victim of a turf war between two gangs, except when he stood up, his nickname seemed somewhat of a misnomer. He was well over six feet tall and almost as wide.

"Lil Shawn?"

"That's me."

"I was just confused about the 'Lil' part."

"My cousin's Big Shawn. He's six feet seven. You'll have to excuse my face."

Blood ran from a gunshot wound in his left cheek, shiny and red against his dark skin.

"I've seen it all before. Uh, you don't want me to avenge your death as well, do you? Because I really don't do that."

"My boys already took care of it."

Thank goodness. "How did you find that out?"

"My mama visits every week." Shawn waved in the direction of a bunch of wilted flowers. "She talks to me, but she don't know I can hear. Guess it makes her feel better. Just wish I could tell her how much I appreciated everything she did."

"I'd offer to help, but she might think it was a bit odd if a stranger suddenly turned up on her doorstep with a message."

"I get that. Yeah, I get that. Who's this missing girl, then?"

"Her name's Emma Cullen. She went outside for a cigarette, and nobody ever saw her again."

"Two years ago, you said?"

"More like two years and four months. Almost five now."

"A redhead?"

"You saw her?"

"Ain't got nothing to do but look at people out here. If she could've heard me, I'd have told her not to get in that fancy-ass Mercedes. There was something off about that guy."

"What do you mean, off?"

"White dude wearin' three-hundred-dollar jeans and a fifty-dollar T-shirt in a place like this? You know he's not comin' for the atmosphere. Looked like a Ken doll and spoke like the asshole in that movie... What's the one with four funerals and a wedding?"

"Do you mean *Four Weddings and a Funeral*? Hugh Grant's character?"

"Yeah, him." The British accent. "My girl made me sit through that shit for hours."

So we'd been right. It *was* him. Tim. I didn't know whether to be relieved that we definitely had one case instead of two or horrified because Emma had become his victim.

"Can you tell me anything else about the man?"

"Didn't get that good of a look at him. Dark hair. Kinda pushy. When he got the girl near the car, she didn't want to go, but she'd had too much to drink and he put her inside. Someone shoulda stopped him, man."

"We're trying. We think he's taken other women too."

"Well, shit. Hey, there was one other thing."

"Yes?"

"He had a tattoo on his left arm, between his wrist and his elbow. Not sure what it was because I only saw it for a second. Maybe one of them tribal things?"

A clue! Another clue! "That's very useful."

"Good luck, lady. Let me know if you find the girl, will ya? And stop by any time. It's been a long while since I talked to anyone but Little Miss Sunshine over there."

"I'll be sure to do that. Thank you for your help."

Reed had been waiting at my elbow, both for moral support and to act as a lookout in case anyone saw me talking to myself.

"Ready to go, sweetheart?"

"Almost. Could you help me with one tiny thing first?"

"What thing?"

"We need to drag this dumpster over there."

Shana screamed blue murder when we positioned the dumpster in front of her, but I ignored her complaints. I'd had plenty of practice at that. Better still, she was short, so the trash muffled her cries and she couldn't see over the top. Perfect.

I gave Shawn a wave as we headed to Reed's SUV, and he grinned and waved back. Yes, today I'd learned a lesson in not judging people by their appearances.

"Did one of the ghosts say you had a fat ass?" Reed asked.

"Shana did. I didn't like her much." Or at all, in fact.

"Don't listen to her. She's talking bullshit."

Perhaps, but it was always easier to believe the bad stuff.

CHAPTER 23 - REED

AFTER OUR VISIT to Illusion, we headed back to Kim's since she had more space than Wyatt. She'd bought a hell of a house for one person. This morning, for the first time in months, I hadn't woken up with a backache, so I couldn't complain about her extravagance, even if worries over Emma kept me from sleeping properly.

On the way, Kim filled me in on her conversations with Shana and Lil Shawn, and my last bit of hope leached away. Emma had been taken by Tim, and if Georgette's fate was any indication, she wouldn't be coming back.

Was it better or worse to know the truth? Before, anger had simmered under the surface every time Emma sent one of her bland messages, but now I felt a mixture of sadness and white-hot fury. More than anything, I wanted to find my sister's body and give her a proper burial, then make sure her killer rotted in hell.

"Shall we pick up groceries before we go home?" Kim asked. Her voice wavered as though she was trying hard to cling to normality.

"Saves going out again later."

The only girl I'd ever been food shopping with was my sister, and while Emma used to rush through the aisles picking out the ingredients for all her favourite foods, Kim studied the calorie contents then added delights like a pre-cooked omelette, pre-chopped vegetables, and pre-grated low-fat cheese to the cart.

"Are you still worrying about the 'fat ass' comment?"

"No." She tossed a package of chips back onto the shelf. "Maybe."

"Ever thought about the reason I always walk behind you?"

Obviously not, but now she did. "Did you just admit to staring at my ass?"

"Yeah."

Her lips twitched as if she wasn't sure whether to be flattered or pissed. Cute.

"Uh, thank you? I think."

I picked up the shrivelled omelette. "You know this is the most expensive way to buy food? And fresh eggs taste much better."

"My smoke alarm thanks me when I buy the pre-made versions."

"I said I'd cook. Just tell me what you want to eat."

"You were serious about that?"

"I'm always serious about food. You feel like having steak? Pasta? Casserole?"

"Can we have sushi?"

"Sushi?"

How the fuck did a person make sushi? I had no idea, but if Kim wanted that, I'd work it out.

"If it's too difficult, it doesn't matter."

"No, we'll have sushi."

Fish and rice, right? How tricky could it be?

***

Wyatt was due in an hour, and I was watching a YouTube video on how to make California rolls while running through facts from the case in my head. I did my best thinking while I cooked. Something about slicing and dicing made ideas click in my brain, and I hadn't had a kitchen to use for months.

"Can I do anything to help?" Kim asked.

"We'll need some way of organising our thoughts later. Paper, pens, Post-it notes."

"A whiteboard? I've seen those on cop shows."

"You have a whiteboard?"

"I organise things for a living. Of course I have a whiteboard."

She did indeed. By the time I'd fiddled around with a bamboo rolling mat, three kinds of fish, vegetables, rice, and seaweed sheets, Kim had replaced a painting in the dining room with the mother of all whiteboards, extended the leaves on the table, and covered it with enough stationery to give Staples a wet dream. She'd already started with the paper clips, and so far, we had a chicken, two dogs, and what looked like a dinosaur.

"Velociraptor?" I guessed.

"It's a parrot." She pointed at the tray of food in my hands. "Are those edamame beans? I love edamame beans."

Psychic, pretty, and easily pleased. What more could a man want?

"Here you go. Wyatt'll be here soon." As if by magic, the doorbell rang. "I'll get it. You carry on with your... cat?"

"Rabbit."

Close.

Wyatt gave a low whistle when he walked inside. "Nice place. Planning weddings must pay well."

"Kim's good at what she does."

He looked back at me. The swelling in his nose had gone down slightly since yesterday, but there was still a definite kink in the bridge.

"And you like her, huh?"

"So what if I do?"

"I didn't think she was your type."

"Neither did I. Did you get the files?"

"Yeah." He gingerly touched his nose. "There's another seven possibles going back three and a half years."

"Fuck. I thought maybe one or two..."

"If this is true, we could be looking at the most prolific serial killer in decades around here, and he's flown right under our radar. I haven't said anything at work yet, but I'm gonna need to go through your evidence so we can decide how to proceed."

Right. All that evidence we didn't have. I'd deal with that later, after I'd seen Wyatt's files.

"Sure. I've made dinner. We can eat while we talk."

"You're still into all that cooking shit?"

"Gotta eat, buddy."

Wyatt rolled his eyes at the sushi, but he still helped himself to a ton of it. Kim lined hers up daintily on a plate and ate it with a knife and fork while we talked.

"I searched the database for any case where a girl in her twenties went missing from a public place in the last five years and hasn't been seen since," Wyatt said.

"Five years?"

"It's a starting point. He may have been active for longer, but right now, we need to find clues and witnesses so we can stop this guy, and that'll be harder for older disappearances."

"Okay, five years. There have to be more than seven unsolved cases in four states."

"Maryland, Virginia, Pennsylvania, Delaware, and I included DC too. Although if that's where he's from, it would be risky for him to hit so close to home. That gave me a list of twenty-seven. But I filtered out working girls, daytime abductions, and any locations that didn't have a parking lot close by. That fits with what we know so far."

"So who have we got?"

Wyatt pulled a stack of files out of his bag.

Gina.

Dawn.

Isla.

Emma.

Georgette.

Jacqueline.

Hailee.

Brianna.

Danielle.

Kimberly.

Tamara.

Seven plus the four we already knew about. Suddenly, I didn't feel so hungry anymore. Instead, I slid the first file towards myself and began reading. Brianna Clifford had vanished late one evening after filling in for a friend as a cocktail waitress at a racetrack in Virginia. An afternoon of horse racing followed by evening drinks, canapés, and live music for anyone rich enough to afford a ticket.

The switch between Brianna and her friend had

been a last-minute thing, suggesting her abduction wasn't premeditated. Colleagues reported no difficulties, no arguments, no complaints about her work that day. Quite the opposite, in fact. Brianna had been a pretty brunette who'd proven popular with the partygoers. Another waitress commented that Brianna had picked up more tips than anyone else. Police speculated that the cash could have been a factor in her disappearance—a robbery gone wrong—but no body had ever been found.

I discounted Danielle, whose boyfriend had disappeared at the same time, and Tamara, because the investigator's notes suggested a neighbour had been a serious suspect in the case before he committed suicide. That left five new possibilities. Nine women in total who'd gone missing in strange circumstances, and one man we suspected of having a hand in those disappearances. The question was, how did we find him?

The tattoo. We had to find out which of the embassy staff had a tattoo on his arm, but how did I explain that to Wyatt when our latest witness had been dead for the last four years?

I read out the names, and Kim wrote them on the whiteboard. Seeing them listed in her neat handwriting made this case seem all the more real. My sister had been just one victim among many, and each had a family out there who missed them. Could we get closure for the surviving relatives who were still suffering?

"So many," Kim murmured.

Wyatt was focused on Emma's name. I still hadn't forgiven him for what he'd done, and maybe I never would, but I knew he'd loved Emma and from the expression on his face, he still did.

A moment passed, and he visibly pulled himself together.

"We need to talk about evidence. If this is what you think it is, I'll need to get my superiors involved, and they'll laugh me out of the room with what we've got so far."

"Yeah, about the evidence..."

Kim stood up, her smile shaky. "I'll just clear away some of these plates."

Thanks, sweetheart.

"Kim came to me a few weeks back, right after our suspect spiked her drink and tried to abduct her in his car. I believe you're familiar with that incident?" I couldn't help a bit of snark creeping into my voice after the way Wyatt had given Kim the brush-off.

"Yes, I did the follow-up. But at the time, we had no reason—"

"Save it, okay?" I ran Wyatt through the way I'd found the footage of Kim in the car, my shitshow of a visit to Brittney, and how I'd seen the diplomatic plate in her friend's picture. The dead end I'd reached after that. "Then we happened to find a witness who placed Georgette Riley and Jacqueline Springer in the same car."

"What? The same witness?"

Shit. "Yeah, the same girl."

"Why didn't she come forward before? Georgette disappeared years ago. Didn't she know that?"

"The circumstances were difficult for her."

"Can I talk to her? Get an official statement?"

Not unless he did it through a medium. "That might

be tricky."

"Buddy, we need more than this. So far, everything's hearsay and coincidence."

"What about Emma? We've got the Mercedes on tape."

"No, we've got *a* Mercedes. We can't read the licence plate."

"Can't the computer geeks enhance it or something?"

"I can ask, but again, I need to have a good reason to make that request. Right now, there's nothing to show she didn't just leave of her own accord like we originally thought."

"Someone's using her debit card. A guy."

"You gonna give me the name of the witness who saw *that*?"

"He wanted to remain anonymous."

Wyatt turned away and huffed. I didn't entirely blame him, but at the same time, I couldn't spill Kim's secrets. I was just trying to come up with an explanation that sounded vaguely plausible when he spoke again.

"Kimberly? What's up?"

I twisted in my seat and saw her standing in the doorway, chewing that lip again. Nervous. "What's wrong?"

"You guys need to see this."

"See what?"

The last thing I needed was more bad news, but I very much suspected that was what we were about to get.

CHAPTER 24 - REED

KIM DIDN'T SPEAK, just walked back towards the kitchen, and Wyatt and I both followed. The TV beside the fridge was on, the volume low, and a sombre reporter from the local news channel spoke to the camera from a dimly lit street.

Wyatt grabbed the remote and turned it up.

Friends say Katia de Bruin was stressed over upcoming exams, but as a diligent student, she'd never have skipped class or done anything to jeopardise her future in business. So the question remains, where did she go after she left Bar One in the early hours of yesterday morning? Police are appealing for anybody who saw her to come forward after one witness reported seeing a girl fitting Katia's description talking to a dark-haired man beside a black car. Katia's parents have offered a twenty-thousand-dollar reward for any information leading to her safe return.

Kim gripped the edge of the counter, her knuckles white. "Did you hear that? A black car. He took another one."

"Sweetheart, we don't know that. A lot of people drive black cars."

Wyatt was still staring at the screen, where an elegant-looking brunette stared out from a "missing" poster.

"I've seen that face somewhere before." He snapped his fingers. "Got it. Her father's a hotel magnate, and there was an uproar a few years back when he built a new resort on a nature reserve. The environmentalists were furious over a bunch of rare frogs or something."

"Frogs?"

"So they said. There were threats. I can't remember what exactly, but we'll have a file."

"And you reckon that might have something to do with Katia's disappearance?"

"I thought it had all died down, but I guess it's a possibility."

"Or Tim took her because he didn't manage to keep me," Kim said. "You said that before, but...but..."

"You didn't want to believe it. Trust me, I didn't either." I unpeeled her fingers from the counter and clasped her hands in mine. "And we still don't know for sure that's what happened."

"Well, I think it's more likely than Katia getting kidnapped by some freaking environmental group!"

A tear rolled down Kim's cheek, and I wiped it away. "I know this is hard." If Wyatt hadn't been there, I'd have cuddled her close to me, but I didn't want to answer questions about a relationship we didn't have. "Don't cry."

"We'll add her to the board as a possible," Wyatt said. "Shall we get back to work?"

In the dining room, Kim grabbed a handful of paper clips, bending and twisting the metal as she stared blankly at the whiteboard. I waited for another grilling from Wyatt.

"Where were we?" he asked.

"Emma. Her debit card."

"Ah, yes. Your mysterious witness."

"Look, I—"

"Wait!" Kim dropped a half-made chipmunk and ran to her sideboard. What was she doing? A few seconds later, she came back with a stack of name cards, those expensive silver-edged ones you get on the table at fancy events, and began writing all the names out again.

"We can do that on the whiteboard..." I began.

"No, look." She shuffled the cards around into a different order. "See?"

Brianna.

Dawn.

Emma.

Georgette.

Gina.

Hailee.

Isla.

Jacqueline.

Kimberly.

Katia.

"See what?" Wyatt asked.

"It's the alphabet. He's going through the freaking alphabet. When Georgette died too soon, he had to get another G. And when I escaped, he needed another K."

I scanned the names again. "We're missing three. Where are A, C, and F?"

"We must have missed some girls. Maybe their families didn't report them. Or they're from another state."

"Hold on," Wyatt said. "How do you know Georgette died too soon? What are you talking about?"

Kim clapped both hands over her mouth, and I let

out a groan. Dammit. How were we supposed to explain this?

Before Emma disappeared, Wyatt had been a friend forever. But he'd never been as open-minded as me, and in the police, he liked to do things by the book. Intuition was a dirty word. The idea of using a...an Electi? Filthy.

But Kim didn't know that.

"I spoke to her," she whispered.

"Spoke to who?"

"Georgette."

"But you said thirty seconds ago that Georgette died."

Kim screwed her eyes shut, and I didn't know whether to hug her or shove Wyatt out the door or laugh off her comments as the ramblings of a woman who'd been through too much.

But before I could make up my mind, she kept talking.

"Yes, she did, but her spirit's still here."

Wyatt began laughing. "For a moment, I thought you were serious." When we didn't join in, his smile faded. "Wait—you *are* serious?" He looked at me. "Is she serious?"

"She's serious."

And brave. It had taken a lot for her to risk ridicule by admitting her abilities to Wyatt.

He laughed again, but this time, there was no mirth in it. "Are you telling me this whole case is based on Kimberly's chats with her imaginary friends? See, this is why we didn't investigate any further after the initial report. Because there's nothing there."

Now I did put my arm around her, and Wyatt's

expression turned to mild disgust.

"You're doing all this just to get in her panties?" He got to his feet. "Man, you must be desperate."

"I knew there was a reason I broke your nose. What about Emma, huh? Are you just gonna walk away?"

"No, I'm not. I'll look for her the old-fashioned way. By finding hard evidence and witnesses who actually exist."

"What do you think I've spent the past two years, four months, and twenty-six days doing? There's nothing. Nobody's seen her. And you know why? It's because some fucker with an English accent's been going around pretending to be E Cullen."

"You really believe that? Then find me proof."

This time, it was Kim who spoke through her tears. "You want proof? Fine, I'll give you proof. Drive me anywhere in the state. Heck, the country. Put me on any street, and I'll tell you who was killed there and how. Then you can look up all the hard evidence you love so much and find out I'm telling the truth."

"Is she for real?" Wyatt asked me.

"What do you expect me to do? Channel her answer? Why don't you ask her?"

"Uh…" Seeing him at a loss for words was strangely satisfying. "Okay, you truly think you can do this? Get in the car."

"I'll just fetch my purse."

"Kim, you don't have to go through with this. If Wyatt doesn't believe you, that's his problem."

"No, it's *our* problem. Because there's a chance Katia's still alive. We need all the help we can get to find Tim quickly, and Wyatt's got access to the police computer."

Wyatt fished around in his pocket then dangled his car keys in front of me. "You heard the lady."

"You've turned into a real dick, you know that?"

"Right now, I'm a dick with a badge, so let's go."

***

I rode in the back seat of Wyatt's truck with Kim as he drove around town, aimlessly it seemed. Through Bethesda, through Chevy Chase, through Silver Spring. She gripped my hand, unspeaking, and I wasn't sure whether her nerves were due to a fear she might fail the test or a worry that she'd pass and her secret really would be out.

"You all right?"

She just stared at me. Okay, dumb question.

Finally, Wyatt drew to a halt outside a boarded-up house in Briggs Chaney, just past Castle Boulevard. Nice choice. Someone would have died around here for sure. He reached under his seat for his gun, and I checked mine was loaded.

"Is that really necessary?" Kim asked.

"Around here? Yeah."

The area was slowly improving—emphasis on the slowly—but it wasn't a place you wanted to spend much time in at night. On the plus side, we wouldn't have to walk far before Kim found someone to talk to.

Less than a hundred yards, in fact. She stopped, and I bumped into her.

"Here?"

"You're standing on his foot."

I stepped back while Wyatt rolled his eyes. Let him. He'd have to change his opinion within the hour, and I was kind of looking forward to rubbing his face in it. With Kim muttering away, I positioned myself so it appeared to any passers-by that we were having a casual conversation, but I made sure to keep an eye on what was going on around us. Right now, that was a drug deal less than fifty feet away, but if they didn't bother us, we wouldn't bother them.

"Kamal Kabede," Kim said, fixing her gaze on Wyatt. "Twenty-four years old, originally from Ethiopia. In March six years ago, a man by the name of Negus Johnson stabbed him once in the chest over there by the abandoned warehouse, and he made it this far before he died. Negus is a pimp, and he blackmailed Kamal's girlfriend into working for him, so they had words, and Kamal's death was the result. What is it with men? Why do they think they can own women?" She turned back to the empty space in front of her. "I'll try to find out about your sister, okay? Thanks for talking to me."

"What *about* his sister?" I asked.

"He gave her money to move out of town. He wants to know if she made it."

"I'll check into it."

"And Negus Johnson is still around. Kamal saw him last week. He should be in jail."

I patted Wyatt on the shoulder. "That one's down to you, buddy. Do you need any other details, or can we go?"

"We can go."

As soon as we climbed back into the truck, Kim punched the door locks and shuddered. Even though she'd put on a long wool coat over her fluffy sweater, she still looked totally out of place in this neighbourhood. I held out an arm then settled it over her shoulder as she squashed against my side. Times like this, I was a Titan to her Tinkerbell, all big and awkward compared to her daintiness. I twirled a lock of silky hair around my finger, wondering what it would be like to have that blonde mane spread out over my chest. Her smooth skin against mine. Every day I spent with this girl, I wanted her more.

Meanwhile, Wyatt was on his phone in the front seat.

"Barb, can you do me a favour?"

Of course Barb would. Well into her sixties now with grey hair and a fondness for saltwater taffy, she'd worked the evening shift for as long as I could remember. As long as you observed her rules, namely bringing her a cup of coffee whenever you fetched one for yourself and keeping the outer door to the squad room closed so the draft didn't blow across her feet, she'd go above and beyond to help.

"I need you to look up a murder for me. Kamal Kabede, out in Silver Spring... Thanks... Just a quick rundown of the details."

He listened, his frown in the rear-view mirror growing deeper with every passing second. Sucked to be wrong, didn't it?

When he hung up, he turned to face both of us.

"Very funny. How did you do that? Does she memorise crime databases or something? News reports?"

"She's told you how she does it. It's just that you choose not to believe."

"Did Negus Johnson ever get tried?" Kim asked.

"He was arrested. There wasn't enough evidence to

charge him, but I expect you already knew that."

"I only know what I told you."

Wyatt went to pinch the bridge of his nose, something he'd done since he was a kid whenever he got stressed. But today, he forgot it was broken, and his face screwed up in pain.

"Fuck."

I snorted out a laugh and turned it into a cough. "You really think it's more plausible that Kim's memorised the details of every murder in the entire state than for her to talk to ghosts?" Okay, so put that way, Wyatt's assumption didn't seem unreasonable. "Why don't you open your mind?"

"What do you think happens after somebody dies?" Kim asked.

Wyatt shrugged. "Who knows? It's not something I've ever considered. I guess they just rot in the ground."

"What about your soul? It's not organic. It can't rot."

"Then what is it?"

"Something intangible. Some sort of energy. It exists quite independently as far as I can gather. Do you want me to find another spirit? Because we can keep doing this all night if you wish."

"One more."

This time, we went back to Chevy Chase, and Wyatt slowed to a crawl as he drove along a side road.

"Let's try a car accident this time. Tell me when you see a victim."

"That won't necessarily work," Kim said. "Single-car victims pass straight over. It's only if somebody else caused the crash that they get stuck."

"You mean there are rules in the afterlife?"

"Rules and procedures, yes."

"All this driving around is stupid, you know that," I told him. "This is why you don't solve more cases. Because your instincts aren't developed properly."

"I got promoted, and you didn't."

"Only because you were better at paperwork."

"Will you two stop bickering?" Kim was already pointing out the window. "Stop here. There's a guy at the side of the road with his head... Actually, carry on. He's wearing an old military uniform, so he won't be in your precious database. Wait. Over there. A woman with a child."

Juanita and Isabella Diaz, we found out. Run over by a drunk driver in the eighties, and they'd been standing there ever since. We huddled in the cool air while Wyatt made his phone call, and this time when he hung up, he nodded grudgingly before a slow smile spread over his face.

"Okay, I believe you now."

"About fucking time," I said.

"But you know what this means?" He grinned at Kim. "This is huge! With your abilities, we'll be able to solve every murder that comes across our desks. We can give you the right questions to ask, and—"

"Oh no. No, no, no." She shook her head. "Solving murders is your job, not mine. I plan weddings."

"But you've got this extraordinary skill..."

"I'm also good at picking out bridal gowns and selecting the perfect flowers for every occasion."

"Don't you want to see murderers get punished?"

"Of course I do, and don't you dare lay a guilt trip on me. I didn't ask for this gift. In fact, I'd rather not have it."

"But when the world finds out..."

"Who's going to tell them? You? Because I'll deny everything and you'll look like a fool. I admitted to what I can do for one reason and one reason only: to get justice for Emma Cullen and ensure the man who drugged me can't hurt any more girls. Once that's over, I'm going back to my world, which is ivory, white, and silver and doesn't involve dead people."

Kim turned on her heel and climbed into Wyatt's truck, then slammed the door behind her so hard the hinges rattled.

And all I could do was smile because that was the moment I officially fell in love with Kimberly Jennings.

Chapter 25 - Kimberly

"IT WON'T DO up!"

I held the phone away from my ear to save my eardrums from Tara Bowman's shrieks. "The designer can adjust the seams a little. That's why we have this final fitting."

"Not this much. There's, like, two inches of gap."

Oh, great. Now we had sobbing.

"I'm coming, okay? Give me half an hour and I'll be there."

Eight thirty on Monday morning, and a simple dress fitting had gone horribly awry. Silently, Reed slid a bottle of Tylenol in my direction. After Wyatt's efforts yesterday and now this, I was tempted to swallow the whole darn lot.

"Problem?" he asked.

"At work? Nothing unusual, sadly."

No, my bigger worry was the investigation. Tim was still on the loose, a problem compounded by Emma's disappearance and now Wyatt's involvement. We'd barely spoken after I threatened him yesterday, and while I was positive Reed would take my secret to the grave, I had no such confidence in Wyatt.

The two men had come up with a plan last night. We knew the culprit must work at the British embassy, and thanks to Lil Shawn, we also knew he had a tattoo.

So starting today, they'd follow each man to the gym, the swimming pool, a sports game, anywhere he might take off his shirt, and eliminate them one by one.

The other possibility was a further line-up with Maria, but none of us had confidence in her ability to recognise Tim now more time had passed, especially since we knew he kept changing his appearance. No, finding the tattoo was our best hope. It wouldn't be the fastest process, but Wyatt concurred with Reed's opinion that getting information from the embassy in a formal manner would be an impossible task. They didn't share.

I stared out the kitchen window at the frost twinkling on my back lawn. If only it were summer. Solving the mystery would be so much easier if the sun was out and everyone was wearing short sleeves.

"Want me to make breakfast before you go?" Reed offered.

"No time."

"Coffee? I can put it in a to-go cup."

"Coffee would be lovely. My travel cup's in the cupboard above the toaster. The pink one with silver stars."

"I could have guessed."

Having a roommate wasn't as bad as I thought it would be. I'd considered renting out a room several times over the years, not because I needed the money, but rather to have some company. So why didn't I? Because I always worried I'd grow to hate the person, and asking them to leave would lead to a level of awkwardness I preferred to avoid.

But Reed cooked. He didn't snore. He left his boots in the hallway. And I'd discovered he was one of those naturally warm people who didn't bother with a shirt if it was hot in the mornings. It wasn't my fault I'd accidentally turned the thermostat up a few notches before I went to bed last night. My hand slipped.

"What time are you meeting Wyatt?"

"Three o'clock. He's got the early shift today. I'm gonna head out to the embassy first."

"Be careful."

"That's usually my line."

"Will you call me and let me know what's going on?"

"Yes, Mom." He closed his eyes for a second. "Sorry. That was insensitive."

Yes, it was, but I pasted on a smile. "It's fine. I shouldn't be so pushy. Annie's told me that many times in the past."

"I like you pushy. In case I forget to mention it later, I was impressed with your comeback on Wyatt yesterday."

"Do you think he'll tell anyone?"

"And risk his reputation at work? I don't think so. Besides, I'll do more than break his nose if he betrays your trust."

"In case *I* forget to mention it later, thank you. Thank you for *your* trust."

He held out my travel cup. "Listen to us. The Reed and Kimberly mutual appreciation society. Get to work, sweetheart."

It would have been so easy to take a step forward, stand on tiptoes, and kiss him. But I couldn't. Not Reed. Not when we were in the middle of hunting a murderer and I was damaged goods. I settled for a wave instead.

"See you later."

***

"I'm so, so sorry. I know we agreed you didn't have to come to the fitting, and I feel really bad for calling you, but the dress just won't do up. Like *at all*. I've tried sucking my stomach in, but I'd have to lose six pounds in five days and I'm just not sure I can do that. I've been living on salad, anyway."

Tara's make-up had smudged where she'd been crying, and I took a deep breath and walked all the way into the fitting room. The dress designer shrugged when I glanced across at her.

"Can you stand up?"

Tara lurched to her feet, holding the half-done-up bridal gown around her chest. Sure enough, the zipper was stuck just below her waist, and with that gap, it wasn't going any farther. Oh, Jiminy Cricket.

The dress had fitted perfectly a month ago, and I believed Tara when she said she'd been dieting. Every other photo on her Instagram was some kind of green stuff.

Just in case, I asked, "How much dressing have you been putting on the salad?"

"Almost none! Only vinaigrette and applesauce."

"Applesauce? On salad?"

"I know that sounds really strange, but one day I got the urge to try it, and it tastes amazing."

"Could you be bloated? Have gas?"

"I don't think so. Apart from feeling a little queasy some mornings, I've been fine."

Queasy? Mornings? Strange cravings? Uh-oh.

"Tara, could you be pregnant?"

She sat down again, the dress poofing out around her. "No, that's not it."

"Are you sure?" I stood back and studied her. If anything, she'd lost weight everywhere but her stomach. "When did you last get a visit from Aunt Flo?"

"A couple of months ago, but I can't have children, Kimberly." She gave a loud sniffle, and the designer leapt forward with a tissue. "I was sick when I was a teenager. Cancer. The drugs they gave me... The doctors said I had ovarian failure, that I'd never get pregnant."

I knelt to give her a hug, and she smeared mascara all over my pastel jacket. The dry cleaner was going to love me. Still, it made a change from the red wine somebody invariably spilled on me at every reception.

"I'm so sorry, Tara."

"It's okay. We've had a while to come to terms with it. Jacob says maybe we could look into adoption once we're married, and at first, I hated the idea, but now... I think I might like that."

Adoption. I'd considered the possibility too, but when I mentioned it to Alan, he'd slammed the idea of "bringing up somebody else's kid" and questioned once again why I refused to have my own. Then after the divorce, I'd have been a single mother, and I was terrified of getting turned down. A psychiatrist would probably tell me that was why I stayed so busy at work —to compensate for what was missing at home.

My heart went out to Tara, but although I wished I could have sat with her all day, we still had a dress that didn't fit and she was supposed to be walking down the aisle in less than a week. I grabbed my phone and consulted Google. Spontaneous reversal of ovarian failure was rare, but it happened, and I couldn't come up with another explanation.

"I'll be back in just a minute."

There was a pharmacy across the street, and I grabbed the nearest pregnancy test off the shelf and ran to the register. What else could it be? Tara's face looked positively gaunt, and that amount of water retention seemed extreme.

"Tara, I understand this is really awkward," I said when I got back. She hadn't moved, and neither had the dress designer. Three months she'd spent on that gown, and the poor woman was probably worried she'd get the blame for it not fitting. "But could you pee on the stick?"

Her incredulous expression told me what she thought of that idea, but luckily, she'd always been one of the easier brides to deal with. The designer held open the bathroom door while Tara squashed herself inside.

"Maybe we should have gotten her to take the dress off first," she whispered.

"Probably. Will those seams go out any more?"

"Half an inch. An inch, max. Not two inches. We could try one of those body-shaper corsets?"

As long as Tara didn't combine it with slimming shakes. No way was I going through that nightmare again.

"I guess. What other dresses do you have in stock? Just in case the corset doesn't work."

"Uh, let me check." She began rummaging through the nearest rack. "How about—"

Tara's shriek cut her off mid-sentence. Was that a

good shriek or a bad shriek? Hard to tell.

"I'm pregnant!"

Relief at being right washed over me, quickly followed by a cold prickle of fear because the wedding plans would undoubtedly descend into chaos, and perhaps I harboured a tiny hint of jealousy too.

"That's good, right?"

She ran out of the bathroom in her underwear and squashed the breath out of me. "I can't believe it. We're gonna have a baby! I gotta call Jacob."

The designer breathed a sigh of relief and tucked a faux-fur cape around Tara's shoulders.

"I'll go and have a look for something with an empire line, shall I?"

***

Two days, Reed had been sharing my house, and already it felt lonely without him. He'd called earlier to say he was following one suspect to a squash club while Wyatt trailed another, which left me at loose ends in the evening.

Tara had been so thrilled about the baby that she'd settled for an off-the-rack dress with extra sparkles, the designer thought she could resell the other one, and I'd caught up on the rest of my work by seven but forgotten to eat lunch. Chicken chow mein was calling out to me, so I ordered that and enough food for Reed as well. If he was out late playing sports, cooking would be the last thing he wanted to do when he got home.

I needed to give him a key too, because when he returned at nine thirty, he had to knock. Sweaty Reed in shorts and a tight T-shirt. It was like having my own calendar model.

"Busy day?" I asked.

"Yeah. I caught up with a few contacts, but Wyatt had to work overtime. Katia's father's upped the reward to seven figures, and every kook and his brother's phoning the hotline. Mothers are accusing their own sons, and one guy's called forty-seven times claiming she's been abducted by aliens from the Andromeda Galaxy."

"It sounds as if her father didn't think things through."

"The captain tried to talk him out of it, but he wouldn't listen."

"Did you have a good game?"

"Got the shit beaten out of me. The chick I tagged along with to get into the squash club played like a demon, but at least we've crossed one suspect off the list." He checked the side of his thigh under the spotlights above the hallway mirror. "Look—bruises."

I was still hung up on the previous sentence. "You went with a woman?"

"It was just work, sweetheart."

Sure. That was what Alan always used to say, and then he spent the evening with *her*. A late presentation one day, a business meeting the next. I shouldn't have let the past get to me, and Reed and I weren't even dating, let alone married, but the thought of him with another girl still stung.

"Work. Of course. There's food in the fridge, and I'm going to get an early night."

"Kim? You okay?"

"Other than the whole murder-hunt thing, I couldn't be better."

Couldn't be freaking better.

Chapter 26 - Reed

SOFT FOOTSTEPS SOUNDED on the stairs as I poured Kim's coffee into her to-go cup. After she gave me the cold shoulder last night, I figured making her a drink rather than breakfast was the safer option. The steps paused, then resumed with a *click, click, click* of heels on tile after Kim put her pumps on.

This morning, she'd gone with a black outfit rather than her usual pastel, a long-sleeved dress that looked more appropriate for a funeral. I almost asked "who died?" but I stopped myself just in time. Probably Kim wouldn't appreciate gallows humour like my ex-colleagues did.

"Sleep well?" I asked instead, then realised her eyes were puffy. Shit.

"So-so."

"How was your meeting yesterday morning? Did your client fit into her dress in the end?"

"Not even close. It turned out she was pregnant and didn't realise."

Kim's previous comments about her lack of kids came back to me, and I realised her touchiness yesterday evening may not have been entirely down to jealousy as I'd first thought. Which was almost disappointing.

"You were okay with that?"

"Of course. Why wouldn't I be?"

No way was I about to open up that can of worms. "I made you coffee. Do you want anything to eat?"

"I'll pick something up on the way to the office. Are you going to DC again today?"

I nodded. "Wyatt too. His suspect kept a sweater on the whole evening, so he's going after the same guy and I get a new one."

"Will you play squash again?"

"No. In his spare time, this dude's the choreographer for an all-female dance troupe, so I'm going to their rehearsal."

Her mouth set in such a thin line her lips almost disappeared, and I swallowed a laugh. Fuck, she was cute when she got mad. And definitely jealous. My cock shouldn't have twitched, but it did.

"A dance troupe? What kind of dance?"

"Samba. Man, the costumes are impressive. Big feathers and sequins."

"Really? I won't wait up, then."

She snatched the coffee off the counter, and she would have marched out of the kitchen if I hadn't snaked an arm around her waist.

"Kim, wait."

"Let go of me!"

"I was just joking."

"Joking?"

"About the dancers."

"Why would you do that? It's not funny."

"Because…" Oh, fuck it. I plucked her out of her stupid pink shoes and kissed her. Hard. What was the worst that could happen? She'd slap me then kick me out of the house.

Perhaps this wasn't such a... Except she was kissing me back, all soft lips and breathy sighs and strawberry-flavoured lip gloss. I sat her on the counter, and she wrapped her arms and legs around me, fingernails scraping on my bare back.

That dainty little tongue flicked out and tangled with mine, and my cock began to harden. This wasn't Kimberly the demure wedding planner with an obsession for order. This was one-night-stand Kim, hungry and wanton.

And late.

I was well on my way to getting lost in her when she pulled back and groaned softly. Checked her watch. Laid her forehead against mine.

"I have to get to work. I wish I didn't, but I have a meeting with a venue manager, and if I skip it, the couple might lose the booking, and—"

"Shh." I pressed a finger against her lips. "I know you have to work, and we'll continue this later, okay?"

Now I got a smile. Not the nervous, flickery smile. Not the tight, professional smile. Not even the friendly-yet-guarded smile I'd been growing accustomed to. No, this was a full-beam, carefree grin. Happy. This was the first time I'd seen Kim truly happy.

"You're really not going to watch a dance rehearsal?"

"I'm going to his gym. I'll be hanging out in a locker room with a bunch of sweaty men, and you'd better believe I'll be leaving that place as soon as possible."

"Shall I order dinner? Pizza?"

"If that's what you want. I'm easy."

"I hope so."

My turn to groan. "Are you sure you can't shift that

meeting? My hands are itching to tear you out of that dress."

"I can't. Not now. Later."

"What's with the Morticia Addams look?"

"I'm going wine tasting with Maria and Annie this afternoon. Last time, I spilled Merlot on my skirt and the stain wouldn't come out, so I thought I'd take precautions. Oh, dammit."

"What?"

"Annie's coming over to watch a movie later. We haven't had a girls' night in ages, and she never stays late, but I could cancel?"

"You have your girls' night. Just save me some pizza, and don't expect much sleep afterwards."

"No sleep. Okay. Reed?"

"Yeah?"

"Kiss me again before I go. And also pinch me because I'm not sure whether I'm dreaming."

I smacked her on the ass instead, which only made her yelp and press tighter against me. Fuck, how did I get this lucky? The scent of her arousal drifted up as our lips met, and this time, it was my turn to pull away.

"If you don't leave now, you'll be naked underneath me in five minutes."

She hesitated. She actually hesitated. But then she untwined her limbs and slid to the floor.

"You'd better take a key in case I fall asleep."

She padded across to the drawer beside the stove and fished one out, attached to a large pink tassel that I'd be removing right away.

"What have I told you about keeping important stuff in the kitchen?"

"As soon as this case is over, you can rearrange

things however you want."

She was planning on me staying here after that? I figured it was too soon to discuss the future, but I liked the direction her thoughts were going.

"Deal. I'll call you at lunch, sweetheart. Don't get too drunk with Maria. I want you sentient tonight."

"That's why I'm taking Annie. She gives me a lecture if I start slurring."

"You know you're meant to spit the wine out after you've tasted it?"

"I don't like spitting."

I couldn't help grinning. "Duly noted."

"You filthy pig. Just leave."

But she was smiling as she said it, and I knew that tonight, Kimberly Jennings was mine.

***

"Looks like the gym's a bust tonight," Wyatt said. "Where do you think they're going?"

"Shared cars? Union Jack balloons? Gift boxes? I'd say someone's having a going away party."

"Stay or go?"

"If they're heading for a restaurant or a club and it gets warm in there, there's a good chance of some of those shirtsleeves getting rolled up."

Wyatt started his truck and pulled out after the last car. We'd parked my SUV with its camera outside the embassy before retiring to watch the video feed from Wyatt's vehicle, parked in a less conspicuous position a half mile down the road. By my calculations, four of our six remaining suspects were in the five cars currently inching along Embassy Row. If we could eliminate them, that would only leave two. And if one of the quartet had the tattoo we were looking for...

"You seem happy considering all our plans just got screwed," Wyatt said, steering around a Honda going ten miles an hour under the limit. "Something happen with Kim?"

Times like this, I wished Wyatt didn't know me quite so well. "A gentleman never kisses and tells."

"Bullshit. You're not a gentleman, and you always kiss and tell."

"Not this time."

"So something did happen?"

"A kiss. That's it."

"But you want more?"

"Yeah, I do."

And in three or four hours, I was gonna get it.

"Are you sure that's a good idea? Kim's... She's different."

"Because she can see ghosts? I'm not sure that impacts on her anatomy, and it sure as hell doesn't put me off her personality. She's smart, she's driven, and she's got a kind heart."

"Just be careful, buddy. I'm only saying that because I care."

"You lost the right to give that speech two years and five months ago."

Wyatt lapsed into silence, and I wondered if I'd been too harsh. But no, that needed to be said. The line of embassy vehicles pulling into the parking lot of a steakhouse up ahead saved us from an awkward silence, and Wyatt began grumbling instead.

"We'll have to get a table for fucking two again."

"Oh, honey. I've missed our little tête-à-têtes."

The last time we'd been undercover, the waitress told us what a cute couple we made and brought us a complimentary dessert with two spoons. Emma had laughed like a fucking hyena when I told her afterwards, but Wyatt didn't see the funny side.

"Shut up."

The restaurant was packed, and we ended up at a table near the back, but the embassy group was between us and the bathroom so I developed a weak bladder. And next to the bathroom was the thermostat, so I took inspiration from Kim and turned it up a couple of notches as I walked past. She sure liked to keep her house tropical, but I wasn't complaining because she also liked to wear slinky tops that showed off her curves, and if she put a sweater on, that would spoil the view.

And soon the restaurant patrons were stripping off too, including three of our suspects. No tattoos.

"Come on, man, take your shirt off," Wyatt muttered right as the waitress walked up behind him. Her eyes widened.

I dialled my laugh down to a grin. "Don't worry, I won't do it." I lowered my voice to a whisper but kept it loud enough for Wyatt to hear. "It's our anniversary today, and he's just feeling a bit excited."

"Oh, congratulations! And how amazing that you chose to celebrate here with us." She patted Wyatt on the shoulder, oblivious to his murderous glare. "Let me bring you out a little surprise."

Today, we got an ice cream sundae with two spoons, chocolate sauce, and a sparkler stuck in the middle, as well as a round of applause from tables either side of us.

"I'll get you back for this," Wyatt promised.

"Sure, honey. I'll bend over when we get home."

Except when we got back to Kim's, Wyatt's revenge was the last thing on my mind.

CHAPTER 27 - KIMBERLY

WHY WAS I so cold? Had Reed turned the heating down? I twisted under the covers, curling my knees up to my chest and tucking the quilt around me. In all honesty, I didn't even remember going to bed, just drinking far, far too much wine with a rather blurry Maria, taking a cab home with her and Annie, and opening a very expensive box of chocolates my father had sent while Annie scrolled through Netflix.

Then I recalled Reed's words before he left this morning. *I want you sentient tonight.* Sentient? I could barely remember my own name. We'd been doing okay until the wine merchant opened the good stuff, and then even Annie had stopped complaining and started drinking.

Yes, I'd messed up big time today. No movie, no pizza, and no sexy times with Reed. What must he think of me? At least I'd given him a key, or he'd be sleeping in his car again tonight. How could I apologise for this? A simple "sorry, I totally forgot what a lightweight I am" really wouldn't cut it. Perhaps I could take him out for dinner? Would that be weird, me asking him on a proper date? Or would he turn me down now he realised what an idiot I was? A low groan escaped my lips.

Then I froze as a voice spoke.

"Are you awake?"

A female voice, but not Annie. No, this voice was higher. Musical, almost. I forced my eyelids to open, and they felt heavy. Sore. Foreign.

And then I realised I wasn't in my bed, and I definitely wasn't in my house. I was in a...a dormitory? A prison? Two dimly lit rows of narrow beds, one row on each side of a long room, and each bed was surrounded by thick metal bars that ran from the floor to the low ceiling. Jail cells with padlocks on the doors. My bed was at the end of a row, and all the others on my side of the room were empty, as was the one opposite. A motionless form lay on the bed beside that, and in the next, I made out a face peering towards me. The owner of the voice?

"Where am I? Who are you?"

"You're in Casa Lunatica. At least, that's what we call it."

"What the...? I don't understand."

Another face, another voice, this one farther along the room. "Welcome to the asylum. I'm Jacqueline, and she's Katia. We also have Isla, Hailee, Gina, Fern, Emma, Dawn, Carolina, Brianna, and Abigail. Plus your friend there, whose name I'm guessing begins with L?"

Oh hell, oh hell, oh hell. My heart began pounding along with my head as her words sank in. "Jacqueline? Jacqueline Springer?"

"You know who I am?" She sounded surprised.

"I've been helping to look for the man who took you." Then the full implications of her words hit. "Emma? Emma Cullen?"

A voice answered from the gloom. "That's me."

Lower pitched than I'd expected. Husky. Emma was alive!

"Reed's looking for you. And Wyatt too. They'll find us."

"You know my brother?"

Not as well as I wanted to. A sob welled up inside my throat, and I swallowed it back down.

"I first met him a few weeks ago when I hired him to find the man who drugged me."

"And that was Peter?"

"Peter? Who's Peter?"

"The man who locked us up down here."

"He told me his name was Tim."

Another voice came from the furthest part of the room, softer this time. "He lies all the time. He's delusional. I'm Abigail Bloom, by the way. Peter's psychiatrist and the first player in this strange little game."

I almost choked. "His psychiatrist? Are you joking?"

"I only wish I was."

"He kidnapped his psychiatrist?"

"Go figure. After I told him I was moving to Hawaii with my fiancé, he just kind of...unravelled." I heard the incredulity in her voice. "Totally missed that one."

"What were you treating him for?"

"Low self-esteem. He had trouble connecting with women."

"You mean this is all the result of his inability to get a girlfriend?"

"Well, it goes a little deeper than that, but basically, yes."

"And he just keeps you in cages?"

"Mostly. He lets us out one at a time to amuse him.

Sometimes two at a time."

"Amuse him?" Oh, freaking hell. The implications of that became clear in my head, and I leaned to the side of the bed and threw up the remnants of yesterday's wine. "N-n-not... Not *that*?"

"Fortunately for us, one of his issues is erectile dysfunction disorder."

"Erectile what?"

Emma cut in. "He can't get it up."

"He controls us in other ways," Jacqueline explained. "Tells us what to do, what to wear, what to say. He makes up these scenes, and we're supposed to act them out with him."

"Last year, he decided we should all learn musical instruments," Emma said. "The noise was horrible."

"At the moment, it's ballroom dancing. He almost broke my toe last week. Uh, if you need Kleenex, there's a box by your Porta Potti."

"My what?"

I looked around my cell properly for the first time. The bed—more of a cot, really—took up most of one side, and a nightstand held a plastic cup of water and a book. *The Art of Ballroom: Step-by-Step*. Wow. Seemed as though Jacqueline was serious about the dancing thing. I'd taken lessons as a child, so I didn't need a manual, but—

Kim, what are you even thinking? No. I didn't want to dance with my freaking kidnapper.

Plastic bottles of water were stacked on a shelf along the back wall, together with crackers, a fruit bowl, a box of chocolates, and a greetings card with a picture of a house on it. *Welcome to your new home!* the message on the front read.

Tim, Peter, whatever—he was certifiably insane.

The aforementioned Porta Potti, a squat cream cube, sat between two short screens for modesty. Nobody would see me poop, at least until Marnie or Mindy or Meryl moved into the cell opposite. Sweat trickled down my spine at the sight of all the empty beds. What was he doing? Collecting us?

"I'm Kimberly, by the way."

"Kimberly?" Jacqueline asked. She seemed the most talkative. Katia just watched me through wary eyes. "But you're in the 'N' room."

I closed my eyes for a second, hoping it was all a bad dream. "My middle name's Noelle. Maybe that's why I'm in here? And my friend's Leanne. Annie for short." A chill ran through me as I realised how Peter found that out. "Dammit, he must've been looking at our company website. The staff page has her full name." I got up and pressed closer to the bars, careful to step around the pool of vomit. "Annie?" I called. Nothing. "Has she moved since she got here?"

Katia finally spoke. "Not yet, but she's breathing."

That was a small plus point, at least. I checked the rest of my cell, hoping for something, anything that I could use as a weapon.

A hairbrush but no mirror. A single wooden chair against the bars opposite the cot. A clothes rail with a few dresses and a bathrobe on plastic hangers, but no underwear that I could see. And no footwear.

"We don't have shoes?"

Jacqueline shook her head. "He's always worried about us escaping. I guess he thinks a lack of shoes'll make it more difficult."

"Has anyone ever gotten out?"

"Fern tried before I got here, but there's a combination lock on the outer door, and she didn't know the number. And he punishes us for disobedience."

Another chill ran through me. "What kind of punishment?"

"It varies. Anything from days without food or loss of clothes privileges to... No, I don't want to scare you. Just don't make him angry."

Scare me? I was terrified. The only reason I didn't puke again was because I'd already thrown everything up, and even then, bile rose in my throat.

"Just tell me, would you?"

A pause, then Jacqueline spoke again. "He's smart. Rather than punishing you, he'll hurt one of the others instead. Would you risk somebody else suffering because of your disobedience? When Fern tried to escape, he raped Emma with a hairbrush."

Jacqueline had been right; I really didn't want to know. And poor, poor Emma. She'd been through quite enough even before she came here.

"People are looking for him. They'll find us. Reed and Wyatt and the police will find us. Does anyone know where we are? What state we're in?"

Silence.

Then I heard another voice, thin and reedy, coming from behind me.

"Y'all are in Virginia."

I turned around slowly, conscious of eleven pairs of eyes watching me. In the shadows on the other side of my cage, I glimpsed another woman hovering in the corner, in her late twenties or early thirties with blonde hair piled on top of her head. She wore a dark-red dress with a long skirt and tight bodice, something from the early twentieth century at a guess, and the colour matched the bloody hole in her neck.

"I'm Josie," she said. "Welcome to High Grove Farm."

This time, I looked beyond my cage in the other direction. This cellar, bunker, dungeon, whatever it was —it wasn't new. Each cell reminded me of one of those tiny showrooms from a branch of IKEA, but the walls themselves were made from rough concrete and old timber painted a dirty cream. A relic from a bygone age, much like Josie herself.

"What was this place?" I asked.

Jacqueline thought I was talking to her. "Who knows? A cellar?"

"An old moonshine distillery," Josie said. "Edgar Schultz ran his bootlegging operation from here during Prohibition. All the barrels got stored in this room, and the still was in the space at the far end where Peter takes the girls for dinner. Used to be thirty men at a time working down here, day and night."

"Moonshine," I murmured. "From one illegal activity to another."

"Moonshine?" Jacqueline said. "What are you talking about?"

"After that, it was empty for years," Josie said. "Decades. Ever gone a lifetime without talking to a soul? I thought I was gonna lose my mind. Then a guy came along and used the place to breed dogs. A cruel man, always unkind to them. He clutched at his chest and keeled over right where the girl with the red hair sleeps, and the hounds in that cage ate most of him before anyone realised he was dead."

At least he'd died of natural causes. Having to spend goodness knows how long with a half-mauled ghost would have made this whole ordeal even worse.

"Then it went deathly quiet until Peter came along," Josie continued. "And the girls. Now we're all trapped, although the company's nice."

"I hear footsteps!" one of the girls said. "He's coming."

Clomp, clomp, clomp on wooden stairs followed by the quiet *click* of a lock, then lights blazed, turning dusk into daylight. What time was it? How long had I been gone? Down here, I had no idea, and I realised Peter had taken my watch. Had Reed even noticed I was missing yet?

"Ah, Noelle. You're awake. Super." Peter strode towards me from the far end of the room and stopped in front of my door, holding the bars as he peered inside. "Did you have a little accident?" He waved at the pool of vomit and tutted. "I'll get you a cloth. Drinking the way you do is dangerous, you know."

Oh, I knew that now. One attempted kidnapping and one actual kidnapping, and with Josie as my witness, I was never drinking again.

"It was a wine tasting," I said. "You're supposed to drink."

"No, Noelle. You're supposed to spit the wine out."

"My name's Kimberly."

"Yes, and if you hadn't got away from me the first time, Kimberly would have been perfectly acceptable. But I replaced you with Katia, and we only had M and onwards vacant."

Vacant? What did he think this place was? A freaking hotel? He took half a dozen paces to my right and peered in at Annie.

"Still sleepy, I see. I had to give her a higher dose than planned because she wouldn't behave either. Propofol's so unpredictable. I much prefer GHB."

He moved on to Katia. "And how are you today, Katie? Feeling any better?"

"Eat shit and die."

"I'll take that as a no. I think we'll stick with crackers and water for a few more days, yes? And Jacqueline? Have you been treating our new guests well?"

"Yes, Peter."

The freak visited each girl in turn, and the responses to his questions got more polite as he moved along the line. The older girls were more conditioned to being here, that much was obvious, although I detected a hint of snark in Emma's reply. Only Abigail broke with the norm, asking Peter how he was instead of the other way around.

"A little stressed lately, Abby. Sometimes, it feels as though the whole world's against me."

"In what way?"

"That one..." He pointed in my direction. "After the way she rejected me, I'm not sure how happy I am about her joining us, but she was causing too many difficulties in town with all her questions. Her and that detective she hired. Honestly..." He walked back towards me. "Noelle, you need to learn when to let things go."

"Hello, pot, have you met kettle? How about you let *us* go?"

"No. No, that's not feasible, I'm afraid. Not after I've put so much effort into gathering you all here. And

I know it's a big change for you, but I'm sure you'll grow to love being a part of our little community. Won't she, girls?"

Silence.

"I said, won't she, girls?"

An edge came into his voice, and a quiet chorus of "Yes, Peter" echoed back at us.

He looked me up and down. "I thought you were more of a pastels girl, so that's what I bought you. What's with the black dress? Did somebody die?"

I wished. "I just felt like a change."

"It's too harsh on you. Now, would you like any more books? Magazines? Specific foods? Hailee here's a vegan, which makes dinner times a bit awkward. Doesn't it, girls?"

"Yes, Peter."

"Noelle?"

No, I didn't want books, not unless it was a copy of *War and Peace* I could hit him over the head with. I just wanted to get out of there.

"I'm fine."

"I'm fine, *thank you*. We do insist on manners down here. The world upstairs is going to hell in a handbasket with all that fighting in Africa and the Middle East. Back in the days of the British Empire, things were so much more civilised."

"Apart from the Boer wars and the Amritsar massacre and the famines in India," I pointed out. "Oh, and slavery. Don't forget slavery."

"You're a history buff? How fascinating."

No, that had been Alan. "I just listened at school."

"But you've only heard one side of the story, no? Britain also promoted trade, improved infrastructure, and taught people to play cricket. And introduced tea to the world. You can't beat a good cup of tea. We'll have tea together when you've settled in."

He walked off whistling, and I slumped back on the bed.

Reed, where are you?

This guy was even more of a fruitcake than we thought.

CHAPTER 28 - REED

"WYATT! GET IN here."

I caught him just before he reversed out of Kim's driveway and right after I found her gold necklace lying on the living room floor, the delicate chain broken. She'd never have taken it off voluntarily. She even wore it in the damn shower. How did I know that? Okay, so she might have left her bedroom door open by accident yesterday. And I might have gotten a quick look before I pulled it closed.

"What's happened?"

"Kim's gone."

"What do you mean, gone?"

"Missing. She's supposed to be here, and she's not."

Yes, there were a thousand and one reasons why the house could be empty. Kim could have gone to a movie, stayed out for dinner, stopped off at the office. But she said she'd be there, and after Emma, my mind went straight from "there could be an innocent explanation for this" all the way to "something bad's happened" without pausing for logic to get in the way.

I already had my gun drawn, and Wyatt reached for his too, but a search of the house revealed no sign of her. I forced myself to look on the bright side. At least we hadn't tripped over a body.

On my second walk-through, more slowly this time,

I spotted a purse that didn't belong to Kim, and I realised the situation was even worse than we'd first thought.

"Wyatt, I think Annie's disappeared too. Kim's assistant from work."

"What makes you say that?"

"Her purse is in the living room, and she was meant to be coming over this evening."

"Shit. And there's a smear of blood on the doorjamb outside the downstairs half-bath. I'll call it in."

The perp had gotten in through the back door. One of the glass panels had a perfect circle cut out of it, right above the handle, and a cold breeze blew through the kitchen as we waited for the cops to arrive. But no chill could have rivalled the ice in my veins.

"Do you think it was the same guy?" Wyatt asked, mirroring my thoughts.

"Either that or it's one hell of a coincidence. Dammit, I should have suspected he'd come back for her. He had her address. She got away, and I bet he didn't like that."

"But he took Katia. He's already got a K."

"Maybe he stopped caring about the alphabet and focused on revenge."

"Or it might not have been him. Coming here would have been a big risk, and a stupid one."

"Yeah, but we've been putting the pressure on," I said. "Maybe he's losing his head, and this time, he felt as if he had no choice but to act quickly. Which means we're getting close." Close, but at what cost? First Emma, and now Kim. But Kim had only been gone for a few hours, and Annie too. Was there a chance they were still alive? "What do you want to do? Split this? I'll work the embassy angle and you treat it like a regular kidnapping?"

My gut told me everything was connected, and I'd learned to rely on those feelings in the past. We'd been stirring up a hornet's nest, and Kim was the one who'd got stung.

"I know we've had our differences, personally and at work, but I trust your instincts." Wyatt gave his head a shake. "Maybe even more than mine."

"Then we've got two suspects left. Kenneth Stern and Hal Bisham, and they've both got diplomatic immunity. As soon as the rest of the cops arrive, I vote we take one each and use whatever means necessary to find out where they were this evening."

"Agreed. Any preferences on who takes which?"

"Give me Bisham. I've got an idea for him."

I pocketed Kim's necklace because with what that meant to her, there was no way I was letting it go into police custody. Wyatt's episode with the coke wasn't the first time vital evidence had disappeared from a supposedly safe place.

A siren sounded in the distance, and I steeled myself for questions from my former colleagues. My explanations would be brief for now. Firstly, I had no way to explain half of the leaps we'd made in the case, from Kim to Georgette to Jacqueline, and secondly, we had no time to lose and following procedures would only slow us down.

When I'd started checking out the embassy staff, I'd followed Bisham to the gym one evening, a twenty-four-hour place on the edge of Chevy Chase. The guy looked as if he worked out regularly—broad chest, narrow waist, tight sleeves. His thighs didn't match, but perhaps he skipped leg day. While Wyatt dealt with his colleagues and dug into Stern's life, I put my car into gear and headed for Esprit Health & Fitness.

How to play this... A sob story? The truth? Or I could cut through all the bullshit and commit a Class 1 misdemeanour. What did twelve months in jail and a fine I couldn't afford to pay matter when Kim and Annie were missing?

At the gym, sorry, the *health club*, I abandoned my SUV in the no-parking zone outside reception, grabbed my fake police badge out of the glove compartment, and jogged towards the doors. At the desk beyond, a young blonde sat playing with her phone.

"Can I help?" she asked as my shadow fell over her.

"Wyatt Banks, Montgomery County PD. I've got a few questions about one of your members."

Her eyes went wide. "I'll call my manager."

"No need to wake your manager up at this time of night. This'll only take a minute."

"Really?"

"Really. The guy's name is Hal Bisham."

"Steroid Hal?" She clapped a hand over her mouth. "I didn't mean that! We definitely don't have any steroids here. There's even a big sign in each locker room saying they're not allowed."

"I don't care about steroids. I just want to know whether Bisham was here earlier this evening."

"He's here every evening. Sometimes he just sits in the juice bar to catch up with friends, which is kind of odd because he's literally the most boring person in the entire world."

There every night? Didn't always work out? Steroid Hal? Asshole was probably dealing.

"And tonight, can you see when he swiped in and out?"

"Uh, sure. Don't you need a warrant or something for that information?"

"I can get one, but it only wastes taxpayer dollars on all the paperwork. Plus it might lead us to take a deeper look into some of his activities."

"Right." She swivelled towards her computer. "Sure. I'll just get you that information... Uh, he arrived at seven and left at nine thirty."

Which may have given him just enough time to drive to Kim's place, but it would have been tight.

"Do you know if he has a tattoo?"

The receptionist giggled. "You mean the one on his butt? SpongeBob? My friend Carla accidentally walked into the locker room while he was changing, and we think he must have gotten it for a bet."

"No, on his left arm."

"Oh. No, nothing on his arms."

"Thanks. You've been very helpful."

"Do you need anything else? A coffee? We offer complimentary two-week memberships for new clients." She twirled a lock of hair around one finger. "I could extend that to a month?"

"Sorry, got to get back to work."

Her face fell. "If you think of anything else, call me," she said as I strode out the door.

**

Every light in Kim's house was blazing when I got back there, hoping Wyatt's luck had been better than mine. A cop tried to stop me from ducking under the crime scene tape at the perimeter, then realised who I was and stepped aside.

"Been a while, Reed."

"Yeah, Norm, it has."

"Sorry about your girl. Wyatt said you're living here?"

"Yeah, I am. Is Wyatt back yet?"

"Five minutes ago. He's inside."

A forensics guy handed me a pair of blue booties at the door, and a woman in a Tyvek suit crouched beside the table in the hallway.

"Have you found something?" I asked.

"There's a shard of china here. Like something broke."

So it had. "There was a vase on that table this morning. A pink one with fresh flowers in it."

And Tim had been calm enough to clear up the mess before he left. So much for my theory about him losing his head.

In the kitchen, Wyatt was talking to another detective. Steve? Stewart? He'd just transferred to Montgomery County from Allegheny Township in Pennsylvania when I left the force. I nodded in his direction, but he didn't recognise me.

"Anything?" I asked Wyatt as Steve/Stewart moved away.

"Stern was with his wife at his daughter's piano recital this evening. I pretended we'd had a noise complaint from one of his neighbours and asked if they'd heard anything."

"It wasn't Bisham either. I told the receptionist I was you and checked the records at his gym. He didn't swipe out until nine thirty, which means we've run out of suspects."

"You impersonated a police officer? That's a misdemeanour."

"If you hadn't acted like an asshole, I'd probably still be a police officer."

Wyatt opened his mouth to speak, then closed it again. Wise move.

"Have the investigators found any clues?" I asked.

"Nothing new. We've canvassed the nearest neighbours, but nobody saw anything. Crazy. Two women abducted on a residential street and not a single witness. Too bad Kimberly isn't around to do her ghost thing."

"Keep your voice down, would you?"

I'd wiped the whiteboard, but Steve/Stewart was still in the room, checking the notes and reminders pinned to Kim's corkboard. *Buy plant food. Make salon appointment.* A shelf next to it held a motley collection of paper-clip animals, and for some reason, those made my gut twist. Kim didn't keep much personal stuff in the house, but those...those were *her*.

"Sorry."

"And it *is* too bad, because according to Kim, there's a ghost in her living room where I found the broken necklace, and she probably watched the whole thing go down."

"A ghost lives in her house? That's freaky, man."

"Not to Kim. They seemed to be friends."

Wyatt rolled his eyes, yet again displaying a remarkable lack of empathy. "Can't you hold a seance or something? Get a psychic in? Late-night cable's full of them."

"One of those fakes? Are you serious?"

"How do you know they're fake? You believed Kim, didn't you?"

"Kim's different."

"How? Because she chooses not to monetise?"

"I don't know, she just is."

"Think about it. Eight billion humans in the world and she's the only one who talks to dead people? If she's the real deal, then statistically speaking, I bet there's more like her."

There were. She'd said as much. At least three more that she knew of, and what if Wyatt was right and one or two of these people who claimed to be psychic weren't actually charlatans? I thought back to the trip to the grocery store in Cincinnati, to the conversation I'd had with Kim about vampires. She'd seen no evidence they existed, but she didn't know for sure. What if the same could be said for true mediums?

"I'll ask around. There's an internet forum I'm on for private investigators, and some of those guys use unorthodox methods."

Wyatt patted me on the shoulder. "Do that. And in the meantime, I'll stick with the forensics. At least we *know* that works."

Asshole.

Chapter 29 - Kimberly

"YOU'RE TRYING TO lead. Let me lead."

I gritted my teeth and squirmed in the stupid ballgown. The seams itched, and the skirt was too long for dancing. Oh, and then there was the teensy issue that Peter couldn't dance in the first place.

"Fine. Just stop stepping on my feet."

"Everyone was a beginner once. Even you, Noelle."

"Stop calling me that. Why didn't you just wait for a girl whose name actually began with the right letter?"

Peter sighed. "I knew you'd be difficult from the start, back when you insisted the barman at the Park Plaza bring a fresh bowl of pretzels in case somebody else had touched them."

"Hygiene's important."

"So is obedience." He gave his head a little shake. "I almost picked an easier girl, but then your boyfriend kept poking around outside the embassy. I tried to distract him by posing as his sister again, but then you got involved and he only dug deeper. You're like a dog with a bone, Noelle. If you'd just quit when you were ahead..."

"Where would the fun have been in that?" I muttered through gritted teeth.

"*Tsk tsk tsk*. This is exactly the attitude I'm talking about. You should take a leaf out of Leanne's book. See how well behaved she is?"

Well behaved? Annie was practically catatonic.

"How do you choose your victims, anyway?"

"Guests. I prefer guests." Of course he did. "And the selection process is part of the fun. Sometimes, I plan the journey in advance, like with Dawn. She used to wait tables at my favourite little lunch spot in DC, and she always gave me extra pickles in my sandwich. Such an angel. We went out for a lovely dinner before we came here, and she certainly made an effort to dress up." He smiled at the memory. "But nothing beats the joy of a spontaneous invitation, like with you the first time around. I only went to that hotel for some waste-of-time meeting about investing in a property development, and there you were. K for Kimberly, waiting for me in the bar. Except now we've had to change your name a tiny bit."

"I wasn't waiting for you."

"Don't you believe in fate, Noelle?"

A month ago, I'd have said I didn't, but that was before I met Reed. The man who believed me. Believed *in* me. Peter took my silence to mean agreement and gave an arrogant little smile I wanted to sandpaper off his pompous face.

"See? We're more alike than you care to admit, Noelle."

"No way. We're not alike at all."

"Don't argue, Noelle. It's not an attractive quality."

Arrrgh! *And stop calling me Noelle.*

Tonight, it was my turn to eat dinner with my captor. Several times over the last three days, he'd apologised for being unable to give us as much individual attention now there were thirteen of us, but he didn't seem sorry for keeping us in his freaking cellar in the first place.

Each morning, he'd stop by with breakfast, which could be anything from a protein bar to a lukewarm breakfast sandwich filled with sausage and egg, served up with a latte from Manny's Delicatessen. What did Manny think when Peter asked for thirteen meals to go? That he was just a real generous guy in the office? I didn't understand Peter either. In a weird way, he did try to look after us—he even brought Hailee a separate vegan option with every meal—but he was also cruel beyond words. Yesterday, I'd tried to reason with him, told him that I had a life and a family and a bride getting married on Saturday, but that had only made him angry. In the evening, when he brought dinner, I'd got a carrot while the others got pizza. Annie tried to pass me a slice of hers, but we couldn't reach through the bars.

Annie wasn't doing well. Understatement of the year there. After she escaped from her ex-boyfriend, she'd withdrawn into herself for months, and I could see her doing the same again now. She mostly sat at the back of her cell, legs drawn up to her chest, muttering about how she'd broken a mirror last week and now she'd have bad luck for seven years. What could I do to help? I'd tried talking to her, but mostly she refused to answer.

Tonight was supposed to be her evening out of the cage with Peter, but she'd looked so terrified at the thought that I'd volunteered to take her place. Which was why I was currently trying to keep my feet out of the way as Peter stumbled through a waltz. Having to touch him made my skin crawl. I wanted to take a shower, to scrub the filth off myself, but it wasn't my turn yet. Showers were once a week, two girls at a time. According to Jacqueline, Peter had fitted one of the storerooms at the far end out as a bathroom with a shower, toilet, and basin, and if we wanted a particular brand of shampoo, he'd buy it for us. How generous.

"Does he watch us? In the shower?" I'd asked.

"Sometimes."

It was all I could do to stop myself from throwing up again.

Lunch was a hit-and-miss affair, usually a salad or a sandwich with fruit. We needed to stay healthy, Peter told us, and he handed out vitamin pills like candy. Dinner might be more of the same or something hot. Abigail and Brianna said that in the early days, he'd put a real effort into cooking, but now there were more of us, he tended to cut corners with TV dinners and packaged food.

The other girls seemed to be resigned to their fate, even Katia although she hadn't been there for long. Abigail in particular seemed fascinated with Peter's evolution, and in the evenings, she gave us long sermons on psychological traits that I tried to block out with a pillow over my head. Only Emma seemed to have any fight left in her, but she was at the far end of the room and we barely got a chance to speak.

The little she'd told me—that she hadn't been outside since six days after her abduction, when Peter found out her brother was a cop then forced her to call Reed and say she'd left of her own accord—made me even more terrified of my fate. Why did she comply? Because Peter had promised to shoot the first random woman he came across unless Emma did as he demanded. How could anybody risk that? Was I destined to spend the rest of my life as the prisoner of a madman?

A smart madman. He'd demanded PIN numbers for debit cards and phones from each girl so he could throw anyone looking for them off the scent. Those who refused to comply went without food until they changed their minds. And Georgette's PIN? He'd bragged about watching her enter it while she paid her share of the drinks in the bar he met her in, the sick freak.

I became strangely grateful for Josie's presence. At night, while my fellow prisoners were sleeping, she told me stories of her life, how she'd grown up as a labourer's daughter then married a farmhand at the grand old age of nineteen.

And tonight, after Peter finally shoved me back into my cage and stared while I changed from the ballgown into a pair of ugly cotton pyjamas, I wrapped my quilt around myself and turned to the wall.

"Tell me about the old days," I whispered. Being in the end cell meant the others couldn't hear me if I kept my voice right down.

"We never had money for anything," Josie said. "Then Prohibition came and Edgar Schultz moved here. The old man who owned the farm died a few years before, and Edgar bought the house off his widow. Such a mess, the whole place. He hired my Charles to help with repairs, and that paid much better than tending cattle."

"Edgar didn't keep cattle himself?"

"No, he grew corn, then ground it down into cornmeal for the still."

"The what?" Hadn't she mentioned that word once before?

"The still. For making moonshine. Edgar was a small-time gangster in New York until he got run out of there by his rivals. In Virginia, he could make big money by selling illegal alcohol, more than he ever did in the city. After the repairs on the house were complete, my husband helped to build this place to hide the equipment. They used a pond up top as a cooling reservoir for the condensing process, fed by an underground spring. You could walk right past and never realise what was going on down here."

Which didn't bode well for us ever being found.

"How did you get in? Is there a hidden door?"

"Yes, in the floor of the barn. If the authorities ever came by, Edgar used to cover it in straw and put a pig on the top."

We were doomed. Even if Reed managed to locate the property, how would he ever find us in here? If we'd been right about Peter having diplomatic immunity, Wyatt wouldn't even be able to get a search warrant to tear the place apart. Peter was the worst kind of monster—his veneer of charm and manners hid a clever, cunning madman. How long before victim number fourteen arrived? I hadn't missed the way he stared longingly at the empty cell opposite mine.

"What happened to you?" I asked Josie, touching my hand to my neck. Peter never turned the lights off completely, just dimmed them, so I could still see Josie's glistening wound.

"I sometimes helped out with the bottling when Edgar was shorthanded. Men would go sick. Pah! Sick. They drank too much of the goldarn product, more like.

Anyhow, I was down here when Charles caught one of the no-good scoundrels stealing a barrel, and I got shot in the argument."

"A guy shot you over a barrel of moonshine?"

"No, Charles shot me by accident. My own husband. Devastated, he was, but I forgave him before I passed. It wasn't long after that this place got raided and shut down. Hearsay was that somebody in Edgar's gang betrayed him."

"Everyone got caught? What happened to Charles?"

"Oh no, they didn't get caught. They all escaped when the men from the Bureau of Prohibition came."

"Escaped how? Did they fight their way out?"

"No, they went through the tunnel in that room over there." She nodded towards the door next to us, between the M and N cells. A new door with a shiny padlock, obviously installed by Peter.

"Wait. Wait! There's a tunnel in there?" I almost sat up, but then I remembered I wasn't supposed to be talking to a spirit. "There's another way out?"

"Not anymore. They filled it in. I heard the shovels."

"Dammit."

"But they didn't find the other ones."

"What other ones?"

"Edgar may have been ruthless, but he wasn't stupid. He built an escape route into each room."

"You mean there's a way out of here? Out of this room?"

She pointed past me, her expression glum. "In the 'R' cage. I suppose y'all will be leaving when Peter gets that far. Such a shame. I've enjoyed having company after all this time."

I squinted into the gloom. "Are you sure? I can't see

anything but a concrete wall."

"It's in the bottom right-hand corner behind the commode. There's a square that isn't solid concrete, just a thin layer over a wood-and-cloth frame. One good kick from steel-toed boots and that thing'll fall right out. My Charles built those hidden hatches, and they've stood up this whole time."

At last, I had a faint glimmer of hope, but Peter kept the unused cells locked. What did he think we were gonna do? Break in and steal a Porta Potti?

"Wait—you said there was an escape route in every room. What about the bathroom at the other end?"

"There should be one, but I'm not sure where. That was where they kept the firewood, and I never went inside much." She shuddered. "Spiders."

My heart began to pound. How long until my turn to shower? Three days? Four? Each pair of girls got half an hour in there, but what if Peter decided to watch? Every night, he'd stared at me as I got ready for bed, and when I tried to change into my pyjamas under my quilt, he insisted I stand up. His creepy eyes roamed over every inch of my body. How could I ever have been attracted to him back in the Park Plaza Hotel? He obviously had money, but beneath his polished exterior, he was just a cesspool.

Never again would I judge someone by their appearance. I'd almost made that mistake with Reed, and he'd turned out to be a true gentleman, a man who cared about me and not my money or my father's connections. What must he have thought when he got home and found me gone? First Emma, now Annie and me.

But I'd get back to him. Somehow, I'd get back to

him.

Chapter 30 - Reed

"'WHILE THE AMBASSADOR is sorry to hear about the disappearances of three Maryland residents, he considers the evidence presented as to his staff's involvement to be tenuous at best.'" Wyatt read from his phone screen. "'The request for a list of embassy staff is regretfully declined, but all of us here at the embassy wish the Montgomery County Police Department the best of luck in their investigation.' That last part's just rubbing our faces in it."

Five days since Kim and Annie disappeared, and we'd added all of our non-supernatural evidence to the police file. Maria's description of Tim and his British accent. The pictures of Kim in the black Mercedes from Luigi at the Italian restaurant and Brittney. The message wishing me a happy birthday on the wrong date. The tape of the car with diplomatic plates at the scene of Emma's disappearance. We'd tried getting Maria to look at photos again, but she still hadn't recognised anyone.

Captain Ward, Wyatt's boss and my ex-boss, had been sceptical, but he'd agreed to write to the ambassador and request his cooperation, if only to rule out an embassy connection. At first, we'd received an overly polite "fuck off" from a low-level staffer, but Kim's father had thrown his weight around and this letter, written on thick cream paper, signed by Robert Turner personally and couriered over, was the result.

"Why won't he help?" I asked, slumping onto Wyatt's sofa. He had the late shift today, so we were still in his apartment. "Is he just an asshole, or does he have something to hide?"

"We know it wasn't him, but somebody borrowed his car. Think he'll have a talk with his staff?"

"After that brush-off?"

"He might want to handle things internally as opposed to causing a diplomatic incident. If only we had something concrete..." Wyatt sighed, which was better than punching the wall like he did after the initial response. The bruises had faded to a yellowish-brown now. "I'll go back to Kimberly's father and see if there's anything else he can do."

Rather Wyatt than me. Kimberly's father had marched into the station the evening after she disappeared, his tan suggesting he'd flown back from someplace far hotter than Bethesda. First, he'd insulted Barb by treating her like a waitress, then he'd demanded someone get the chief out of bed to explain what was going on when any one of the dozen detectives there working on the case could have filled him in.

Mr. Jennings had brought his current girlfriend along too, a bottle blonde who perched on the edge of a chair in the lobby, giving dirty looks to everyone who passed after she'd first complained about the lack of a cappuccino machine. Between his stuck-up attitude and what he'd done to his ex-wife, no wonder Kim had little to do with the man.

I rolled my eyes at Wyatt. "Good luck with that. Did

any of the forensic results come through yet?"

"Still backed up, but only one set of fingerprints in Kim's house got a hit on AFIS, and they belonged to the guy who repaired her dishwasher two months ago."

"What did he do?"

"Assault and battery on his ex-girlfriend."

If Kim came back, I'd be vetting everyone who set foot in her house in the future, as well as getting her a new alarm that monitored the perimeter when she was home. No, not if. When. *When* Kim came back. I had to think positive. Until we found a body, I wasn't giving up, although with Emma having been gone for over two years, fighting off the inevitable feeling that the worst had happened was becoming more difficult with every passing minute.

We were out of clues. One neighbour thought she'd seen a blue minivan driving slowly past Kim's house, and another said a light-coloured van with some kind of logo on the side paused at the kerb for a while. But Kim's front yard was hidden from view by a high wall, so nobody saw either girl being taken out of the house, and despite TV appeals, no one had come forward with any information.

"I can't believe there's nothing."

"Seen it before," Wyatt said. "A respectable man driving in a decent car around a middle-class neighbourhood. People don't even notice. If he'd been a black man in a pimped-out truck, we'd have gotten fifteen phone calls 'just in case.'"

Speaking of phones, mine pinged with an email. Another notification from that damn PI forum. Over thirty posts and counting taking the piss out of me over that thread asking for a reputable psychic. I wished I'd never posted the damn request.

Except this one wasn't the usual sarcastic reply; it was a private message.

Saw your post about communicating with the dead. Always been fascinated by that area myself. How does it impact on your case?
Will Lawson
L&A Investigations, London

I almost wrote it off, but two things made me pause. First, he was from England. Could he have any connections that might help to identify our cagey diplomats? And second, I recognised his username: LA-Law. With a handle like that, borrowed from a US legal drama, I'd written him off as another wannabe at first, but over the past year, he'd boasted a solve-rate even the most experienced investigator envied. Although I'd never realised he had an interest in the paranormal.

Unless of course his message was a joke, in which case... No, he'd always been serious on the forums. Never courted controversy.

But how the hell was I supposed to answer him?

Me: You wouldn't believe me if I told you.

The green dot beside his name showed he was online, and a message popped up seconds later. What time was it there? Ten p.m. here, so it must be the early hours in the UK.

LA-Law: Try me.

At this point, what did I have to lose? Only the woman I'd fallen in love with.

Me: My client believes there's a ghost in her living room. A crime was committed there, and we have no other witnesses. Sounds crazy, right?

Yes, it definitely sounded crazy. In fact, I could hardly believe I'd typed those words.

LA-Law: What makes her think there's a ghost in her house?

Shit. I couldn't spill all of Kim's secrets. Even though she'd gone AWOL, it wasn't my story to tell.

Me: I can't go into the details. Client confidentiality— you know the drill. Have you ever tried using a psychic?

"What are you doing?" Wyatt asked.
    "Replying to a message about a psychic."
    He grimaced. "I saw that thread, man. Brutal."
    Before I could agree, Lawson replied again.

LA-Law: Have you got a number I can call you on?

Well, that escalated quickly. But like I said, what did I have to lose? I typed out my mobile number, and thirty seconds later, it rang.
    "RC-DC?"
    My username, thought up after I'd watched one of

the Star Wars movies while under the influence. "Also known as Reed Cullen."

"So..."

"So..."

Lawson laughed. "This conversation feels like it's gonna be awkward."

"I don't even know where to start."

"Ghosts. They're not something that usually gets mentioned on the PI forum," Lawson said. "Most people are pretty sceptical."

"Are you?"

"I'm...open-minded. You?"

"Same. Open-minded. Recent events have been... interesting."

"In what way?" he asked.

"Hmm. How do I put this? A client has told me certain things that she claims were revealed to her by ghosts, and initial fact-checking backs up those claims."

"So if your client can talk to ghosts, why doesn't she have a chat with the one in her living room?"

Okay, this was where it got difficult. "Because she's been kidnapped." A lump came into my throat. "I found her gold necklace by the sofa, which suggests a struggle happened there, and if what Kim said is true, the ghost must have watched it happen and she's the only witness. Yeah, I know this sounds insane, so please, go ahead and laugh if you feel the need. I won't be offended."

"A gold necklace? What kind of gold necklace? You're sure it was hers?"

"A flat piece with weird symbols on it, and it was definitely hers. She wore it every day."

"Can you send me a picture?"

"Of the necklace? Why? Can you read hieroglyphics or something?"

"Because I'm curious."

And I was worried we were wasting time. High solve-rates or not, Lawson sounded like a kook, but it was faster to send him a damn picture than argue. How could it hurt? There was no mention of jewellery in the contract I'd signed with Kim. I took the necklace out of my pocket, snapped a quick photo of it in the palm of my hand, and messaged the picture over. Almost immediately, Lawson sent it back again.

"What was that for?" I asked.

"The photo I sent?"

"No, the photo *I* sent. Why did you just message it back to me?" More time wasted.

"Look again."

"What? Why?"

"Just look again."

Okaaaay. My eyes rolled all of their own accord as I put the phone on speaker and lined the screen up next to Kim's necklace. Two gold... Hold on. What the...? The pieces were similar, but not identical. The pendant in Will's hand had subtle differences in its shape, and when I looked closer, the symbols were different.

"Where did you get that?" I asked.

"I think that should be my question." A pause. "Does the word 'Electi' mean anything to you?"

Holy fuck. I'd heard the phrase "heart-stopping moment" before but never truly experienced it.

"You've heard of the Electi?"

"What are you talking about?" Wyatt asked. "What's an Electi?"

I didn't even bother trying to explain, just walked

into the kitchen and kicked the door shut behind me. Wyatt, I could apologise to later, but I couldn't afford to let Lawson go. He had information on the Electi? I was kinda surprised he'd come right out with his question, but then again, it wouldn't have meant anything to the average person. They'd have experienced mild curiosity at most.

"They've shown up on my radar," Lawson said. "I take it from that reaction you've come across them too?"

"I've heard the name."

"From your client?"

"She was the person who mentioned them, yes."

"Is she one of them?"

"I can't—"

"You said she'd been kidnapped?"

"Yes."

"And you're desperate. You must be to have posted that message online and then left it there through all the ridicule. So stop with the bullshit. I know how difficult this is to talk about, believe me. I've been there. So I'll ask again; is your client a member of the Electi?"

Blunt. Will Lawson didn't mess around, did he? And he'd been there? Was he telling me what I thought he was telling me? That one of his clients was a member of the Electi too? Or something more... Suddenly, his high solve-rates made sense.

"So she claims. You're working with one of them?"

He laughed. "You could say that. Whereabouts are you in the USA?"

"Maryland."

"We're on our way. Send me your email address,

and I'll let you know when we get to the airport."

"You'll help?"

"Mate, I'm as curious about the Electi as you are."

CHAPTER 31 - REED

"SO LAWSON'S BRINGING his partner?" Wyatt asked.

He'd come with me to Dulles International, quick to forgive me for shutting the door in his face when he realised we could be a step closer to finding the man who took Emma. After she disappeared, I'd been fast to assume he didn't care about her anymore, but during the past few days, I'd come to learn the opposite was true. Even though he'd redecorated, he still had reminders of her all over his apartment. Her picture sat on his nightstand. Her clothes took up half of his closet. He had a packet of Graham crackers in the cupboard even though he hated them, because my sister had loved s'mores. And the night before last, he'd confessed he still loved her and until now, he'd never given up hope that she'd come back if he gave her the space she'd asked for.

"Yeah, he's bringing his partner."

"And this guy can see ghosts too?"

"Tell the whole world, why don't you?"

I glanced around the arrivals area, but luckily nobody was listening to us. The girl standing next to me squealed and flung herself into the arms of a shaggy-haired guy carrying a backpack.

"Sorry."

"Lawson didn't give me any details, just said 'they'

were coming right away. I was too grateful to interrogate him."

And they must have driven straight to London Heathrow, because I'd gotten an email an hour and a half later saying they were boarding a plane. With a flight time of seven hours, they'd be here before eight p.m. our time.

Wyatt nodded at the arrivals board. "Flight's landed."

I didn't even know what Will Lawson looked like, so I'd written his name on a bag from the fast-food place where we'd grabbed a late lunch, and now I was holding it up like a bargain-basement cab driver. The uniformed chauffeur a few feet to my right had already given me a filthy look and taken a pace farther away.

Fifteen minutes passed, and I clenched my teeth as an image of Kim came into my head. Not happy Kim, twisting her paper clips as she compared wedding invitations and flower arrangements, but Kim lying cold on the ground, her lips blue. My fists balled up of their own accord, itching to pound Tim's face into a bloody pulp.

Then two people veered away from the throng of businessmen and vacationers and walked in our direction. A man around my height but thinner, with brown hair and an assessing gaze, and a woman six inches shorter with dark hair, dark skin, and dark eyes. Exotic looking. I glanced down at their joined hands. More than partners. He was dating her? A gold necklace glinted through a gap in her jacket. This was one of the Electi?

"Reed Cullen?" the guy asked.

"That's me. And this is Wyatt Banks. He's a cop

working the investigation, and he's also a...friend."

Lawson held out a hand for me to shake. "Will Lawson. And this is Rania Algafari."

She reached out as well, her skin cool to the touch. Rania was no Kim, that was for sure. Where Kim was outgoing and a little nervy, Rania was suspicious, guarded. Closed off.

"You're...her?" I asked.

Lawson cut his eyes in Wyatt's direction. "Does he know?"

"Yeah, he knows." I'd filled him in on everything else I knew about the Electi after I got off the phone earlier. If we were going to work as a team, we couldn't keep one member in the dark. "We think the person who took Kim has taken more girls. My sister was one of them, and Wyatt was dating her."

"Kim?" Rania spoke for the first time, and her accent was a mix of English and something else. Something Middle Eastern. "Her name's Kim?"

"Kimberly. Kimberly Jennings. Shall we go? We can talk in the car on the way."

They hadn't brought much luggage, just a duffel bag for Will and a backpack for Rania. My offer to carry it was met with a shake of her head.

"Want me to drive?" Wyatt offered when we reached my SUV.

I tossed him the keys. At least with Wyatt behind the wheel, I'd be able to concentrate on the case rather than the road. Will opened the nearest back door for Rania then walked to the passenger side.

"So," he said when we were underway. "It's been an interesting day so far. Want to fill us in on the rest?"

I gave him a recap on the case, from Kim getting

drugged to our trip to the car wash where she spoke to Georgette, then our realisation that Emma was involved in the same case and Kim's subsequent disappearance. In return, Will told us how he and Rania met—while he was investigating a murder case, how else?

"I'm still having trouble with this ghost stuff," Wyatt admitted.

Will nodded. "I can understand that. Rania's best mate basically tries to pretend they don't exist most of the time."

"How many people know about Rania?"

"Just me and two other friends. And now you guys."

"And all ghosts are murder victims?"

This time, it was Rania who answered. "Not all of them, but they've died at the hands of another. Some were killed by accident. I think that's why we exist; to differentiate. If black souls were automatically banished, some good people would slip through."

"But if you don't kill the killers, the ghosts are trapped permanently?"

"Yes."

"So say a mom accidentally ran over her kid, you'd have to kill the parent?" Wyatt asked. "Or the kid's stuck here forever?"

"Nobody said it was fair. It wasn't me who came up with the system."

"How do you know it even works? I guess I can believe in ghosts because I've seen some evidence now, but this legend? Honestly? It sounds like bullshit to me."

"It's true."

"You've tested it?"

"Yes."

That shut Wyatt up. But Will looked pissed, and I couldn't blame him. He didn't fly four thousand miles for his girlfriend to get interrogated by an out-of-jurisdiction cop. I opened my mouth to tell Wyatt not to ask any more questions, but Will got there first.

"Don't worry. She got cleared in the police investigation, and we're here to look at your case, not one we've already closed. Do you have a plan?"

"Not much of one," I admitted. "Go to Kim's house and see what this ghost's got to say. We need something that'll put pressure on the British embassy, enough that they'll start cooperating. They won't even give us a list of employees right now, and having to piece one together person by person has taken weeks."

"A list of employees? Let me see if I can find someone to help."

"You have a government connection?"

"I have a computer-hacking connection."

Back in the old days, Wyatt would have made a comment about ethics and legality, but today he just gripped the wheel and kept driving. Perhaps there was hope for him yet.

"Has the crime scene been released?" Rania asked.

"Not exactly, but I've got a key."

And a penknife I used to slice through the tape sealing the door. Hopefully by the time anyone noticed, we'd have enough evidence to justify a few minor procedural violations.

In the living room, I pulled the drapes closed, then turned on the lights. Rania headed straight for the corner beside the window, near where I'd found the necklace.

"Hi," she said. "Yes, that's right. I'm Rania. No, I don't know Kim, but I'm here to help find her."

Watching Rania talk to thin air was a strange experience. Yes, I'd seen Kim speak to ghosts, but she barely moved her lips and always tried to pretend she was doing something else. In a room full of people who knew her secret, Rania didn't have to hide her abilities.

"Margaret saw what happened," she told us, and I sagged in relief along with Wyatt. Now all we needed was a clue. "If it's any consolation, Kimberly slept through the whole thing. Margaret thinks she may have drunk a bit too much."

We already knew that. When I'd spoken to Maria the day after the girls vanished, she said the three of them shared a cab to Kim's place after the wine tasting. Apparently, the sommelier had encouraged Kim to spit out the champagne, but she'd refused. Annie and Maria helped her inside when they got back because she wasn't too steady on her feet.

When I'd first talked to Maria, I hadn't liked the woman, but I had to say she'd come through. Kayla had gone into a full-on meltdown when she heard the news of Kim and Annie's disappearance, and Maria had stepped in to help run whatever wedding was on this weekend. She said that after two of her own, she'd had some practice.

"Kimberly and Annie were watching a movie, then Annie left the room... Margaret's not sure why... Maybe a bathroom visit. Then she heard a commotion in the hallway, and a man chased Annie past the door, there was a crash, and everything went quiet." Rania listened again. "She thinks the man drugged Annie. He had a syringe in his hand." Another pause. "After that, he came for Kimberly."

My blood froze. I'd gotten an idea of what happened from the trace evidence, but to hear it narrated so matter-of-factly left me cold.

"He drugged her too, but when he lifted her up, the necklace snagged on the corner of the side table and he didn't notice."

"What about the man? What did he look like?"

A back-and-forth discussion ensued, and when Rania summarised it for us, it was clear she'd been assisting Will because the description she'd managed to tease out of Margaret blew Maria's, Lil Shawn's, and Grocery Store Guy's out of the park.

"He was an inch or so shorter than Will and Reed, so around five feet eleven. Not fat, but soft around the middle like he doesn't take much exercise."

"His hair? We've had reports of blond and brown."

"Blond, but Margaret could see darker roots coming through. Brown eyes, wide-set, and a sharp nose. Straight. His face was square like Wyatt's, but with a weaker chin."

"Any accent?"

"He didn't speak."

"Not a word?"

"Nothing. Hold on..." Rania suddenly smiled. Good news? "He was driving a big black car."

"A Mercedes?"

"Margaret doesn't know what a Mercedes is. Have you got a piece of paper and a pen? I'll have to draw the badge."

I remembered seeing a pad of paper in the dining room when Kim got more paper clips out of the sideboard. Her secret stash of stationery. Two minutes later, Rania had drawn a slightly lopsided Mercedes logo, but Margaret's answer was obviously in the negative.

"Can you describe it for me, then?" Rania asked.

Line by line, a chunky cross took shape on the paper. A Chevrolet. Our man was driving a Chevrolet.

"It sounds like a four-by-four from the description."

"A what?"

"An SUV," Will filled in.

"Something like a Tahoe or a Suburban?"

"Can you get me pictures?" Rania asked.

After some dithering as Rania thumbed through images on my phone, Margaret finally settled on a Suburban. Eighty percent sure. Which gave Tim plenty of room to load both girls into the trunk and drive them to wherever he wanted, the sick fucker.

And then came the kicker.

"Margaret couldn't see most of the registration plate because there was a bush in the way, but she said it was light blue with a red line at the top. A curved red line. Concave. She glimpsed it when the security light came on."

A diplomatic vehicle. Another fucking diplomatic vehicle.

CHAPTER 32 - REED

WITH KIMBERLY'S HOUSE technically still a crime scene, we retired to Wyatt's apartment while we worked out our next move. We were so fucking close, but that last step... It seemed impossible.

"I wanna ram the ambassador's face into a wall," Wyatt grumbled.

While it was good we were starting to agree on things again, I wished I didn't share his sentiment. What kind of prick put politics above women's lives?

"Hey." Rania laid a hand on Wyatt's shoulder as he paced the living room. "We'll find her. RJ's good at what he does."

"RJ?"

"Our friend in England. Most of his work with computers is legitimate, but he likes to test the boundaries as sort of a hobby."

Thank goodness Will and Rania were here. Their confidence gave me hope, whereas otherwise, I'd probably have been up on a murder charge before morning. Fucking diplomats.

"How did you arrive so fast, anyway?" I asked in an attempt to keep my mind off manual strangulation. "Didn't you have to get a visa to enter the US?"

"I took Rania for a break in New York a couple of months back, and the visa from that was still valid."

"New York?" I recalled what Kim had said about visiting the site of the former Twin Towers. "You didn't go near ground zero, did you?"

"No way, mate. Steered well clear of that one. At least the Statue of Liberty and Empire State Building tend to have suicides rather than murders."

"And suicides are...okay?"

Rania nodded. "They don't hang around."

These rules of the afterlife would take some getting used to, but at that moment, the only thing worse than the prospect of having to plan future vacations around local murder rates was not needing to plan them at all. Where the hell was Kim?

"Any messages yet?"

Will glanced at his phone. "Sorry. Why don't we get some food while we're waiting? I've got a feeling we're in for a long few days, and we need to keep our strength up."

Wyatt paused his pacing to stare incredulously. "You really think I can eat right now?"

I wasn't hungry either, but I saw Will's point. "Why don't we order pizza? You can eat something later if you feel like it."

The first email from RJ arrived right after the delivery guy from Benny's Italian, and fuck me, the man had struck gold. RJ, not the pizza dude. Not only did we have a list of all the staff who worked at the embassy and their positions, but he'd also found the registration records for the embassy's diplomatic plates. The deep-pans with everything went cold as we pored over the lists, cross-referencing what we knew. Twenty-two people in Robert Turner's department. Eleven Chevrolets on the list, but only three were SUVs.

One was allocated to a woman, although she could have lent it out, but...

"Peter Turner? Who the hell is Peter Turner?"

He drove a Chevrolet Suburban registered to the embassy, and he didn't appear anywhere on the staff list. But with that surname...

"He's got to be a relative of your friend Robert, surely?" Will said, taking a bite of pizza. "A son?"

"His kids are both too young to drive." I went back to the embassy website and called up the staff page. "See? Unless... Oh, fuck." Dread settled in my stomach like a lump of lead. "What if he has an ex? More children?"

A bitter divorce and a new wife would explain why he didn't want to parade Peter around in public. And if they were related, it also explained why the ambassador was being so cagey. A senior staff member's son killing women around DC under the cover of diplomatic immunity wouldn't look good on TV, would it?

And I'd missed it. I'd fucking missed it, and now Kim had paid the price.

"We'll find out." Will's distance from the case allowed him to remain calm and dispassionate while Wyatt and I climbed the damn walls. "RJ?" he said into the phone. "Focus on a guy called Peter Turner, and can you find out if he's any relation to Robert?"

Wyatt began calling people too, everyone from my former colleagues in the police department to informants to contacts in Washington. I'd never felt so helpless—most of my sources came from the streets, not the higher echelons of government, and the chances of them having crossed paths with the embassy staff were slim. Unless...

I dialled Jacob Morgan, an old hack hanging on by his fingernails until retirement. Yes, he had a slight drinking problem, but he'd been around the political scene forever, selling salacious gossip to the highest bidder, and more importantly, he owed me a favour.

"Jake? It's Reed Cullen."

"Thought you were dead."

"I could say the same about you."

The old man chuckled, then went into a coughing fit bad enough to bring up not only his lungs, but most of his internal organs too. Did I mention he was also a chain-smoker?

"What d'ya want, Cullen? You never call to shoot the damn breeze."

"Peter Turner. Do you know anything about him?"

"Who?"

"Related to Robert Turner, big shot at the British Embassy?"

"Oh, *him*. Nobody talks about Petey-boy anymore, not least his father."

"Why? What happened?"

"Junior's got issues. His mother died from an overdose when he was thirteen, fourteen, something like that, then his daddy married his mistress. Debra. A real looker. Have you seen a picture?"

"Yeah." But she wasn't a patch on Kim.

"They already had a kid together, which was probably what drove the first Mrs. Turner to over-medicate in the first place—a little girl. And when Peter was fifteen, Debra caught him in the kid's room and refused to have him in the house anymore."

"What did he do?" I asked, even though I didn't

honestly want to know.

"Nobody ever said. It was all rumour. But whatever he did, it was bad enough that Robert sent him off to boarding school, and he's been in exile ever since."

"In exile where?"

"I've never cared enough to find out. Peter turns up at functions with his father occasionally, but he keeps his nose clean. No juicy stories, nothing that'll sell papers." Oh, if only he knew. "Why do you ask?"

If I told Jacob the truth, unconfirmed gossip would be all over the internet in minutes, but luckily, I'd gotten plenty of practice at fibbing as a PI.

"The name came up in conjunction with a gang selling stolen puppies, but I'm not sure it's even the same guy. From what you've said, probably not. The family doesn't seem short of a buck or two."

"You're not wrong there, and Robert Turner's the type of man who gives out cash instead of affection. But call me if it comes to anything? I'll keep your name quiet, and there'll be a drink in it for ya."

"Sure. I'll do that."

I ended the call, and Wyatt paused his steps long enough to raise an eyebrow. "Well?"

"It's got to be him. Peter Turner was a deviant even as a teenager."

A freak who preyed on women weaker than him, be they too young or too drunk to resist. Men like him deserved to be buried alive.

On the other side of the room, Rania was sitting cross-legged on the sofa with her laptop, and now her lips curved into a hesitant smile. Did she have good news?

"I think we might have found him."

"What? Where?"

Three men were breathing down her neck in an instant, but I took a half step back when I noticed her shrink closer to Will. Something bad had happened in her past, hadn't it?

"According to RJ, Robert Turner owns three properties in the USA. An apartment in Washington, DC, a beach house in Florida, and a farm near Bluemont, Virginia."

"The farm? You think it's the farm?"

"The utility bills are in Peter's name."

Holy shit. We had him!

"We need to get over there," I said.

"I need to call the captain," Wyatt said at the exact same time.

For fuck's sake. "Are you serious? The whole Turner family has diplomatic immunity. The cops can do exactly nothing."

"They can put pressure on the ambassador through the proper channels. And if there's a patrol car sitting outside Peter's gates, he'll know we're onto him."

"Precisely. And if Kim and Annie aren't dead already, that'll give him plenty of time to get rid of the evidence."

"All right, Cullen. What do *you* think we should do?"

"Sneak into the farmhouse and find them ourselves."

"That's illegal."

"And kidnapping fourteen girls is totally above board?"

"I'm going with Reed," Rania announced, scrambling to her feet, and Will rolled his eyes.

"Nia, no. Are you crazy?"

Her look said he already knew the answer to that.

"We're tourists in a foreign country," he tried.

"Yes, and I don't want to attend a funeral while I'm here."

"We can take my car," I told her. Although I didn't know her well, and from the outside, she looked pretty and delicate, a core of steel ran through her centre. Something told me Rania Algafari knew how to take care of herself.

Will grabbed his jacket too. "I'm not letting you go without me."

That left one holdout. "Wyatt?"

"Fine. But for the record, I think this is a terrible idea."

"Noted."

"Just let me get my handcuffs."

Handcuffs? Who needed handcuffs? I had a fully-loaded semi-automatic, and even if it meant spending the rest of my life behind bars, I wasn't afraid to use it.

CHAPTER 33 - KIMBERLY

"NOW, WHICH OF you is going to come with Noelle and show her where everything is in the bathroom?"

Finally, a week after my abduction, it was my turn to shower. My hair hung around my chin in rat tails, and my armpits smelled disgusting. At least Peter didn't skimp on the beauty products, and we were allowed safety razors to shave our legs.

Emma raised her hand. "I'll go."

"Thank you, Emma. It's so awkward having an odd number, but don't worry—we'll be back to evens soon."

Oh, hell. He'd found his M, hadn't he? Another victim to come and join us in the dungeon. Who would it be this time? As well as a psychiatrist, we had a medical doctor in Fern, an artist in Brianna, and a scientist in Gina to name but a few. And how long before he swooped on his prey? A day? A week? He was escalating, wasn't he? Did he feel time was running out? Or had taking three girls in such a short period of time emboldened him? One thing was for sure—there were thirteen empty cells in the old distillery, and Peter wouldn't stop voluntarily until he'd filled them all.

What would happen then? Would we have to shower in threes?

He unlocked my cage first, then went to Emma's. Oddly, he seemed to give us leeway down here, probably because he thought we couldn't get out. Even if we somehow disabled him, we couldn't get past the combination lock on the door, plus he was a big guy and, according to Jacqueline, he carried a knife. He'd never used it, but the threat was there.

The bunch of keys jangled as he opened Emma's door, each one labelled with a letter. Two larger keys, one with a blue sticker, one with green, opened storerooms at either end of the distillery where Peter kept supplies. Bedding, toiletries, Band-Aids for our damaged toes. More freaking protein bars.

This was the first time I'd seen Emma without bars between us, and up close, I realised the toll this ordeal had taken. Only twenty-four years old, yet she already had a network of fine lines around her eyes and pale, pale skin from the lack of sunlight. I'd assumed her dark-red hair, almost cherry, was dyed, but now I realised it was her natural colour. Except today it hung dull and lank, the ends chewed ragged.

Peter followed in our footsteps—our bare footsteps —as we headed for the shower room. Bathrobe only— that was the rule, and he'd stared at me while I changed. As the others said, he didn't touch us, but his gaze was like an army of venomous slugs, crawling its slimy way all over my body.

Emma took my elbow once we got through the door. Well, not a door, exactly, but a doorway with two rusting hinges on one side where a door had once hung.

"The shower runs on spring water, but it's hot. Just be careful with the dial. A fraction of an inch too far and it burns. The waste water goes into a dry well, and it can be a little slow to drain, so don't worry if it looks blocked. That always happens. We've all got our favourite brands of products, and each of us has a basket over here..." She gestured towards two shelves on the far wall. "Oh, look. Yours already has stuff in it. Shower gel, shampoo, face wash. No conditioner, but you can borrow mine."

"I had to improvise," Peter said. "I haven't been to the store since you came. But you can put an order in next time along with the other girls so long as you behave."

Emma nudged me. "You have to say 'thank you, Peter.'"

The words physically hurt as I forced them past my lips. "Thank you, Peter."

"Over here, we have the blow dryer. And if you want to fetch your toothbrush from your room, you can brush here with running water. The dental floss is beside the toothpaste, and if you need a beaker..."

Peter tapped his watch. "Tick tock, Emma. You both get fifteen extra minutes since it's Noelle's first time, but that's all. I have a function to attend this evening."

I'd hoped he'd leave, but no, he leaned against the doorjamb, watching. Waiting. Emma was clearly used to it because she dropped her robe without hesitation, then nodded at me.

"Do you mind if I go first? My hair's thicker than yours, and it takes ages to dry."

"Go ahead."

I brushed my teeth, stalling for time, searching the wall in front of me for any sign of the escape tunnel Josie had claimed was here. About two feet square, she'd said. Somebody had painted, but not recently, and yellowed paint peeled off in flakes, making the job even more difficult. Nothing. I could see nothing. No crack, no seam, no change in texture. And as Emma turned the heat up, steam rolled through the air, and I almost cried.

A *thump* sounded, then a gasp, and I turned to see purple conditioner splattered all over the shower.

"I'm so sorry, Peter. I dropped it."

"You need to be more careful, Emma. I only have one bottle spare."

"We can manage without."

"No, no. I'll get it."

Peter disappeared, and Emma jumped out of the shower. "Quick, get in before that fucker comes back."

"Huh?"

"You were looking uncomfortable, so I got rid of him for a few minutes. If you turn the heat up as hot as you can bear, he can't see much through the steam."

She'd done what? Emma had sacrificed her dignity for me? She clenched her teeth, somehow looking determined and defeated at the same time.

"Quick!"

I dropped my bathrobe and leapt into the shower cubicle. The glass door didn't shut properly, and the whole thing looked to have been built by a drunken monkey with no plumbing qualifications whatsoever. Peter had just shoved a shower tray into a corner and cobbled together some piping and a heating unit that ran off a portable gas canister connected by a rubber pipe. For a moment, I wondered if we could blow the place up, but we'd all die too, which kind of defeated the purpose.

The water was blessedly warm, and after a week of festering in my own sweat, the shower felt better than it should have. I grabbed a bottle of shampoo, but as I straightened up, I saw the faintest crack in the wall. A line, too straight to be a natural imperfection. Ohmigosh! I'd found it. I'd found the freaking exit. I tapped on that section with my knuckles, detecting where the hidden door ended and solid concrete began. Yes, about two feet square. I gave it a thump. Nothing. It didn't budge, not even a little.

So I kicked it and hurt my foot.

Dammit.

If I couldn't break through the wall today, another week would pass, another girl might get taken, and Peter would probably fracture one of my toes.

I poked my head out of the shower door.

"Uh, Emma?"

She looked around from her spot by the sink.

"I realise we've barely met, and this might sound crazy, but could you help me to pick up that gas canister?"

"What? Why?"

"Don't ask me how I know, but there's a hidden passage in here, and we need to use the canister to break through the wall."

"You're right. That *is* crazy."

"If we don't do this right now, Peter's going to come back and it'll be too late."

"Are you really dating my brother?"

"Yes." At least, I hoped so. He was living in my house. That had to count for something, right? "Why does that matter?"

"Because Reed would date crazy, but he wouldn't date stupid." She dropped her hairbrush and hurried across the room. "Okay, let's do this."

"We need to unscrew the nozzle thing." It was tight,

but panic strengthened my grip and I managed to twist the canister free of the rubber pipe.

"You really think this'll work?"

"I hope so. What's the worst that can happen?" She glanced across at the hairbrush, and I realised I'd said something really, really stupid. "I'm so sorry. If you want to—"

She grabbed one side of the canister. "Just get it over with, okay?"

Three...

Two...

One...

Shit, the crash was louder than I anticipated. But a dusty hole opened up, just wide enough for a person to crawl through.

"Get in there!" Emma gave me a shove.

Don't think about the spiders, Kim. Or the rats. Or the beetles. Freaking heck, I hated spiders.

I scrambled inside on my hands and knees, and several decades' worth of detritus tore at my skin.

"Hurry up!" I yelled at Emma.

But footsteps came running, and all I got in reply was a scream. A hand grasped at my ankle, but my skin was still slippery from the shower, so Peter couldn't get a grip.

"Go!" Emma yelled. "I'll hold him off."

I almost turned back when she screamed again, but my head fought to overrule my heart and won. What if we never got another chance at escape? A hiss followed by a decidedly male shriek made up my mind. Did Emma just attack Peter with a can of hairspray?

Another shout came. "Don't stop!"

Into the darkness I went, desperately trying to

ignore the cobwebs and whatever just skittered over my leg as my heart threatened to beat out of my chest. A sudden panic gripped me—Josie said these passages were well built, but what if the roof had fallen in? When was Prohibition? The 1920s?

Then I rounded a corner, and when a faint glimmer of light showed, I almost cried with relief. Daylight. For the first time in a week, I saw daylight.

I fought my way through a prickly bush and found myself in a wooded area, surrounded by twiggy undergrowth. Too late, I saw a stray, dead leaf clinging to a twig and realised where I'd ended up. Right in the middle of a patch of poison freaking oak. Even in winter, the stuff could be vicious since the oil was in the stems too—I'd found that out as a child when a walk in the woods with my mom went very, very wrong.

To paraphrase Reed—oh, fuck.

I leapt to safety as quickly as I could, but the itching started almost immediately. Where was I? I looked around, but all I could see was trees, trees, and more trees. Was there a road nearby? If Peter had brought Annie and me here in a car, there had to be. How many motorists would stop for a wild naked woman with wet hair and blistered legs?

Only one way to find out.

I stopped to listen for a second, but I couldn't hear any traffic, only the wind as it blew through the bare branches above. Which way should I go? I didn't even have a coin to flip.

A deer ran past, and I followed. What was it I'd heard on the Discovery Channel? If there's a fire, always follow the animals. Well, there may not have been any flames, but there was certainly danger.

"Hey, Bambi. Wait for me."

I stumbled forward, the chill air nipping at my exposed skin. I'd have given my Hermès Birkin bag for a blanket right now. Or a pair of tennis shoes. The ground was littered with twigs, and most of them seemed to be covered in thorns.

Bambi disappeared, but I kept going. How long did it take for hypothermia to set in? I couldn't have been out for longer than ten minutes, but the shivers had started already. This was a nightmare, pure and simple. I was naked with a deranged diplomat chasing me, and all I knew for certain was that I was in Virginia.

Then I heard it.

"Tsk tsk tsk."

I almost wet myself with fear. But then I bolted, screaming into what felt like a void.

"Help! Somebody help me!"

"Nobody's coming, Noelle." Peter's voice taunted me as he followed.

Through the trees and bushes I crashed, running for my life, but my desperation wasn't enough. Peter was taller and faster than me, plus he had the advantage of boots. I tripped, and I would have fallen if he hadn't grabbed my hair and yanked me back against him.

"Didn't the others tell you what happens when you try to escape? You get sanctioned, and one of your friends gets punished too. Who do you want to suffer for your sins, Noelle?" He leaned closer, his voice a harsh whisper in my ear. "Emma? Leanne? Jacqueline?"

"Stop!"

A voice came from straight ahead of me, and a

familiar figure stepped out of the shadows. Reed. Oh, Reed. He looked mad as hell, and he had a gun aimed at Peter.

Too late, I felt the point of the knife digging into my neck. After all this, I was going to die anyway? Reed couldn't shoot Peter without the bullet going through me first, and now the freak began backing away.

A second figure appeared beside Reed, a man I'd never seen before with a phone pressed to his ear. "We've located the suspect, but he has a hostage. Yes, High Grove Farm, near Bluemont."

"Drop your weapon," Reed said, his voice eerily calm. "The game's up. The police are on their way."

Peter began laughing. "They can't touch me. I've got diplomatic immunity. They're not even allowed to set foot on the property."

"Funny things, boundary lines. Out in a forest like this, it's sometimes difficult to work out where one property ends and another begins. But I'm sure if anyone makes a mistake, we can sort it out after you're dead."

Peter's grip loosened infinitesimally. "Well, I'm telling you, the edge of this property is a quarter mile behind where you're standing, so you're trespassing."

"Sorry? I didn't quite catch that. I've been having trouble with my hearing lately. Probably because my ears have gotten blocked up with all the bullshit your father and his cronies have been spouting."

Reed took a step forward, and Peter's arm tightened around my waist as he pressed the knife in harder with his other hand. I felt a sting as the point broke my skin, a warm tickle as blood ran down my neck.

"Let her go and walk away, and I'm sure the British

government will find some way to cover this up."

"Don't you understand? Noelle's mine now."

"My name isn't—"

"Shut up!" he shrieked. "Why can't you—"

He never got to finish the sentence. Blood and brain matter splattered over me, and my ears rang from the gunshot. I twisted in Peter's arms, and for the first time, I saw a black soul rise from a person's body and scatter on the wind as he crumpled to the ground.

The gunshot hadn't come from Reed. No, he lowered his pistol and looked to my right. A woman stood beside Wyatt, another stranger, but somehow I felt as though we knew each other. And that wasn't all. She had an aura around her, a white light that shimmered as she moved.

I felt myself drawn to her. Despite everything that had just happened, with Reed in front of me and Peter's body lying behind, I staggered in her direction. This beautiful but dark girl who opened her arms and lit up the gloom from the inside out.

When she hugged me, I realised I didn't know who she was, but I knew what she was. She was a part of me.

And then I cried.

CHAPTER 34 - KIMBERLY

REED TUCKED A jacket around me, and his arm settled into place over my shoulders. I didn't have to look to know it was him—I'd recognise him even in the pitch black. His musky smell. His gentle touch. The calming vibes that washed over me.

"He's gone, sweetheart."

"I know."

"This is Rania. She's another—"

"I know."

His arm tightened, and he bent to kiss my hair. "Fuck. I thought you were gone too. After a week... We couldn't find you. What happened to your legs?"

"Poison oak."

He called out to the guy on the phone. "Will, make sure there's an ambulance coming too."

I reached up to Rania's face, and my fingers passed through her weird aura and touched smooth skin.

"You've got this glow. A white light."

"So have you, but pink."

"I do?"

To me, my skin looked perfectly normal. Well, pale and a little pimply because I hadn't showered for a week, but it wasn't glowing pink. But the ghosts had told me I glimmered and that was how they recognised me. Was I now seeing what they saw?

Rania read my mind. "This must be how they see us. The spirits."

"No wonder they always shout at me when I walk down the street." I screwed my eyes shut. "You killed him."

"Yes."

"Wyatt, why did you give her the gun?" Reed asked. "Is that your service piece?"

I opened my eyes and saw Wyatt in my peripheral vision, wiping the butt of his pistol with his sleeve.

"Yeah. We'll tell them I did it, but it had to be Rania. It was the only way to set Emma free." His voice hitched as Rania nodded her agreement. "If what the girls say about trapped souls is true, I didn't want her to be stuck here on earth forever."

Freaking heck, they didn't know!

"Emma's alive," I croaked, emotion getting the better of me. "They're all alive except Georgette."

Reed stiffened. "Emma's alive?"

"She helped me to escape. I-I-I think she might be injured. I heard them fighting as I crawled away, and I wanted to turn back and help, but she yelled at me to keep going."

"Where is she? Kim, where is she?"

"Underground. There's an old moonshine distillery, and I found a hidden tunnel in the bathroom, but then I kept walking because I wanted to find a road, and it was just trees, trees, trees, and I don't know how to get back there." I looked down at my legs, now blistering nicely. "The exit was in the middle of a patch of poison oak. That's all I can remember."

"Fuck. We'll get a search party out here."

I shook my head, trying to clear the fuzz.

Everything was jumbled up inside. "No, wait. There's another entrance. The one Peter used." What had Josie told me? "An old barn, and there's a trapdoor in one of the animal stalls."

"Guys, spread out!" Wyatt said. "We're looking for the remains of an old barn."

"Wait! Get Peter's keys first."

Reed hesitated. "Fuck. Kim, you should get to the hospital."

"Are you kidding? I'm not going anywhere until we find the others."

I didn't even know which direction I'd come from. Reed picked me up, cradling me in his arms so I wouldn't be left behind as they searched. The rest of the girls would be okay for a few days—they had food and water—but what about Emma? How badly had she been hurt?

To our left, Rania stopped suddenly, looking up. I followed her gaze and almost vomited. A man hovered six feet above us, spinning gently with his neck at an unnatural angle as he hung from a tree limb that no longer existed.

"Hey," she called. "We're looking for a barn. Do you know where it is?"

Silently, he extended one arm in front of him, pointing.

"Over there," I told Reed. "Towards Wyatt."

Rania was already moving in that direction, followed by Will. Who was he? How did they meet? I had so many questions, but they'd have to wait until we found the other girls.

A shout came from Wyatt, and Will began running with Rania at his side. Reed followed, carrying me as if

I weighed nothing, and I clung to his neck and buried my head against his shoulder as the branches whipped past.

Out of the murk, a building began to take shape. From the outside, the barn was a ramshackle ruin, sagging at one end where decades of the elements had taken their toll. But inside, new timbers propped up the roof, and a line of footprints on the dusty floor showed us where we needed to go. Wyatt was already pulling the trapdoor open, and Will flicked on a flashlight as they ran down a set of wooden stairs with Rania.

"Do you want to go down there too?" Reed asked.

Not in a million years, but at the same time, I had to. "Yes."

Except when we got to the bottom, our way was blocked by a solid wooden door and the combination lock that had thwarted Fern. Wyatt gave it a kick, and it barely even rattled. Peter may have had a screw loose, but I had to hand it to him—he was reasonable at DIY, the shower excepted.

"We can't shoot the lock," Wyatt said. "Not with people on the other side."

"What about knocking out the hinge pins?" Will suggested, shining the flashlight around the edges of the door. "Anyone have a multitool?"

"Hang on," Rania said, hurrying past us, back up the stairs. "I've got an idea."

A minute later, she came back with an axe. "I saw it as we came in."

Wyatt grabbed it off her and attacked the door like a man possessed. Woodchips flew everywhere, and Rania covered my eyes with her hand.

"Can you stand for a second?" Reed asked me.

"Okay."

I hung onto Rania as the three men charged at the door once, twice, three times. There was a splintering crash, and it flew open, smashing off the wall as light spilled out of the dungeon. Startled faces looked out at us, and Wyatt was the first inside.

"Emma? Where's Emma?"

"She's here," Fern called out. "I'm a doctor. Let me out, and I can help her."

The monster had locked Emma back into her cage, and while all the other girls had their faces pressed against the bars, Emma didn't stir. Bruises blossomed on her pale flesh, and the mattress was stained red. Peter had done a real number on her in the short time before he came after me.

Wyatt's hands trembled as he unlocked her door, and Reed was so tense I feared one touch would shatter him.

"Go to her," I whispered. "I'll be fine."

He hesitated, but then Rania stepped in. "I'll take care of her."

"She stepped on poison oak. See if you can find some water to wash the oil off her legs."

"There's a shower room," I told them. "To the right."

And inside, it looked like a slaughterhouse. Blood splattered the walls, dripping down into the mess of toiletries that littered the floor. It seemed as though Emma had thrown everything she could get her hands on at Peter. And he'd thrown the gas canister at her, judging by the crimson stain on one edge.

"So that's how you escaped?" Rania asked, nodding at the gaping hole in the shower wall.

"There's a spirit in the other room. She told me about it. You know, until now, I've mostly avoided talking to them, but this last month..."

"I used to hate it too, but some of them aren't so bad." She smiled for a second. "I met Margaret in your living room. Hold on a second, I saw a stool outside."

Rania came back a moment later and helped me to sit in the shower. The water ran pink from all the cuts on my feet as she picked out thorns with her fingernails.

"I don't understand how you got here. You're from England? Or somewhere else? I can't place your accent."

"From Syria, originally, but I live in England now. With Will. He's a private investigator—we both are—and Reed was asking online for a medium who could speak to Margaret. Will got curious and called him. Of all the ways I imagined finding another of the Electi, this wasn't it." She adjusted the stream of the water. "Is that any better? We don't have poison oak in the UK."

"A little, but it still itches like crazy. Can you go and see how Emma is? Please?"

Rania nodded and moved towards the door, and I willed myself not to puke in the shower because the water was already pooling around my ankles. If Emma was badly hurt, or worse, I'd never forgive myself for leaving her. And for Reed, it would be like losing her all over again. Plus I wasn't sure of the logistics. If Peter's actions had caused her death, and he'd already been killed by one of the Electi, what would happen to her soul? Would she get a free pass? Or would she be stuck here forever with no hope of freedom? Did Rania know? It had always bugged me that I was supposed to live by a set of rules I didn't fully understand.

"She's mumbling a bit," Rania said when she came back. "The girl who's a doctor thinks she's broken her arm, but the emergency services are on their way. Will's gone up top to direct them."

Thank goodness.

"But she'll be okay?"

"I think so. Wyatt won't leave her side. Is something still going on between them? I get the impression Will and I are missing huge chunks of the backstory here."

"Wyatt and Emma used to date, but they had a huge argument right before she disappeared. I honestly don't know anymore."

Then above the running water, I heard the most beautiful sound in the world. A siren. Running feet and gasps audible even above the rest of the noise told me the cavalry had arrived. We were free. We were all free, even Georgette.

I gripped Rania's hands. "Thank you for coming. For everything that you did."

For shooting Peter and setting one troubled spirit free. I wasn't sure I could have done that, even in such dire circumstances. Rania had guts, that was for sure.

She hugged me again, ignoring the water all around. "I'm so glad I've found you. I didn't know what it would be like if I ever met another one of us, but it feels...it feels like coming home. I can't explain it."

"I can't explain it either, but I feel it too."

Chapter 35 - Reed

THE CROWD IN the hospital barely gave us room to breathe. I sat on the hallway floor beside Will and Rania while Wyatt paced in the tiny space available, unaware of the dirty looks as he bumped into people.

Two steps, turn. Two steps, turn. Two steps, turn.

I wished he'd stop, but pacing had always been a nervous habit of his, and with my sister currently in the operating theatre having her arm pinned back together, I understood his fear. At least the head injury hadn't been worse. Emma had gotten away with a mild concussion.

When we arrived, a nurse had taken Kim away to treat her legs and feet. As well as the poison oak, she'd cut herself on whatever rocks she'd run across, and her wounds were still filled with thorns and bits of grit despite Rania's efforts. Plus she'd scraped up her knees and palms crawling through the tunnel. Once the adrenaline had worn off, the pain started to hit, and by the time we got to the emergency room, her face had been twisted up in agony.

Fuck. The two girls who meant the most to me, and they were lying side by side in the hospital.

A nurse fought her way through the crush and stopped in front of me. Over the past three hours, the place had filled up with relatives, then news of the rescue broke on social media and reporters descended en masse. They'd been confined to the waiting area, and according to Will, every news website in the world had the story front and centre.

"Your fiancée's back in her room now," the nurse said.

Okay, so we'd embellished the truth slightly. The nurse manager hadn't been impressed by the sudden influx of people into her hospital, and she'd kicked out anyone who wasn't family or at least betrothed. Which was why Emma was about to be Mrs. Banks as well.

Luckily, Kim's father had come and gone, so he wasn't around to correct the fib. Not that the medical staff had much respect for him anyway if one nurse's muttered comment about him being "that asshole who lobbied against cheaper cancer drugs" was any indication.

"Can I see her?" I asked.

"Yes, but one at a time." She glanced at Will and Rania. "Her brother and sister will have to wait."

I followed the nurse along the hallway and into a private room. It seemed Fern's father also worked at the hospital, and he'd made sure all the girls were getting the best treatment.

"Reed," Kim murmured, sounding drowsy. "You're still here."

"Of course I'm here, sweetheart. I'll always be here."

"They told me Emma's in surgery?"

"She is, but it should be over soon. How are you feeling? How are your feet?"

She pulled the blanket back to reveal swaths of bandages, all the way from her toes to her thighs.

"Itchy. They put cream on them and gave me something to help with the pain, but I still want to scratch my skin off."

"Good thing they wrapped your legs up, then."

"At least they let me take a proper shower first. They didn't want to, but I begged." Her face crumpled. "I smelled so bad. He kept us like animals, all in cages."

"I saw, sweetheart."

I sat on the side of the bed and wrapped Kim up in my arms as she cried against my shoulder. And while I knew we'd had the best outcome with Rania pulling the trigger because that had allowed Georgette to pass over or pass on or whatever it was spirits did, at that moment, all I wanted was to turn back the clock so I could shoot the son of a bitch myself.

"The fucker who took you's gone now, and I'm not leaving your side. Promise."

"Will you stay with me? At my house? I know the case is over, but..."

Which part of "not leaving your side" did she not understand? "Don't you think this was a drastic way of getting me to move in with you? You could have just asked. We both know what the answer would have been."

"You'll stay permanently?"

"If you'll have me." A sudden shiver of worry ran through my torso. What if I'd jumped the gun and Kim had been thinking of a more temporary arrangement?

"Well, somebody needs to learn how to work the waffle maker, and it won't be me, will it?"

Thank goodness. A hospital wasn't the best place for a proper reunion, but I couldn't resist one kiss. That bullshit in movies about melting hearts and fluttering pulses? It was all fucking true. Nothing else mattered when Kim's lips met mine. She tasted of mint toothpaste and heaven, but I pulled away before my cock burst through my damn zipper.

"I can't believe you found me," she said, eyes teary. "Some of the girls had been there for years, and I thought—"

"Don't think about it."

"I still don't understand how you knew where to look."

"Rania spoke to Margaret, and she helped us to identify Peter Turner's car. Then a friend of Will's hacked into the British embassy's computer system and found the owner."

"Peter Turner?"

"Yeah."

"*Turner*? As in Robert Turner?"

"Peter was his son by his first wife. The black sheep of the family, by all accounts. From what we can ascertain, daddy dearest just gave him money and otherwise pretended he didn't exist."

Too late, I realised what I'd said, but before I could apologise, Kim got in first.

"I know how that feels."

"Sorry. I need to think before I speak."

"It's okay. I'm used to my father acting like that now, and I never got the urge to kidnap anybody." She managed a flicker of a smile. "And he cares in his own strange way. I'm not sure what he plans to do back in Washington, but I wouldn't want to be in Robert Turner's shoes right now."

"Maybe I should send him a thank-you card."

"Uh, I didn't tell him about us yet."

That hurt more than it should have. A little stabbing pain right in my chest. Yeah, I knew I wasn't the kind of guy a girl wanted to take home to Daddy, especially a girl like Kim, but—

"I didn't want my father to scare you off. When I was eighteen, he interrogated my prom date so rudely the poor guy climbed out the window in the downstairs bathroom and didn't come back."

And breathe again.

"Seriously? You got stood up for prom?"

"Yes, but I honestly couldn't blame him. And I didn't tell Father I was dating my ex-husband until we were engaged." Kim pressed tighter against me, her breasts pillowing against my chest. *Down, boy.* "But enough about my dysfunctional family. How did you find me in the woods?"

"Pure dumb luck. We couldn't knock on the front door of the farmhouse because of diplomatic immunity, so we thought we'd sneak in the back way, then we heard you screaming."

"If you'd been five minutes later..."

"Like I said before, don't think about it. We arrived right on time, and all the girls are going home. You were so fucking brave, sweetheart."

"And so was Emma."

"Yeah, and Emma." She always had been. Crazy too, but nobody could question her courage. Sneaking out of a sixth-floor apartment and climbing down the balconies to the ground? No problem. Whacking a gas station robber over the head with a fire extinguisher? She'd done that too. "But you two need to promise you'll take it easy for a while. I don't think my heart'll take any more drama."

***

"We've put you in the honeymoon suite, ma'am. Is that okay? It's wheelchair accessible."

Kim grimaced, and I hoped that was because of her mobility situation and not at the thought of sharing a bed with me.

The hotel receptionist frowned. "Ma'am?"

"The honeymoon suite's great. Thank you."

As long as it didn't come with a ghost in the fucking bedroom this time.

A porter grabbed the suitcase Kayla had thrown together for Kim while we finished up with the doctors, and Kim smiled up at Annie, who'd shared a cab with us from the hospital.

"At least we don't need to eat protein bars now, huh?" Kim said.

Annie managed a tight smile. She'd still barely spoken, and I'd overheard one of the doctors muttering about therapy. Kayla had offered to stay with her in a twin room until she began to process things properly.

Right now, we were at the Hampton Park Hotel and Spa, the jewel in the crown of Katia's father's hotel empire. He'd cleared out an entire wing so the girls could undergo their interviews in peace and slightly more comfort than the police precinct.

"Stay as long as you want," he'd said as he shook my hand for the twentieth time.

It sure beat the prospect of bunking down on Wyatt's sofa, which he'd offered while we were waiting at the hospital before I agreed to move in with Kim.

In the honeymoon suite, the staff had left us a fruit

basket, a fancy box of chocolates, and a chilled bottle of Veuve Clicquot, but Kim took one look at the champagne and asked the porter to take it away.

"I'm never drinking again. Not after what happened the last two times."

"It's probably not a good idea with your painkillers either."

She stared out the window at the golf course beyond, lit by strategically placed spotlights.

"I'm so sorry. You must think I'm a total train wreck."

"Kim, you're anything but a train wreck. You're a smart, determined, courageous woman who's been dealt some bad cards recently."

"I managed to sleep through my entire freaking kidnapping!"

"Okay, so that was a first. But if it hadn't been for you, my sister and eleven other women would still be trapped underground, and we wouldn't have gotten some kind of justice for Georgette."

"Every day, that vile animal would undress me with his eyes, and every night, I dreamed of you tearing my clothes off." She smiled hesitantly, the corners of her lips flickering even as tears pooled in her eyes. "But look at the state of me... I'm a mess."

I didn't say anything, just picked her up out of the wheelchair and kissed her shiny pink lipstick into oblivion.

"You're my mess now. Every other man who wants you can fuck right off."

"What about all my baggage? It's not only my remarkable ability to get abducted on a regular basis. There're the spirits, and I'll never want to have biological children."

"I can live without kids. Or we could adopt. I don't think I can live without you."

"And the rest?"

"Tell me there aren't any dead people watching us at the moment."

"No, we're good."

I kissed her again, more deeply this time, and she wrapped her legs around my waist as I carried her to the bed. This was the honeymoon suite—surely there had to be condoms in here somewhere? I struck gold in the nightstand drawer and held up my prize.

"You good with this, Mrs. Cullen?"

"Just hurry up and give me your cock." She clapped both hands over her mouth. "I'm so sorry! I don't know where those words even came from."

"It's yours, sweetheart. It's all yours."

I pressed my lips against the thundering pulse in Kim's neck, then trailed my tongue along the edge of her jaw. I swear she didn't realise how stunning she was. Pale skin, glossy hair, a slim waist, and curves not even Photoshop could compete with. I never wanted to stop touching her.

"You're beautiful," I said, just in case I forgot later. My mind was already drowning in her fucking aura.

When she tangled her fingers in my hair, I no longer cared that I hadn't gotten it cut. But I loosened her grip for long enough to get her out of her fancy dress. Diane von something-or-other, but I didn't care about the name, more the fact that I could open the whole thing by tugging on the tie at the waist. Ten seconds, and she was naked underneath me, soft in all the right places and blushing nicely. Too fucking cute.

It shouldn't have surprised me, but Kim tried as hard with her underwear as she did with everything else in her life. Scraps of pink lace barely covered the good bits, and I tugged her bra down so her nipples poked over the top. That little gasp when I sucked one into my mouth nearly made me come in my boxers.

"This isn't fair," she mumbled.

"What isn't fair?" I kissed my way down her stomach, and her eyes rolled back into her head. I liked that she didn't try to hide who she was anymore, that she was unashamedly hot and bothered.

"You're still wearing clothes."

"Then take them off."

Slender, trembling fingers reached for my belt, and after a few fumbles, I paused to help her because I couldn't wait a moment longer either. Wanton Kimberly turned me into a horny teenager again.

Then she closed her dainty fist around my cock, and the only thing that mattered was getting inside that sweet warmth.

In the past, I'd treated sex as a mind-numbing pleasure. Something to indulge in at the end of a night out without worrying too much about what came next. With Kim, it was different. My hot little mess. Perfectly put-together on the outside, mixed up on the inside, and, as I quickly discovered, totally wild between the sheets. When she said she didn't spit, she meant it.

The moment I slid into her, I got the strangest feeling of coming home, as though we were meant to be together. And when she gasped my name and locked onto me with those baby blues, there were only three words I could say.

"I love you."

Her eyes got wider. And wetter.

Oh fuck. "Don't cry, sweetheart."

"Are you crazy? How can I not cry? I'm so freaking happy."

"So these are good tears?"

She pulled me closer, mashing her wet cheek against mine as she whispered into my ear.

"These are good tears, Mr. Jennings. I love you too."

CHAPTER 36 - KIMBERLY

I'D NEVER BEEN so tired in my life. A week of police interviews in the daytime and Reed's attentions at night had left me drained. And I couldn't walk very well either, but luckily everyone thought that was due to the poison oak.

"Happy Wednesday," Reed said, holding out a pink paper carrier bag. "I got you these."

A gift? For me? I tore off the tissue paper and opened the box. Tennis shoes? He'd got me pink tennis shoes? I hated tennis shoes. But for the next few weeks, I couldn't wear anything else, so they were absolutely perfect.

"Thank you. They're exactly what I need."

"Ready to go to the hospital?"

Was I ever. I could finally get these bandages off and take a long, hot shower. Reed had been washing me with a sponge for a week, but I still felt icky. With anyone else, I'd have felt mortified too, but he'd seen me at my worst and he was still here, so I figured I'd manage to live with the embarrassment.

After my check-up, we'd be going home. The hotel was lovely and everything, and it was weirdly nice being with all the girls somewhere that wasn't a dungeon. Despite being from different backgrounds, we'd bonded over non-alcoholic cocktails and a shared love of daylight. Well, apart from Abigail. When the police told the others that Peter was dead, they'd squealed with delight and hugged and high-fived, but not her. She'd cried. Stockholm syndrome, the police psychiatrist told me in a whisper.

The porter knocked on the door of our suite, and I took one last look around. I'd miss the place. It held good memories, and better still, no ghosts. But soon I'd be back in my house, in my bed—our bed—to make new memories with Reed.

Will and Rania would be staying with us for another week or two before they returned to England. Neither of them had visited Virginia before, so they thought they'd do some sightseeing before they went home. Two new friends, one new soul sister. I finally had people I could talk to about my gift, people who took me seriously and discussed the spirit world as if it were merely another town or city, not like my father. Where was he in this whole sorry tale? I hadn't seen him since his visit to the hospital, but he'd had his assistant send a card and two tickets for an all-inclusive break in Hawaii. I'd gifted the vacation to Kayla. She deserved it. I'd missed Tara's wedding, but Kayla and Maria had been keeping Just Imagine going until Annie and I felt up to working again.

Even though my father's parenting skills were woefully lacking, at least he knew what he was doing in Washington. At first, the British government had been reluctant to chastise Robert Turner, who claimed to have no knowledge of his son's misdeeds, even when it turned out he'd been paying the credit card bills when Peter bought large quantities of women's clothing and thirteen freaking pizzas a day. His son had always been generous with gifts, he claimed, as well as having a high metabolism.

But then my father had done his thing, and the British government had recalled Robert after several senators, a gang of congressmen, and the media verbally eviscerated him. The now ex-ambassador had offered an insincere non-apology on TV the day before yesterday—along with citizens of America, staff at the British embassy were shocked to learn of the heinous actions of an individual who decided to imprison thirteen young women, yadda yadda yadda—which was kind of insulting, but at least he got his butt kicked back across the Atlantic with Robert.

It was over.

Two more figures appeared behind the porter. Katia and her father, who'd treated us like royalty for the last week.

"Are you sure you don't want to stay longer?" she asked.

"I just want life to get back to normal."

Or whatever passed as normal these days.

"I guess I can understand that," Katia said. "We're building a new resort in California, so I'll be flying out there in two weeks to oversee the work."

"With her bodyguards," her father said.

She rolled her eyes. "Yes, with my new bodyguards. All three of them."

"And you're sure about the reward?" her father asked Reed.

A million dollars, that was how much he'd offered for the return of his daughter, but Reed, Wyatt, Will, and Rania had asked for it to be split among the girls instead to help them get back on their feet. Even though Reed needed the money, he still refused to take a cent. Yet another reason why I loved him.

"Yes, we're sure."

"Well, remember you're always welcome at our resorts. Any time, any place, we'll give you the best room."

"That's much appreciated, sir."

Annie and Kayla were staying at the hotel for another week to take advantage of the spa facilities, or so Annie said. I'd been worried at first that she wasn't recovering, but then Reed had pointed out the way she looked at the waiter who served us breakfast every morning. The sneaky glances. The shy smiles. Somebody had a crush.

"Has Emma decided what she's doing yet?" Katia asked.

"Not officially," Reed said. "But fifty bucks says she'll move back in with Wyatt."

"Aw, they make such a cute couple. I've seen the way he looks at her."

Reed sighed. After Emma came round from her operation, the tears had flowed. Mostly from her, but also from Wyatt and even a few from Reed. Emma had apologised for being, in her words, a bratty little bitch, and promised she'd never act like that again. I got the impression she'd done a lot of thinking during her time with Peter. The pressures she'd placed on her brother and Wyatt, the way she'd taken them for granted, the drugs, her acting out when she didn't get her own way. I'd only known her for a week, but that wasn't the Emma I'd seen. She'd changed.

And despite everything, it was clear there was still a spark between her and Wyatt. He'd stayed with her in the hotel, and even though she swore at first that he was sleeping on the sofa, yesterday she hadn't been able to stop smiling and I knew he was back in her bed.

Wyatt would be returning to work next week too. Officially, he was on a temporary suspension, having received a rebuke for shooting a diplomat's son on a property covered by sovereign immunity. Unofficially, he was a national hero, and his colleagues were taking him and Reed out for drinks on Saturday.

Katia's phone pinged, and she glanced at the screen.

"Your car's waiting outside. You promise you'll both come over for dinner on Sunday?"

I gave her a quick hug. "We promise. No pizza, no sandwiches."

"Got it. The chef's promised to create something special."

Reed helped me out to the elevator, and I smiled as the doors closed. I'd done better than I ever thought possible out of this ordeal. Peter was dead, and I was alive, properly alive, whereas before I'd just been going through the motions. In the past, I'd only had a handful of friends—Annie, Kayla, and perhaps Maria—but now I'd more than doubled my little circle. Yes, I'd always hate Peter for what he was and what he did, but a tiny part of me wanted to thank him too.

I pulled Reed down to my level so I could kiss him on the cheek.

"I love you, Mr. Jennings."

"Love you too, Mrs. Cullen."

***

Three weeks had passed since we left the hotel, and at times, I'd thought today would never end. Only my third full day back at work, and I'd had a budget meeting with a new client, gone venue hunting for Bridezilla's fiercer cousin, undertaken a tense negotiation with a DJ who also happened to be the groom's nephew and thought the entire wedding revolved around his set, then drawn up a minute-by-minute timeline for Maria's wedding day. But now everything was finished, and I couldn't wait to get home, not least so I could take my shoes off. My feet still hurt, but the swelling had gone down enough for me to wear pumps again.

"Are you almost done?" I called out to Emma.

"Five minutes. I promised this guy I'd get back to him today."

As predicted, Emma had moved back in with Wyatt, but when he went to work, she hated being home alone. Reed and I couldn't take time off either, not when our phones were ringing off the hook after all the press coverage, so we'd come up with a different solution. A week ago, I'd promoted Kayla from receptionist to wedding planner to help deal with the extra work, and Emma came to work at Just Imagine. We had Reed's calls diverted through our switchboard so she could do his admin too. A perfect solution, even if she didn't share my love of pastels.

I should have been happy, but today I was struggling to smile because after extending their trip, Will and Rania were finally flying home tomorrow morning. Saying goodbye would be hard, even with Skype and email and the fact that Reed and I had promised to take a trip to England soon. Somehow, I'd get myself onto that airplane.

On the surface, Rania and I couldn't have been more different. She'd grown up in Syria, a victim of the civil war that had torn the country apart, and when she told me a bit about her teenage years, I'd wept along with her. And now I knew why she was so tough. Out there, she *had* tried to fulfil her Electi duties, even though she hated the curse, as she called it. While I agonised over what shoes went best with which dress, she'd been fighting for her own survival and the freedom of spirits. Now she still fought, but in a different way—by helping Will to get justice by more legal means.

And it made me think... Perhaps I could do the same with Reed? Not by becoming an actual investigator, but surely I'd be able to manage the occasional interview of an other-worldly witness? He'd confessed that he sometimes found working solo frustrating, especially the loneliness aspect, and maybe I could ease that a little, along with Wyatt now that they were friends again.

And I could help the spirits in other ways—start bringing the Electi into the twenty-first century, if you like. With Reed and Wyatt's help, I'd found that Kamal Kabede's sister had indeed left town, and relayed the news that she was living happily in West Virginia. And Lil Shawn was thrilled to hear we'd caught the man responsible for Emma's abduction. Said he'd be able to sleep easier now, metaphorically speaking.

Yes, I'd talk to Reed about my ideas later, but for now, I was determined to enjoy the time I had left with Rania.

That evening, we sat at the table with our gold

necklaces side by side, the curved edges slotted perfectly against each other. Two pieces missing. Two more girls out there somewhere.

"Have you ever thought about trying to find the others?" I asked Rania.

"A few times, but I always wondered what the point would be. I never wanted to do my duty, so I figured they wouldn't either. But now I've met you, I know there's something else there. A deeper connection."

"An energy? As if the four of us were once one soul and then we were split? Oh, listen to me. I sound like one of those late-night weirdos off the TV."

"No, I get it. I do. And at least now we know we can recognise the other Electi if we ever see them."

"Yes, because they'll glow, right? And it's also good to understand why I was always drawn to the colour pink."

"Will's probably thanking his lucky stars that I got the white aura. We bought a new house last year, and I went minimalist. Grey and white. It's okay apart from when it rains, then we get muddy footprints all over the tiles. You promise you'll come and visit?"

"In April. I've already got two weeks blocked out in my schedule. Reed wants to visit Windsor Castle and the Tower of London while we're there."

"You're going to the Tower of London? Do you know how many people died there?"

"No, I'm going to Harvey Nichols instead. And the Tate Galleries."

"I'd love to see the art, so I'll play tourist with you. And you can meet Shannon and RJ."

Ah, yes. RJ, the friendly computer hacker who was dating Rania's best friend. At least, when they weren't trying to kill each other. According to Will, they had a weird love/hate relationship, but somehow it worked for them.

"I can't wait. And you're coming back here too?"

"Will's started planning our road trip. He wants to rent a vintage muscle car over the summer and drive halfway across the country."

I made a face because driving a car without AC through California or Nevada wasn't my idea of fun, but Rania just laughed.

"At least I've got a driving licence now," she said.

"Really? You don't mind going?"

"Honestly? No. Will changed my life for the better, and I realise it sounds corny, but I'm happy doing anything as long as he's along for the ride."

"That's kind of how I feel about Reed."

"Why don't you come with us? Even part of the way? If you can't live without your creature comforts, you could rent a more comfortable vehicle, like a Lexus, or a... Okay, not a Mercedes. A BMW?"

I'd have to learn to pack light, but I *had* kind of enjoyed that trip to Ohio with Reed. And if my soul sister was in the US, I wanted to see her.

"I'll check my schedule and speak to Reed."

We hugged each other tight, two women bound by a strange gift and dramatic circumstances. Over Rania's shoulder, our two necklaces glinted under the spotlights. Was it just my imagination, or did they glow a bit too?

WHAT'S NEXT?

The Electi series continues in _Possessed_...

Geneticist Nicole Bordais has one goal—to find a cure for her supernatural powers so she can walk the streets of California without the spirits of the dead constantly harassing her. At least, until her scumbag of a boyfriend steals a precious family heirloom and skips town. Now, along with her best friend Lulu, she's on a mission to get it back.

Part-time bounty hunter Beckett Sinclair doesn't want to hunt down escaped felon Corey Haynes. No, he'd rather stick with his regular job as a nightclub bouncer and his hobby researching the paranormal. But family obligations send him west, where he finds more than he bargained for in San Francisco...

For more details: www.elise-noble.com/possessed

And if you also enjoy romantic mysteries without magical elements, why not give my Blackwood series a try? The story starts in *Pitch Black*...

What happens when an assassin has a nervous breakdown?

After the owner of a security company is murdered, his sharp-edged wife goes on the run. Forced to abandon everything she holds dear—her home, her friends, her job in special ops—she builds a new life for herself in England. As Ashlyn Hale, she meets Luke, a handsome local who makes her realise just how lonely she is.

Yet, even in the sleepy village of Lower Foxford, the dark side of life dogs Diamond's trail when the unthinkable strikes. Forced out of hiding, she races against time to save those she cares about. But is it too little, too late?

Pitch Black is currently available FREE.
For more details: www.elise-noble.com/pitch-black

If you enjoyed *Spooked*, please consider leaving a review.

For an author, every review is incredibly important. Not only do they make us feel warm and fuzzy inside, readers consider them when making their decision whether or not to buy a book. Even a line saying you enjoyed the book or what your favourite part was helps a lot.

Want to Stalk Me?

For updates on my new releases, giveaways, and other random stuff, you can sign up for my newsletter on my website:
www.elise-noble.com

Facebook:
www.facebook.com/EliseNobleAuthor

Twitter: @EliseANoble

Instagram: @elise_noble

If you're on social media, you may also like to join Team Blackwood for exclusive giveaways, sneak previews, and book-related chat. Be the first to find out about new stories, and you might even see your name or one of your ideas make it into print!

And if you'd like to read my books for FREE, you can also find details of how to join my review team.

Would you like to join Team Blackwood?

www.elise-noble.com/team-blackwood

END-OF-BOOK STUFF

I can't remember when I drafted this book, but it was either at the end of 2017 or the beginning of 2018. Fast forward through the editing process, and just before release date, there's possibly the biggest diplomatic scandal of all time—the murder of Jamal Khashoggi in the Saudi Arabian embassy. Back when I first penned the story, I wondered if the concept of a diplomat being such a murderous little shit was a bit farfetched, but I guess it wasn't. Sometimes, life imitates art in the worst possible way.

For me, the whole concept for this book started with the characters and the first line. *My date was going well until the dead girl in the back seat started talking to me.* Because how much worse could a date get? Much worse, it turned out, because I have a warped mind and it's fun making life difficult for my characters.

In Kimberly, I wanted a girl who was a contrast to Rania. I love contrast. While Rania has a dark side she tries to smother, Kim's all about the light, although she's full of contradictions too. A rich woman who likes to work. A trophy wife who refused to conform. A power she calls a gift that she refuses to use. And Reed... He's a kindred spirit for Will, albeit on another continent.

I've already written the next book in this series, and Nicole takes Rania's abdication of her duties and Kim's avoidance of ghosts and goes one better. She believes in science, not the supernatural. Her new friend Beckett, on the other hand... Well, you'll have to wait and see what happens.

I'm writing this in November, although by the time you read it, Christmas will have come and gone. So I hope you had a great time and also that there's snow. And that neither of us ended up in too much of a food coma.

For me, a new year is an opportunity not so much for a new start, but for a push to change all those little things that have been bugging me over the last year. In 2019, I'm hoping Trev the horse stays sound so I can ride more often, and I need to spend more time out of the house before my ass permanently moulds to my desk chair. I'd also like to publish eight books—that's my goal—so I guess I'd better get writing.

As always, thank you to all those who assisted me with this book. Abi for designing another cover I love, Nikki for editing, and Lizbeth, John, and Debi for proof reading. And at the beginning, my awesome beta readers: Jeff, Renata, Terri, Lina, Musi, David, Stacia, Jessica, Nikita, Quenby, and Jody. I couldn't do this without you guys!

Thank you for reading, and thank you for reviewing. See you in the next book!

Elise

OTHER BOOKS BY ELISE NOBLE

The Blackwood Security Series

For the Love of Animals (Nate & Carmen - prequel)
Black is My Heart (Diamond & Snow - prequel)
Pitch Black
Into the Black
Forever Black
Gold Rush
Gray is My Heart
Neon (novella)
Out of the Blue
Ultraviolet
Glitter (novella)
Red Alert
White Hot
Sphere (novella)
The Scarlet Affair
Spirit (novella)
Quicksilver
The Girl with the Emerald Ring
Red After Dark
When the Shadows Fall
Pretties in Pink (TBA)

The Blackwood Elements Series

Oxygen

Lithium
Carbon
Rhodium
Platinum
Lead
Copper
Bronze
Nickel
Hydrogen (2021)

The Blackwood UK Series
Joker in the Pack
Cherry on Top (novella)
Roses are Dead
Shallow Graves
Indigo Rain
Pass the Parcel (TBA)

Baldwin's Shore
Dirty Little Secrets (2021)
Secrets, Lies, and Family Ties (2021)
Buried Secrets (2021)

Blackwood Casefiles
Stolen Hearts
Burning Love (TBA)

Blackstone House
Hard Lines (TBA)
Hard Tide (TBA)

The Electi Series
Cursed

Spooked
Possessed
Demented
Judged

The Planes Series
A Vampire in Vegas
A Devil in the Dark (TBA)

The Trouble Series
Trouble in Paradise
Nothing but Trouble
24 Hours of Trouble

Standalone
Life
Coco du Ciel (2021)
Twisted (short stories)
A Very Happy Christmas (novella)

Books with clean versions available (no swearing and no on-the-page sex)
Pitch Black
Into the Black
Forever Black
Gold Rush
Gray is My Heart

Audiobooks
Black is My Heart (Diamond & Snow - prequel)
Pitch Black
Into the Black
Forever Black

Gold Rush
Gray is My Heart
Neon (novella)

WANT TO STALK ME?

For updates on my new releases, giveaways, and
other random stuff, you can sign up for my newsletter
on my website:
www.elise-noble.com

Facebook:
www.facebook.com/EliseNobleAuthor

Twitter: @EliseANoble

Instagram: @elise_noble

If you're on social media, you may also like to join
Team Blackwood for exclusive giveaways, sneak
previews, and book-related chat. Be the first to find out
about new stories, and you might even see your name
or one of your ideas make it into print!

And if you'd like to read my books for FREE, you
can also find details of how to join my review team.

Would you like to join Team Blackwood?

www.elise-noble.com/team-blackwood

END-OF-BOOK STUFF

I can't remember when I drafted this book, but it was either at the end of 2017 or the beginning of 2018. Fast forward through the editing process, and just before release date, there's possibly the biggest diplomatic scandal of all time—the murder of Jamal Khashoggi in the Saudi Arabian embassy. Back when I first penned the story, I wondered if the concept of a diplomat being such a murderous little shit was a bit farfetched, but I guess it wasn't. Sometimes, life imitates art in the worst possible way.

For me, the whole concept for this book started with the characters and the first line. *My date was going well until the dead girl in the back seat started talking to me.* Because how much worse could a date get? Much worse, it turned out, because I have a warped mind and it's fun making life difficult for my characters.

In Kimberly, I wanted a girl who was a contrast to Rania. I love contrast. While Rania has a dark side she tries to smother, Kim's all about the light, although she's full of contradictions too. A rich woman who likes to work. A trophy wife who refused to conform. A power she calls a gift that she refuses to use. And Reed... He's a kindred spirit for Will, albeit on another continent.